THE ALPHA

by Brooklyn

The contents of this work, including, but not limited to, the accuracy of events, people, and places depicted; opinions expressed; permission to use previously published materials included; and any advice given or actions advocated are solely the responsibility of the author, who assumes all liability for said work and indemnifies the publisher against any claims stemming from publication of the work.

All Rights Reserved
Copyright © 2021 by Brooklyn

No part of this book may be reproduced or transmitted, downloaded, distributed, reverse engineered, or stored in or introduced into any information storage and retrieval system, in any form or by any means, including photocopying and recording, whether electronic or mechanical, now known or hereinafter invented without permission in writing from the publisher.

Dorrance Publishing Co
585 Alpha Drive
Suite 103
Pittsburgh, PA 15238
Visit our website at *www.dorrancebookstore.com*

ISBN: 978-1-6480-4092-4
eISBN: 978-1-6480-4904-0

THE ALPHA

FOR DEONTA

CHAPTER ONE

Dream A Dream of Me

Pandora stepped out of the woods and into a clearing. The setting sun made the tree line look as if it were on fire. In the middle of the clearing stood a cottage with a pond to the right of it. The cottage itself was nothing special. It was made of redwood and had a porch just big enough for two rocking chairs on one side and a porch swing on the other. There was a light coming from the windows as if someone was home, waiting for her.

Pandora walked towards the cottage, careful to not make any noise. About halfway towards the cottage, a wolf came to the front of the cottage. Its fur was white as snow and its eyes were glowing blue. The wolf's black nose turned up, as if the wolf was looking down on Pandora. Its hair was standing on its back.

She froze where she stood and held her ground, staring at the wolf intensely, challenging it. The wolf growled and barked at Pandora, conveying that it did not believe that Pandora belonged there. Pandora held her ground still, determined to make it to her goal.

The wolf snarled, showing its razor-sharp teeth to Pandora. Pandora questioned herself, wondering if she should just turn back as she had so many times before, but she knew she may never get this far again. Pandora took a tentative step forward and regretted it immediately. The white wolf took her step as a challenge and charged at Pandora, and once close enough, leapt at her, jaw wide and ready to swallow her whole.

Pandora woke in a cold sweat and sat up quickly, scanning the room for the wolf that had attacked her. The only other living being the room was Abby, her roommate. Seeing Abby's sleeping form calmed Pandora enough to lay back down and take a few deep breaths. She thought over her dream and all the other times that she had dreamt the same thing.

When she was younger, she would just dream of being lost in the woods and being terrified and wishing someone would find her. As a teenager, she walked through the same woods, finding peace in the quiet around her. Once she started her senior year of high school, she found the cottage in the woods. She marked her path every night to find her way there, finding landmarks to point her way.

She told her psychology teacher about her reoccurring dream and how it changed. He encouraged her to pursue it and write down every change that she would find. He told her to go in different directions and try to approach the cottage. So far, now at the age of twenty-four, she would only ever get lost or find the cottage. Every time she took a step towards the cottage, the wolf appeared. It appeared later the older she got. The redwood cottage was basically mocking her. It seemed inviting and homey, like a mother welcoming her child into her arms after a long day. The wolf was always guarding it like a dragon guards a princess in her tower. Some nights she would run from the wolf and it would chase her. Other nights she held still and would wake up on her own. Other nights, like tonight, she challenged the wolf.

Pandora pulled her dream journal out from under her pillow and turned on her book light as to not wake Abby. She began writing the details in her journal, careful to not leave anything out. Once she had finished, she put her journal back and picked up her phone to check the time.

4:08 A.M.

Pandora sighed and soundlessly climbed out of her bed and slid her slippers onto her feet. She changed into her workout clothes and tennis shoes, then strapped her iPod to her arm and stuck her headphones into her ears. Locking the door behind her, Pandora took the stairs down three floors and snuck out of the side door that was always propped open.

She looked to the sky and, just barely making out the storm clouds above through the still dark sky, smiled as she began her morning run. She jogged around the campus, pacing herself and smiling at the sights around her as she made her way towards the track field. Once there, she sat at the start of the third row, remembering her years at the school.

Pandora had grown up in Conway, South Carolina. Her parents had met at Coastal Carolina College. Ever since she first heard the story of how they met, she had dreamt of going to the same school. When they died in a car accident when she had just started school, she began pushing herself to reach her goal. Pandora had a 4.0 GPA in high school, a 34 on her ACT, did charity work, and was on the track team. She got an athletic scholarship to the school easily. She majored in management and minored in business, receiving her master's degree in five years.

Pandora sat on her row and listened to her music, watching the sun lazily rise into the sky. She didn't know how long she sat there, but time seemed to always slow for her when she was on the track. It had a way of clearing her head, which is what she needed at the moment as she was about to graduate. Time had gone so quickly in college that she wasn't sure what to do with herself now that her dream had been fulfilled. She supposed it was time for a new dream, not just in her real life, but in her sleeping state as well.

At some point during the sunrise, Abby had joined her. Abby stayed silent to not interrupt Pandora's thoughts but sat close enough that Pandora knew Abby was there for her, their knees just barely touching. Pandora smiled, happy that her best friend had stayed consistent at every point in her life. They had grown up together and lived next door to one another most of their lives. They had the same teachers and classes throughout grade school, both on the field and track team, and dormmates since the beginning of college.

"We're lucky," thought Pandora as she rested her head on Abby's shoulder with a small smile gracing her lips. "Lucky that we've always had each other."

CHAPTER TWO

TO GRANDMOTHERS HOUSE WE GO

"Okay." Pandora smiled. "Everything that we don't need is packed and in the truck to take home, right?"

"Stop worrying, Pandora." Abby smiled to her best friend. "My parents live, like, seven blocks from campus. If we have to take more than one trip, I think we'll live."

Pandora stuck her tongue out at Abby and then smiled at her. Pandora worried about everything, but Abby always knew how to calm her down. It was a bonus of growing up together. Abby's boyfriend, Mason, came into their room and looked around.

"It looks so empty," he commented.

"There's still clothes in the closet and sheets on the bed," Abby stated, trying to make the room still seem full.

"Yeah," Mason agreed. "It still looks weird though."

Pandora smiled, knowing Mason was sad that college was almost through. They had finished their finals a week ago and only had two more days until graduation, three more days until they went home for good. The three friends left the room and headed towards the truck. Once to the parking lot, Pandora smiled at her dad's old truck, remembering how she used to sit on his lap as he would drive down Main Street with her, showing her how to drive the truck at such a young age. Her grandmother had kept the truck, having a mechanic look at it a few times a year so it stayed in working condition until it was time for Pandora to drive.

Pandora climbed into the driver's seat as Abby climbed into the middle, Mason following close behind. With the truck weighted down in the back by their few boxes each, the trio took off, windows rolled down and the music loud. Pandora breathed in the salty air. The warm breeze lifted Pandora's spirits as they rolled through the campus and towards Pandora's and Abby's childhood homes. Mason began singing along to a love song terribly, pretending to have a microphone and pointing to Abby. Pandora smiled at their antics, loving how in love her friends were.

Once they reached their homes, Abby's parents came out and helped unload the truck. Mason and Abby worked on Abby's boxes as Pandora and Abby's father worked on Pandora's. Once all of the boxes were in their respective rooms, Pandora went to her grandmother's backyard. Taking her seat next to her grandmother, Pandora took her grandmother's wrinkled hand in hers and smiled. Abby, Mason, and Pandora stayed on campus throughout the weekdays during classes since having dorms made tuition cheaper, but they were home every weekend.

Shannon, Abby's father, started lighting citronella candles as Mason and Abby brought out mason jars and a pitcher of sweet tea. Candace, Abby's mother, began asking the girls and Mason questions about graduation and their final grades. Grandma just smiled and nodded along to the conversation.

Grandma hadn't spoken a word since Grandpa had passed away ten years earlier. The house that had once been full of laughter and music sat eerily quiet ever since his passing. Grandpa always brought light into the room with open bay windows and a warm smile, wind chimes playing a soft melody as the tubes and bells tolled in the wind. When Grandpa died, the wind chimes came down and the windows closed. The record player gathered dust from not being used and the records sat untouched.

Grandma still smiled and interacted with everyone as she had before. She was just a little more broken inside than she wanted everyone to know. First, she had lost her daughter and son-in-law, then her husband followed seven years later. It had drained her more than she would ever let on. Pandora was happy that she had been so young when she had lost her family. She felt that if she had been older, the memories would have drowned her until she became mute as well.

Pandora shook her head and abandoned her sorrowful thoughts to join the conversation happening around her.

"What was your final score in psychology, Pandora?" Candace asked.

"I think it was a ninety-four," Pandora stated, not quite sure.

"Yeah, a ninety-four." Abby rolled her eyes. "Highest grade in the class."

"In some defense, it was a tough class." Mason smiled, placing a small kiss on Abby's head.

Abby smiled and sighed, content. The conversation continued flowing as Shannon cooked burgers on the grill he always left on Grandma's back patio. After everyone got their fill on burgers and chips and had finished catching up on final grades and graduation talk, Pandora walked Mason and Abby's small family to the gate door that connected their backyards and wished them goodnight. Then, Pandora walked her grandmother into their home and into her grandmother's bedroom. Her grandma placed her small hand on Pandora's cheek and smiled gently, a small twinkle in her eyes. She shut the door behind her and headed to the backyard to collect the dishes and clean them. Once everything was in order, Pandora went to her room, ready for sleep to overcome her.

Pandora couldn't tell if it was day or night, as the sun was shut out of view by the oak and maple trees surrounding her. She sighed, knowing exactly where she was and knowing that the dream had resurfaced after a week of peaceful sleep. She turned towards the jagged rock that pointed her in the direction of the cabin. She rolled her eyes at the mocking rock and began her hike, moving at a faster pace than normal, ready to be awake. Once to the cottage, she didn't hesitate to look at her surroundings and continued walking. The wolf came around the cottage halfway through her journey again. She stopped upon seeing it and stared into its hypnotizing eyes.

"What?" she asked it when it growled. "What do you want?"

It growled louder. Pandora, annoyed by the wolf, growled back. The wolf bent down and whimpered, shocking Pandora. She took a step back, eyes wide in disbelief. The wolf looked at her, tilting its head as if curious on what Pandora would do next. Pandora took a step forward and, seeing the white wolf stay down, approached it. She held her hand out towards it, and the wolf smelled her hand as a dog would.

The wolf stood suddenly, causing Pandora to jump back. The wolf pushed her towards the woods with its head. Pandora turned and began walking back to the trees, the wolf falling into step just a little ahead of her. They passed the jagged rock together and started climbing a steep hill. The wolf seemed to climb effortlessly, as if it made this climb all of the time. Pandora was sweating and out of breath halfway up the rocks. She stopped for a moment, holding herself up and catching her breath. The wolf yipped at her, catching her attention. The wolf looked like it was defying gravity the way it stood proud at a horizontal level.

Pandora began her climb again. When they were almost to the top, the wolf let her catch up and helped push her the rest of the way up and over the ledge. Pandora rolled to her back once she was on level ground again and tried to catch her breath. The wolf laid next to her, waiting patiently for Pandora. Once Pandora was breathing again, she looked to the wolf. The wolf stood and began walking on what looked like a trail. Pandora stood and followed, curious about where they could possibly be heading.

She didn't have to wonder long as the wolf stopped in front of a tree with two signs nailed to it. Pandora hurried over and looked at the signs.

"WOLF ROCKS BYPASS A.T. JCT. 1.0 MI."

"SPRINGS 250 FT."

"Wolf Rocks?" Pandora questioned, looking to her guide with a smile. "Really?"

The wolf barked with what looked like a smile on its face. Pandora rolled her eyes and studied the signs, determined to not forget them. When she looked back in the direction of the wolf, she noticed that it had disappeared. She looked around frantically, trying to find it. She heard a rustling from a bustle of bushes next to her and turned to it, ready to run if needed. Suddenly the wind picked up, knocking her over from how rough it was.

Right before she hit the ground in her dream, Pandora awoke, sitting up instantly. She looked around her room and saw her grandmother standing in her doorway. Pandora jumped, almost falling out of her bed as she threw her hand over her mouth to not scream.

"Grandma?" she questioned, standing and walking towards her. "What are you doing in here? You scared me."

Her grandma stood in her spot, staring at Pandora with wide eyes. Suddenly her mouth opened wider than she should be able to, as if unhitched from her jaw. A loud, rumbling moan escaped her grandmother's throat, causing Pandora to retreat further back into her room. Her grandmother's arm raised, pointing to her as the deep moan morphed into a scream that shook the windows. Pandora threw her hands over her ears, terrified of what was happening in front of her.

Suddenly, her grandmother leapt at her, her teeth as sharp as the wolf's had been in her previous dream.

Pandora woke up, a scream ripping from her vocal cords. She stopped screaming once she realized she was still in her bed. She sat up quickly and looked at her door. Her grandmother was standing there again, a grave expression on her face that could just barely be seen through the sunlight coming through Pandora's open windows.

"Grandma?" Pandora questioned, standing and walking further away from her stand-in guardian.

"The white wolf waits for you," her grandmother stated in a gravelly tone before walking out of Pandora's doorway and back into her own room, closing the door behind her.

Pandora stood rooted to the ground, unsure of what to do. Her grandmother had just spoken for the first time in ten years, and the first words that she had said were about a dream that she had only ever told one other person about. The nightmare from before the words were spoken still weighed heavily on her mind.

Slowly, Pandora walked to her grandmother's bedroom door. Once there, she knocked twice, hoping on some level that her grandmother would not answer. When she received no reply, Pandora gently twisted the doorknob and looked into her grandmother's room. Her grandmother was lying in her bed, fast asleep, as if she had not been walking and talking just moments before. Pandora watched her for a few moments, wondering if she had still been dreaming.

Pandora shook her head violently, trying to figure out the difference between her dreams and reality. She shut her grandmother's door quietly and went straight back to her room, locking the door behind her. She opened her laptop and did an internet search on the words from her first dream. Her computer quickly dinged, indicating that it had found a match. She clicked the first link that appeared and began reading.

"Wolf Rocks Trail is a loop trail near Somerset, Pennsylvania. Features a river and is rated as moderate," Pandora read to herself quietly.

Next she looked up the distance from Conway to Wolf Rocks, curiosity eating away at her. Seeing that it was just over nine hours away made Pandora even more curious than before. She clicked on the images of the trail and was surprised when she immediately recognized the place on her computer screen. As she clicked through photo after photo, she felt herself becoming afraid. When she was just dreaming of the place it was one thing. To know that her dream may actually be real, disturbed her beyond belief.

"How could I have dreamt of a place I have never heard of before?" she thought. "How is this possible?"

A knock at her door caused her to jump and slam her laptop closed.

"Pandora?" she heard Abby call. "Why is the door locked? Are you okay?"

"Yeah," Pandora called. "I'm coming."

Pandora stood and unlocked the door. She opened it to reveal Abby staring at her questioningly.

"I must have accidentally locked it," Pandora lied, heading towards her dresser to pull out clothes for the day.

She changed silently as Abby sat on her bed, looking around at all of Pandora's dream catchers.

"You never told me why you have so many of these," Abby stated, pointing at one that looked like a chandelier.

"Grandpa said they would help with my nightmares after my parents died," Pandora shrugged. "I've just kind of collected them ever since."

Abby smiled sadly, wishing she could help Pandora more. Abby couldn't even begin to understand how Pandora was so strong. If she had lost so much of her family, she didn't think that she could go on so well.

"Hey, so, I wanted to run an idea by you," Pandora stated suddenly, pulling Abby back to her friend in front of her.

"Yeah?" Abby smiled. "Must be important if you want my opinion. Typically, you just do whatever is on your mind and drag me through the adventure with you."

"Shut up." Pandora smiled. "At least my adventures benefit you. I remember you meeting a certain Mason during one of them."

"And that same night all three of us ended up in the county jail," Abby stated laughing.

"It was only for a few hours!" Pandora defended. "I was just seeing if Mason could hang!"

Abby and Pandora both laughed at the memory before Pandora got serious again.

"But, for real though. It's my turn to pick the summer road trip," Pandora stated.

"Did you finally pick a place?" Abby asked.

"Yeah," Pandora said, not sounding very confident.

"Where is it and what's wrong?" Abby asked the questions together.

"It's called Wolf Rocks Trail. It's about nine hours from here up in Pennsylvania," Pandora explained, ignoring the second half of Abby's question.

"So, what's wrong with it?" Abby asked.

"Nothing," Pandora shrugged. "I just feel like it might be boring to Mason to go hiking in some mountains up north."

"I'm sure he'll be fine." Abby smiled. "When do we leave?"

CHAPTER THREE

Departure

"Abby Michaels."

Mason and Pandora cheered loudly from next to each other as Abby walked across the stage, accepting her diploma from the dean.

Mason smiled brightly, proud of his girl. Pandora smiled at the look Abby was receiving, again happy for her two friends finding each other. Mason and Pandora waited impatiently for their row to stand. Finally, the last row with them both in it stood.

"Mason Weatherly."

Pandora cheered as Mason stepped onto the stage in front of her. He accepted his diploma and smiled brightly for his photo.

"Pandora Williams-Anput."

Pandora smirked as she walked across the stage and accepted her diploma, a smile gracing her lips as she looked towards the camera. Pandora finally moved her tassel to its new side and took her seat next to Mason again. The dean asked everyone to stand and congratulated them. All of the graduates took off their hats and threw them into the air, smiling and laughing as they did so. Mason and Pandora hugged each other tightly before releasing each other and turning towards where Abby had been standing. Abby was already over halfway towards them, smiling from ear to ear.

Once Abby reached Pandora and Mason, Mason picked her up and spun her around while kissing her. Pandora pulled out her camera and recorded it on her phone to edit later. Pandora stopped recording once Mason released Abby. Abby turned to Pandora and threw her arms around her neck in a fierce hug. Pandora squeezed her tightly, so happy that they had made it so far together.

They headed out of the school and met with their families at their vehicles. Once everyone had finished hugging, the four cars pulled out of the parking lot slowly, wishing for lighter traffic. Abby was in the leading car with her parents, Mason in the middle car with his mother and younger brother, and Pandora and her grandmother in the rear. Pandora and her grandmother hadn't been alone since the morning of her nightmare. Pandora sat quietly, feeling awkward in the driver's seat.

Pandora's grandmother reached over and placed her hand on Pandora's as they waited in the long line trying to exit the campus lot. Pandora smiled weakly, taking her grandmother's hand in hers. Her grandmother squeezed her hand to get her attention, so Pandora turned to her since they were at a stop. Her grandmother looked at her questioningly. Pandora turned away from her grandmother and looked forward again.

"Grandma, do you remember a few days ago when I stayed the night at home? I brought boxes home that night?" Pandora questioned, looking back at her grandmother to see her nod.

"Do you remember standing in my doorway and speaking to me?" Pandora asked.

Her grandmother smiled and nodded to her. Pandora breathed out slowly.

"What did you mean? You said that the white wolf was waiting for me."

Her grandmother just smirked and pointed her head towards Pandora, as if trying to say that Pandora knew what she meant.

"How did you know about my dreams, Grandma?"

Her grandmother just smiled, frustrating Pandora more. Pandora let go of her grandmother's hand and looked away from her.

"I know that you can talk so just talk," Pandora stated, her annoyance showing. "What aren't you telling me?"

Her grandmother sighed and looked forward, still not speaking. Neither spoke as they drove home, letting the air fill with tension. Once they reached their home, Pandora walked her grandmother to the living room and then went straight to the backyard to unlock the gate, ignoring the look that her grandmother sent her way. After she unlocked the gate, Pandora turned on the grill and pulled the longer folding table from the back shed onto the patio. She opened the table and set up enough chairs for everyone around it.

Pandora finally went back inside the house to gather the dishes. Her grandmother was sitting at the dining room table, waiting for Pandora. Pandora looked into her grandmother's tired eyes and sighed. She sat down next to her, putting her task of the dishes aside for the moment.

"I want to tell you a story," her grandmother croaked from the years of not speaking.

"Hold on," Pandora stated, rising quickly and getting her grandmother a glass of water.

Once the water was in front of her grandmother, Pandora sat back down to listen, patiently waiting for her grandmother to drink about half of her water before she started speaking again.

"This story is very old, passed down from generation to generation," her grandmother stated, her voice a little less rough than before. "You know your ancestors were nomads on your grandfather's side and Indians on my side. There's a legend that we've always told about, back during the Civil War, the Indians, slaves, and nomads coming together.

These three different types of people all believed in the old magick. The Indian elders and nomad leaders brought their magick together to form a blessing upon the three peoples. The Africans, as it was their idea, and as they were the only ones that did not practice magick, only worshiping it instead, chose an Egyptian god to pray to. His name was Wepwawet, and he was a war deity and looked like a wolf. His name meant 'opener of the ways,' and they hoped that he would lead them all to their freedom.

During the Wolf Moon, with snow on the ground and temperatures so low that they all should have died from frostbite, the three peoples met together in the woods. They performed the ritual as the full moon began to rise in the sky, reaching the apex of the ritual at the same time that the moon reached the highest point in the sky. Slowly, the people began to kneel over and die. By the time that the morning came, they were all unmoving. Not a single soul was alive. No one found their bodies through the forest, as it was too cold to search during the day. That night, as the moon climbed into the sky again, the people began to awaken.

They all began to stand, completing the ritual by giving themselves to the god Wepwawet. Once everyone had awoken from the dead, a select few began to morph into terrifying creatures. They turned into huge wolves, the leaders with fur as white as the snow beneath their paws and eyes glowing as blue as the moon above had been. The wolves attacked their abusers in the night, traveling as fast as the wind to the south to seek their revenge for their people. They took out half of the Confederates that night. No one understood how wolves that had never been seen before had taken so many lives. By the next morning, the wolves had returned to their woods up north and returned to their human forms.

The people never transformed again but passed down the legends to their children along with the wolf gene in their blood. The legend states that once the descendants reached twenty-five years of age, they too die and give themselves to Wepwawet. As time went on, the legends just became stories that grandchildren received from their grandparents before bed at night. However, the legend also tells of a great leader to lead the wolves in a time of great danger—a leader who dreams of the great white wolf that they are meant to become at the site of the ritual."

Pandora's grandmother drank the rest of her water with a small smile, letting Pandora soak in everything that her grandmother had told her.

"Are you saying that I'm supposed to die on my twenty-fifth birthday next week in Pennsylvania and turn into some wolf, Grandma?" Pandora deadpanned.

Her grandmother just smiled and stood from her seat, setting her empty glass into the sink.

"Grandma?" Pandora questioned.

Her grandmother did not answer, as if she had gone mute again. Her grandmother began pulling out the plates and cups that Pandora had put off, smiling and not speaking. Pandora huffed and walked over to her grandmother. She took the plates from her grandmother's wrinkled hands and set them on the counter. She crossed her arms over her chest and turned to her grandmother.

"I'm not dying while hiking. That's ridiculous. Have you gone insane?" Pandora questioned.

Her grandmother simply patted Pandora's shoulder gently and picked up the cups and headed out the back door where Abby's and Mason's families were coming through the gate door. Pandora ignored the questions she felt rushing through her mind and grabbed the plates. Once outside, she set the table and acted like her grandmother hadn't spoken to her in ten years, wishing it was true.

The next week, two days before Pandora's birthday, Pandora, Mason, and Abby piled into Pandora's truck with their luggage in the bed. They promised to call when they got to Pennsylvania and to send pictures. Pandora had kissed her grandmother's head at the front door before climbing behind the wheel of her truck. They turned on the GPS and set out for their adventure, Pandora with a heavy heart that her two friends were clueless of.

CHAPTER FOUR

BIRTHDAY PARTY GONE WRONG

"So, where did your mom set us up at, Mason?" Pandora asked curiously. "Some fancy hotel in Richmond called The Jefferson. When I told Mom we were going to Pennsylvania for your birthday, she wanted to spoil you a bit," Mason explained, rolling his eyes at his mother's favoritism.

"Why does she like me so much?" Pandora asked, confused.

"I don't know." Mason sighed.

"Beats me." Abby laughed.

Pandora smacked Abby's arm with a Twizzler, a smirk on her face. They continued their drive, heading towards Fuller's Old Fashion BBQ for lunch, as they did every time they went through North Carolina. Pandora's father had taken her to Fuller's when she was younger every weekend since it was only an hour and a half from Conway. It gave Pandora's mom a break on the weekends to enjoy herself with her friends and no children. From Fuller's, they would only have four hours to go to get to the hotel, then they would drive the last four hours to the Days Inn in Somerset.

"Why are we going all the way to Pennsylvania for a hike?" Mason questioned.

Before Pandora could answer, Abby spoke up.

"Because it's Pandora's turn to choose the location, and it's her birthday the day after tomorrow. This is where she wanted to go."

Pandora smirked at Abby's defense of her. Mason just looked out the window, still confused as they pulled into Fuller's at twelve thirty in the afternoon.

Once they got their fill on the best BBQ they had ever tasted, Mason drove the rest of the way through North Carolina, stopping at the welcome center so that everyone could empty their bladders, then continued to Richmond.

Once there, they checked into their hotel room, marveling at how gorgeous the building was. The high ceilings and chandeliers made the hotel seem too good to be true.

"How did your mom swing us a place in here on such short notice?" Abby asked.

"I honestly have no clue," Mason admitted, leading the girls to the elevator and then towards their room for the night.

The room was a little less extravagant then the lobby, but still beautiful nonetheless. Pandora fell onto the bed closest to the air conditioner and sighed, content to just lay there all night. Abby plopped down on the second bed in the room, ready to do the same as Pandora. Mason just smiled at his girls as he took a quick picture on his phone of them both smiling to send to his mom, so she knew they had made it safely.

Mason set the girls' bags in between the beds and his on the other side of the bed Abby had chosen. He began looking up places in Richmond to explore, asking the girls' opinions as he searched. They set their minds to visit Belle Isle for the day and then eat dinner at the hotel as Mason's mother had paid for their meal in advance.

Belle Isle was a twenty-minute taxi ride with the traffic. Abby took pictures on her camera the whole way as their driver gave them a brief history of the landmarks and bridges that they were passing. Once to Belle Isle's pedestrian bridge, their driver gave them a few tips on where to explore. They got out of their taxi after paying and followed the directions that they had been given and crossing the bridge. There they saw people sunbathing and rafting through the James River. They explored the abandoned buildings that were only half standing near the water and found a few geocaches while there. They ended up sitting on a rock in the sun and people watching until five thirty rolled around. They walked back across the bridge where a new taxi was waiting to take them back to The Jefferson.

Once there, they had a delicious meal in the hotel restaurant named Lemaire. They were served jumbo crab cakes as their appetizer before each getting a different main course that they shared with one another. Pandora was served pan-seared scallops, Abby was given black angus filet mignon, and

Mason finished off with herb-roasted cobia. For dessert, they each received a glazed blueberry mousse. All of their food was served with a white wine that none of them could pronounce but tasted like heaven in a bottle. Once they had finished eating, they headed back to their room, all too full to explore the breweries around Richmond and ready to be back in their beds.

The next day, Mason checked them out of their room as Pandora and Abby waited for Pandora's truck. While waiting for Mason to join them, Abby's curiosity got the better of her.

"So why Pennsylvania?" she asked Pandora.

Pandora shrugged, "I opened my map and pointed to a random spot."

"And you just happened to land on a hiking trail?" Abby laughed.

"I'm magical like that," Pandora smirked.

"Alright." Abby smiled. "Keep your secrets then. I'm sure it'll be beautiful."

"Me too." Pandora smiled softly, hiding her real reason from her best friend.

Once Mason, Abby and Pandora were all safely in the truck with Pandora driving, they drove towards Pennsylvania, deciding to eat snacks until they had made it to their next destination only four hours away. Once they reached their cheaper hotel in Somerset, the city where Wolf Rocks was located, they went to the Dairy Queen for burgers before exploring the historical district, including the county jail, sheriff's residence, and Lansberry House. After their small adventure, Mason drove the hour to Pittsburgh so that they could celebrate Pandora's birthday at Howl at the Moon. It took everything in Pandora not to laugh at the irony.

Once they were in the bar, they ordered a few drinks, receiving bucket cups with wolves howling on them and crazy straws. After a few drinks, Abby took Mason's hand and dragged him to the dance floor. Pandora laughed as Mason tried so hard to dance with Abby, but his two left feet kept getting in the way. Pandora continued sipping from her bucket, keeping an eye on her friends and their drinks. Pandora finished two of her drinks and, while the bartender made her another for her bucket, a man slid into the chair next to Pandora. Slightly buzzed, Pandora turned to the man.

Pandora smiled to him politely and he nodded in return. Pandora looked back to the bartender that was pouring her drink, and the man tapped her arm. She turned to him, trying to continue being polite. He pointed to the dance floor, as if silently asking her to join him.

"I don't dance!" Pandora yelled over the music. "Thank you though!"

The man frowned, and his brown eyes seemed to darken a bit.

"Oh great," Pandora thought.

He pointed towards the dance floor again. When Pandora shook her head no, he stood and grabbed her arm, trying to drag her with him. Pandora pulled her arm from him and searched for her bartender, but the bartender had moved on. She looked towards her friends, but they were too lost in the music to notice her trying to fight off some creep. The man grabbed her arm more forcibly, causing her to come off of her stool and just barely land on her feet. She tried to pull her arm away again, but it didn't work. The man began dragging her towards the bathroom, Pandora yelling at him to let go of her in the process, hoping to catch someone's attention. As luck would have it, someone must have heard her, because as soon as Pandora and the man reached the bathroom door, another man appeared and pushed the creep, causing him to let go of Pandora but knocking her to the ground in the process.

A few heads turned towards her once she was on the ground. Her savior was punching the man who had dragged her through the bar and four more guys had appeared as if out of thin air. Two of the guys gathered around the fight, ready to help her savior if he got into some trouble. The other two turned towards Pandora, both reaching out a hand to help her up.

Pandora took the taller man's hand and was easily lifted from the ground. He pulled Pandora close, tucking her under his arm as if to protect her. She swore she felt him smell her hair in the process and pulled away from him, desperately seeking out for Abby and Mason. She didn't have to look long. Abby and Mason were pushing through the crowd, trying to get to Pandora as fast as they could.

Pandora looked to the fight to see her savior being pulled off of the creep by the four other men who had followed him. Seeing the creep with blood all over her face, Pandora ran to her friends, afraid of what would happen if the other men couldn't pull the savior off of him. Abby hugged Pandora hard once they reached each other.

"Can we go, please?" Pandora asked Mason, tears welling in her eyes.

Mason nodded and took each of the girls by their hands and led them to the bar. Mason paid for their drinks quickly and they ran out of the front door. Pandora took a few deep breaths of the warm air and kneeled, trying to control her tears. Abby bent down next to her, not sure what to do as she had never seen Pandora so upset before.

"Let's get to the truck and get back to the hotel," Mason said after Pandora had taken a few deep breaths.

"Are you okay?" a deep voice with a slight British accent asked from behind them, causing Pandora to jump up immediately and stand in front of Abby.

Once Pandora had turned to face the voice, she recognized him as the other man who had offered to help her up. She took a step back, but accidently stepped on Abby's foot, her buzzed state getting the best of her.

"Ow," Abby complained.

"Sorry," Pandora grimaced before turning back to the man. "I'm fine. Thank you for trying to help me."

"It was no problem, sweetheart," another voice, this one with a southern accent, stated, coming out of the bar, followed by the rest of the men who had helped her, including the man who had beaten up the creep until he was unrecognizable.

Pandora locked eyes with the man, not sure if he was a savior or another creep.

"You didn't have to hurt him that badly," Pandora stated, feeling herself become angry.

"Oh, but I did," he responded. "You have no clue what he could have been trying to do to you."

"You could have just pushed him and left it at that. The message would have been clear at that point," Pandora stated, venom in her voice.

All five of the men seemed to cringe a bit at her tone. Pandora rolled her eyes before finally asking their names.

"I'm Jordan," the British one answered and then pointed to each man individually. He pointed to the southern man who had smelled her hair, "That's Warren. Bit of an ass. Sorry about him." He pointed to the two men who hadn't spoken yet, "That's Loren and Nature." Then he turned to the "Savior,", "And this is…"

"Sam," the man interrupted, holding his hand out for Pandora to shake. "Sam Anubis."

"Anubis, like the Egyptian god?" Abby asked, causing all five men to turn towards her and Mason.

It was like they hadn't even noticed her friends there, but Sam smiled warmly to Abby anyways.

"Yes," he stated. "Do you know anything about the Egyptian gods?"

"Not much," Mason stated as Abby shook her head.

Mason turned his attention back to Pandora.

"Anubis was the god of death," Pandora stated. "Just because your last name is a god of death, doesn't mean you should beat someone almost to theirs."

"He'll be fine," Loren stated. "Probably need some ice for his face and a few stitches, but he shouldn't have been trying to hurt you."

"Well, I do appreciate your help," Pandora said to Loren before turning back to Sam. "Thank you, but we really need to head back to our hotel. Stay out of trouble."

Pandora, Mason, and Abby turned away from the five men and headed towards where Mason had parked her truck. Sam yelled after them.

"You never told us your name!" he called.

Pandora turned back to him for a moment, debating if she should answer. She made up her mind quickly.

"Pandora," she stated, just loud enough for him to hear. "Pandora Anput."

She climbed into her truck, taking the passenger seat and allowing Mason to drive with Abby between them. Pandora didn't look back to see Sam's reaction as they headed back towards Somerset.

CHAPTER FIVE

Admittance

Pandora only got a few hours of sleep, her mind racing from the events of the night she'd had. She ended up quietly rising from bed around seven in the morning, careful not to wake Abby and Mason in the bed next to hers. She changed into her running clothes and put her headphones in, grabbing a key on the way out the door, leaving a note to not worry Abby or Mason if they woke up before she returned.

Pandora ran for a while, using the exercise to clear her mind. She ran through Main Street, passing the Historical & Genealogical Society building and Coffee Springs Farm without even realizing how far she was going. She continued running until she was outside of Olde Towne Bakery and Café. She looked at her watch and realized she'd only been running for twenty minutes but felt like she needed to stop.

Pandora headed inside, intent on grabbing donuts for Abby, Mason, and herself. She had looked down to her phone, stopping her music when she walked in. She didn't noticed Sam in front of her in line until she almost ran into his back. She cursed under her breath and had almost turned around to leave, but he had heard her and turned to face her. The confused look on his face to her presence made Pandora almost smirk at him.

"Well, hello there, darlin'," Warren's southern accent rang out from beside Sam.

"Hello, Warren." Pandora smiled, rolling her eyes.

"What brings you to our bright little town?" Warren asked her before flinching as Sam elbowed him in his rib.

"Actually." Pandora smiled, "It's my birthday. I've always wanted to go hiking at Wolf Rocks. Abby, Mason, and I all just graduated college, so we decided to come here."

"How old are you?" Sam asked, a slightly worried expression on his face.

"Twenty-five at nine-o-seven tonight," Pandora smirked, walking past the two men in front of her to cut them in line.

"How can I help you today?" the girl behind the counter with strawberry-blonde hair asked.

"Can I order a dozen donuts, please?" Pandora smiled. "I'll need half glazed and half maple bacon."

"I'll get right on it. Your total will be $11.50 after taxes."

"Thank you." Pandora smiled, pulling out fifteen dollars cash and telling the girl to keep the change.

Pandora turned back to the boys as she waited for her food.

"You cut us." Warren glared playfully.

"You were taking too long," Pandora shrugged.

"So, you're hiking today? At Wolf Rocks? On your twenty-fifth birthday?" Sam questioned.

"Yes," Pandora stated. "Why is that so stressful for you?"

This time, Warren elbowed Sam.

"No reason," Sam said quickly.

"Oh-kay," Pandora said slightly, turning to collect her donuts. "Can y'all tell me how to get to Harmon Street from here? I'm not sure how I got here honestly."

"I'll drive you," Sam offered.

"Ditching me?" Warren questioned.

"I'll be back before you finish eating," Sam rolled his eyes at Warren before turning back to Pandora. "I'm in the Impala out front."

"The black four door?" Pandora asked, heading towards the door.

"That's the one." Sam smiled, taking Pandora's box from her and holding the door open for her.

"So polite," Pandora commented.

"My momma raised me right," Sam shrugged.

Sam held the passenger door open for Pandora and handed her the box of donuts. Once he was behind the wheel, he started his Impala and Pandora listened to it roar to life. For a moment she wondered what year it was before the radio caught her attention.

"Are you listening to 8 Graves?" Pandora asked excitedly.

"You know 8 Graves?" Sam questioned, disbelief in his eyes.

"'Bury Me Low' is basically my lifeline," Pandora stated.

"That's my favorite 8 Graves song." Sam laughed, pulling out of the parking lot and turning south down Main Street.

"What's your favorite song?" Pandora questioned.

"'Horns' by-"

"Bryce Fox!" Pandora exclaimed. "Mine, too!"

"No way?" Sam asked in disbelief.

"Really." Pandora laughed.

"That's crazy," Sam stated. "Typically, whenever the guys get in my car, they immediately change the music. They say my music is for creepy, emo kids."

"Well, I mean, not completely wrong, but doesn't make it bad music."

"True."

Pandora smiled as Sam turned left onto Harmon Street.

"Are you staying at the Comfort Inn?" Sam questioned.

"Yeah."

Sam pulled into the parking lot of the hotel slowly, careful not to cause Pandora to drop her donuts. He parked the car and climbed out immediately, opening Pandora's door for her and taking her box again. He held out his hand and Pandora stepped out of the car. When their hands touched, Pandora felt a spark in her hand. She stood quickly, ignoring the feeling in her hand. Sam stared at her for a moment, as if captured by her. Pandora cleared her throat.

"I'm this way," Pandora stated, walking towards the stairs.

"Yeah," Sam said, following Pandora with her box.

They walked slowly, both feeling a bit awkward.

"So, Mason is Abby's boyfriend?" Sam asked.

"Yes," Pandora answered.

"Where's yours?"

"My what?"

"Your boyfriend."

"I don't have one." Pandora shrugged.

"Why not?" Sam questioned.

Pandora laughed as Sam realized what he said may have seemed rude.

"I...I mean." He started tripping over his own words.

"It's okay, Sam." Pandora smiled sweetly to him as they stopped in front of her door. "I've never had a boyfriend. I tend to keep to my small circle."

"Why?" Sam asked.

"Just always have. Abby's mom said I used to have a lot of friends, I just haven't kept very many," Pandora shrugged again.

"Abby's mom? Not yours?" Sam asked.

"Yeah. My parents died before I started school, so I live with my grandmother. Abby's parents are basically mine."

"I'm so sorry," Sam said, looking at her sadly.

"It's okay." Pandora smiled lightly. "I don't remember them all that well in all honesty. My grandfather and grandmother took care of me until my grandfather died. Now it's just my grandmother and me. Plus, Abby lives next door, and we went to school together all the way through elementary and college."

"Your own little family." Sam smiled.

"Yeah." Pandora smiled. "You mentioned your mom raised you. Any other family?"

"I never met my father, and my grandfather died before I was born. I have a little sister, but she lives with my mom still, so I don't see her very often."

"Where do they live?"

"Ohio," Sam said, seeming sad.

"How'd you get all the way here from Ohio?" Pandora asked.

"You want the truth?" Sam asked with a smirk.

"Always." Pandora smiled mischievously.

Sam hesitated for a moment before speaking again.

"I used to have this weird dream all of the time growing up. I was in the woods, and there was a wolf that would chase me. One day, I saw a sign saying Wolf Rocks Trail and looked it up. Decided to come to school in Pennsylvania for photography and haven't left since."

Pandora's smile faded as she listened to Sam describe a dream much like hers.

"Was the wolf white?" Pandora asked, knowing the color had probably drained from her face.

"No," Sam answered. "It was black. Why?"

"No reason." Pandora smiled quickly, trying to get out of the conversation as quickly as possible now. "I should get inside. Abby and Mason may begin to worry."

"Yeah," Sam agreed, a bit of tension in his voice.

Pandora took out her room key and opened the door. She took her box from Sam and headed inside. Once she set the box down, she turned towards the door, but Sam was already gone. A little confused, Pandora looked out of her door to see Sam already almost back to his car. She shut the door and turned around to look for Mason and Abby.

Mason was sitting on his and Abby's bed, a strange expression on his face. Pandora could hear the water running in the bathroom, signaling that Abby was in the shower.

"Was that one of the guys from the bar?" Mason asked.

"Yeah. Sam."

"Huh. He lives here?"

"I guess," Pandora shrugged. "I ran into him at the bakery."

"Like, actually ran into him, or he was there as well?" Mason smiled.

"Almost ran directly into him." Pandora laughed. "You know how I get when I've been running."

"That I do." Mason smiled. "What kind of donuts did you bring?"

Once Abby was out of the shower, Pandora took her turn. She let the water roll down her back as she tried to relax. It was taking everything in her to not hunt Sam down and demand more information from him. Did his family believe in the legends? How was he related to the wolves? She was so confused as to how they had both had dreams about the same place. She didn't understand what was happening.

She rolled her eyes and told herself to get it together. She finished in the shower quickly, not wanting to waste any more time. She needed to tell Abby and Mason what was going on with her. She needed to tell them about her dreams and her plan to find the cottage. Pandora didn't want to keep lying to her family anymore, and today she was finally going to open up to them as she should have years ago.

Mason and Abby were sitting on their bed when Pandora exited the bathroom. They both looked at her with concern, as if they knew Pandora was hiding something.

"Dora?" Abby used Pandora's nickname to try to draw her out of herself.

"I need to tell you guys something," Pandora stated. "But I need you guys to stay open minded."

"We promise," Mason stated, and Abby nodded in grievance.

"Where to start?" Pandora asked herself, sitting down on her bed across from them.

"How about I ask a question and you answer it?" Abby suggested, knowing how Pandora could get lost in her own thoughts.

"Okay," Pandora agreed.

"Why are we here?" Abby asked.

"A dream," Pandora answered.

"What dream?" Abby questioned.

"I've been having this reoccurring dream since I was seven. In the dream there's a wolf that chases me down. The most recent dream though, the wolf showed me where the dream was happening."

"And it was happening in Wolf Rocks?"

"Yes."

"Kind of ironic." Mason smiled.

"That's what I told the wolf." Pandora smiled.

"You could talk to the wolf?" Abby asked.

"Not really," Pandora stated. "It mostly attacked."

"So, why are we looking for a wolf that attacks you?" Abby continued.

"I think…" Pandora stopped to think for a moment. "I think I am the wolf."

"What do you mean?"

"My grandmother spoke to me the day of graduation," Pandora admitted.

"What?" Abby asked in shock.

"She spoke to me. She told me of a legend from the Civil War where the nomads from my grandfather's side of the family, the Indians from her side, and a group of African slaves got together at Wolf Rocks and did magick. The magick killed them all, but they all came back alive and some of them turned into wolves. The wolves took out half of the Confederate Army and then returned to their people as humans again."

"That's crazy," Abby stated with wide eyes.

"I know," Pandora stated. "My grandmother told me that there's a white wolf waiting for me when I turn twenty-five though. I think the wolf is me."

"So, you may be a werewolf?" Mason asked.

"No," Pandora rolled her eyes. "I don't think it's that literal. Maybe the legend was embellished as the years went on. I'm not sure. It might just be an inner thing. But I want to see if I can find the cottage."

"What cottage?" Abby asked.

"So, the dreams start in the woods. I travel through the woods to a cottage in a clearing. That's where the wolf always is."

"So, we're looking for a cottage in the woods?" Mason asked.

"And hopefully we don't get eaten by wolves in the process?" Abby added.

"Yes," Pandora answered both questions.

"So, why was Sam dropping you off?" Abby asked with a small smile.

"Sam is weird," Pandora said, confused about her conversation with him from earlier.

"How so?" Abby asked with concern.

"He had a dream like mine. He said he moved here because he dreamt of a wolf chasing him through the woods and ended up seeing a sign saying Wolf Rocks Trail."

"So, you told him about your dream, but not me?" Abby asked, offended.

"No," Pandora answered quickly. "I asked why he moved here from Ohio and he told me about his dream. My wolf was white. His was black. I didn't tell him anything about my dream."

"Oh," Abby said, sounding a bit relieved.

"It's so strange that our dreams were so similar." Pandora sighed. "I don't understand."

"Well, don't try to. We'll find the cottage first, and then we'll talk to Sam. Maybe he's from the nomads or Africans. You never know," Abby stated, trying to calm Pandora.

"Okay," Pandora nodded. "Okay."

"So, get dressed for a hike. We need to pick up water and granola bars before we explore Wolf Rocks," Abby stated.

Pandora smiled and stood. She grabbed her clothes from her bag and went to the bathroom to change, letting out a relieved sigh. Once she had her boots on, she met Mason and Abby at the truck.

"Ready?" Abby asked.

"Definitely."

CHAPTER SIX

WOLF ROCKS TRAIL

"Okay. This article says the trailhead is at the top of Linn Run Road off of Laurel Summit Road. We're supposed to park to the left at parking lot D," Abby explained.

Pandora parked her truck easily once they reached the parking lot, as no one else was around yet.

"Think it'll be easy to find?" Mason asked.

"Well, I brought rock climbing equipment for a reason Mason," Pandora stated.

"How steep is it going to be?" Abby asked.

"In my dream, I was out of breath while going up pretty easily. It's probably going to be terrible at first," Pandora answered honestly. "We need to get to the end of the trail and climb over the edge carefully. It's seventy feet down."

"Easy-peasy," Mason joked, helping Abby out of the truck.

"Everyone have their bags?" Pandora asked as she rounded the front of the truck.

Mason and Abby nodded to Pandora, and the three friends began their quest. The trail itself wasn't hard. The elevation didn't change often for the first two miles. Pandora pointed out the sign from her dream as they passed it, indicating that they were close to the climbing point above the valley. Once they reached the edge, Mason and Pandora set up their gear, anchoring to a thick tree as Abby looked over the valley, curious if she could see the cottage from where they were. Due to the trees that Pandora had pointed out to the left; they couldn't see anything.

"Down we go." Pandora smiled, stepping over the edge carefully to begin her free climb.

Abby and Mason followed soon after. Pandora was calling to them where to step and where to watch for possible snakes. When Pandora was almost to the bottom of the climb, she rappelled down the remainder of the way, landing on her feet effortlessly. She unhitched herself from the rope and took a look around. As she moved forward, towards the woods, she felt like she was being drawn closer to the cottage within. Pandora snapped out of her trance as Mason landed on his feet behind her, catching Abby once she was close enough.

"It's this way," Pandora stated, just barely above a whisper to her friends.

Abby and Mason followed close behind Pandora, careful of where they were stepping since the terrain was a bit muddy. They entered the woods, and Pandora led them to where she and the wolf had climbed the mountain. Mason whistled loudly at the distance before they continued their search. About an hour after they had reached the bottom of Wolf Rocks, Pandora spotted the rock that her dreams always began at. She sat upon it for a moment, feeling a bit frightened.

"Is everything okay, Dora?" Abby asked gently, kneeling down in front of Pandora.

"I'm terrified," Pandora stated. "My dreams always begin here, on this rock. I'm afraid that we won't find the cottage after this point. But, I'm also afraid that we will. What are we going to find when we get there?"

"Stop overthinking it. It's going to be alright." Abby smiled patiently. "We're going to be here for you either way. Besides, your dream hasn't been wrong yet. We found the sign. We found where you and the wolf climbed. You're sitting on the rock that you always dreamt about right now."

Pandora let out a small breath, deciding to tell Abby and Mason the thing she was most afraid of.

"I think I'm going to die," Pandora said shakily.

"Don't be ridiculous," Abby said, a little taken aback. "Why would you say something like that?"

"Grandma said that the white wolf only goes to a great leader who is supposed to save the descendants when they're in danger. She said that, at the age of twenty-five, the descendants could give themselves to the god that turned their ancestors into the wolves. In the stories, the people had to die," Pandora explained, trying to control her breathing. "What if we get there, and something happens, and one of us gets hurt? Grandma has me so paranoid that some Egyptian god is going to take my life. I don't even think the legend is all that true, but there's so much that she told me that makes sense."

"Then don't give yourself to the weird guy in the sky," Abby stated plainly. "Your grandmother said you can give yourself to him. That means that you have a choice. Did you ask her if you had to die?"

"I did."

"And?"

"She stopped talking."

"Of course." Abby sighed. "The woman hasn't talked in forever and the first thing she does is freak you out and not give you any real answers. Everything is going to be fine, Dora. We're right here with you. We've got you."

Pandora let out a long breath she hadn't realized she'd been holding in.

"Let's rest here for a while. It's quite beautiful honestly." Abby smiled.

Pandora nodded to her and scooted over on the rock to make room for Abby and Mason. They sat next to her, stripping their packs off their backs and setting them at their feet. Abby pulled out a water bottle for each of them as Mason passed out granola bars. Pandora soon followed their lead and passed out trail mix. They sat and ate their snacks and drank their water, staying quiet to enjoy the nature around them. Pandora felt content where she was but could still feel something inside of her stirring. The feeling inside of her wanted her to go forth, towards the direction of the cottage. She shoved the feeling down and enjoyed her time with her friends, taking in everything around her. Once they had finished admiring everything around them, the trio slipped their packs back on and headed on their way again.

"What time is it?" Abby asked.

"It's six," Mason stated. "We'll have to hurry to get back to the truck before dark."

"Unless the cottage is there, and the people in it will let us stay for the night." Abby smiled. "Maybe Sam lives there. Who knows?"

Pandora rolled her eyes and then froze in her place. She could swear something was watching her. She looked around carefully, ignoring Abby and Mason's looks of concern.

"What is it?" Abby finally asked after Pandora had turned in three slow circles.

"I thought I heard something," Pandora explained.

"It was probably just a bunny," Mason explained.

"Or a snake," Abby moaned.

"Or a wolf," Pandora shrugged before leading her friends forward again.

They stayed silent as they walked through the woods. They stepped over rocks and fallen-over trees. Pandora helped Abby navigate the muddy spots to keep her from slipping. Pandora was starting to lose hope until she saw a break in the trees ahead. She quickened her pace a bit, trying to see ahead of her. Once she reached the opening in the trees, she gasped.

There, in the middle of a clearing, stood her cottage next to its pond. Pandora felt herself drop to her knees as Mason and Abby reached her. Abby gasped when she saw the cottage, knowing it must be the one from Pandora's dreams. Mason kneeled next to Pandora and put a firm hand on her shoulder.

"It's real." He breathed. "It's real, Pandora."

Pandora could only nod as she stared forward. The cottage looked exactly how she had dreamt it would. The setting sun. The trees looking as if they were on fire. The light inside the cottage, welcoming her.

"What do we do?" Abby asked.

"We go forward," Pandora whispered, rising to her feet. "Stay behind me. If we see any animals, we run. Do you understand me?"

"Yes," Abby and Mason stated together, sounding stronger than any of them actually felt.

Pandora looked around again, waiting to see if a wolf would appear before stepping into the clearing and towards the cottage. She took a few more tentative steps before looking back towards Abby and Mason who had been waiting for her signal. She nodded to them, letting them know that everything was clear so far and they could follow her now. Mason took the first step, protecting Abby with his own body just in case danger was present.

Mason and Abby followed Pandora as she slowly continued her approach to the cabin. Pandora stopped when they got to the halfway point.

"What is it?" Mason asked.

"This is the farthest I've ever gotten," Pandora explained.

"Take your next step then," Mason urged her. "One more step and you'll be closer than you've ever been before."

Pandora let out a shaky breath and took her step. She felt as if a weight was lifted from her chest once that step was taken. Everything seemed easier than it had in her dreams now. She took another step. Then, another. She continued moving until they reached the five stairs leading up to the cottage door.

Being this close, she noticed the designs in the wood now. Each step had a wolf burned and painted into it. The bottom step had a red wolf. The next step, a grey one. A grey and white wolf, followed by a wolf with spots, led up to a black wolf as Sam had mentioned. The wood itself looked morphed, like it was in transition for something. The door was as red as the rest of the cottage but beautiful, like it belonged on the front of a luxury cabin.

Pandora took the steps one at a time and stepped up to the door. She could hear Abby and Mason waiting at the bottom of the steps for her. Pandora raised her hand, ready to knock when she heard creaking coming from both sides of her. She lowered her hand and turned her head to the left quickly. Pandora almost screamed as she stepped away from the cottage and towards the steps.

"Pandora?" Abby asked shakily.

Pandora turned to her friend and felt as if she was going to faint. Surrounding Mason, Abby, and Pandora were five wolves. The one to Pandora's left was red, the one to her right was grey and white. The one next to Abby had spots and the one next to Mason was grey. The four around them were huge, but not as big as the pure black one that was stalking slowly towards them from across the clearing.

Pandora took the steps down two at a time to reach Abby and Mason. She looked back and forth from each wolf as they all got closer to the three humans.

"What do we do?" Abby asked.

"We can't run," Pandora stated. "There's too many of them and they would just pick us off."

"Maybe we shouldn't keep eye contact?" Mason suggested, looking at the ground.

"Stand your ground," Pandora said, feeling her anxiety rising in her.

The wolves continued their approach, three of them growling at Pandora, Abby, and Mason.

"I'm so sorry," Pandora whispered to her friends. "I'm so sorry that I brought you out here. Now we're probably going to die, and it's all my fault."

"Stop talking like that. We aren't going to die," Abby said strongly. "This is your dream, remember? What did you do in your dream?"

Pandora thought for a moment, remembering how she had been attacked in every dream except for one. She thought back to her most recent dream. She knew what she needed to do. The wolves were completely around Pandora, Abby, and Mason now, each of them growling and ready to pounce. Pandora stood tall, facing the black wolf. She made eye contact as it took a defensive stance. The wolf growled at her and steadied itself. Right when Pandora felt like it was about to attack, she growled back at it.

All of the wolves froze immediately and collectively stopped growling. Slowly, each wolf began to kneel in front of her. Pandora's eyes went wide as the black wolf seemed to smile at her as it lowered its head.

"Holy shit," Mason whispered. "What do we do now?"

"We go inside," Pandora shrugged, heading back up the steps quickly, wanting to distance herself from the wolves as quickly as possible.

Abby and Mason followed close behind Pandora, careful to keep an eye on the still bent wolves. Pandora reached the door and turned the handle gently. The door opened easily, and Pandora stepped over the threshold, feeling safer and at home than she ever had before.

CHAPTER SEVEN

THE COTTAGE

The interior of the cottage was beautiful. Walking through the front door transported you into the open floor plan containing the living room to the right and kitchen to the left. The living room was a step down and had two black, leather couches on either side of it with a coffee table in between them. There was a fireplace on the center of the wall where a small fire was lit, making the room look cozy. The kitchen had an island in it to separate it from the rest of the room with six bar stools around it. Casement windows went all the way around the kitchen, giving it plenty of natural light and all the appliances looked new. There was a hallway that lead to what Pandora guessed were the rooms and bathrooms.

"Wow," Pandora heard a familiar voice say from behind her.

Pandora, Abby, and Mason all turned towards the voice quickly, finding Sam standing in the doorway. He was looking around the cottage as if he'd never seen it before. Nature and Jordan were standing behind him with expressions that matched Sam's.

"Have y'all never been in here before?" Pandora questioned. "The door wasn't locked."

"It was for us," Warren's voice rung out as he looked around Jordan into the cottage.

"Why are you standing out there instead of coming inside?" Pandora asked.

"Where'd the wolves go?" Abby asked suddenly.

"And what do you mean it was locked for you?" Mason added on.

"We have to have the White Wolf's permission to enter her home," Sam stated, looking into Pandora's eyes.

"I'm not a wolf," Pandora explained quickly.

"Not yet." Warren smiled. "But it is your birthday."

"I'm not dying for some god," Pandora said defensively.

"We all did," Loren stated.

"What?" Pandora, Abby, and Mason all asked in surprise.

"Not all of us on purpose," Sam stated.

"What do you mean?" Pandora questioned.

"May we come in?" Sam asked Pandora, keeping eye contact with her.

"Where are the wolves?" Abby asked again.

The men all rolled their eyes and let out sighs.

"Come in," Pandora said, looking directly at Sam.

Sam stared at Pandora as he took a small step into the cottage. He stood tall in the doorway, a small smile gracing his face for Pandora. Pandora sent Sam a small smile back as he stepped aside to let his small crew through behind him. The men quickly filled in and took spots on the bar stools. Sam remained standing, taking the spot next to Pandora as Abby and Mason sat on bar stools opposite of the four sitting men.

"So, do you know the legend?" Sam asked Pandora.

"Yeah," Pandora rolled her eyes. "Civil War. Nomads, Indians, and slaves. Ritual for Wepwawet. Everyone died and came back like zombies. Leaders turned into wolves. Now, at the age of twenty-five, descendants can die and become wolves. Blah, blah, blah."

Sam smiled and rolled his eyes.

"Those would be the SparkNotes." Sam smiled. "It's true by the way."

"So, you're a werewolf?" Pandora asked.

"Yeah," Sam shrugged.

"I don't believe you."

"You don't have to."

"Good, 'cause I don't."

"You will."

"Get a room." Warren laughed.

"You guys seriously think you're werewolves?" Abby questioned the sanity in the room.

"We are, and you're an outsider," Loren said to Abby.

"She belongs here more than you do," Pandora defended, finally looking away from Sam.

She sent a glare towards Loren, as if daring him to argue with her. Loren remained silent.

"You turn twenty-five in twenty minutes," Sam stated. "What are you going to do?"

"I'm not dying," Pandora stated.

"I didn't have the choice," Sam stated.

"So, this god is just going to murder me?" Pandora asked, annoyed at her lack of choices.

"I was shot three years ago," Sam stated. "Drive-by. Woke up in a hospital morgue."

"Rock climbing went wrong, a week after Sam was shot" Loren stated.

"Stabbed in a mugging last year," Jordan added.

Pandora looked to Warren and Nature.

"Mine was on purpose," Warren stated. "I always believed the legends, so I willingly gave myself."

"You killed yourself?" Abby asked.

"Yes and no," Warren stated. "My father killed me for me after I did a ritual. It killed him in the process. It's been two years."

"That's sick," Abby whispered.

"What about you?" Mason asked Nature.

"He doesn't speak," Jordan stated, his British accent heavy.

"Why not?" Mason questioned.

"He can't." Jordan shrugged.

Nature smiled gently at Pandora.

"You're the red wolf?" Pandora asked him, to which he nodded.

Pandora nodded back, realizing that he had been the only wolf not growling earlier, which reminded her.

"What was the growling about?" Pandora turned to Sam as she asked the question. "Very rude."

"That was my idea." Warren smiled, then wiggled in his seat under Pandora's glare. "I just wanted to test you as the wolf. The moment you growled, we all fell into submission though, so it kind of worked out."

"Submission?" Pandora asked the room.

"We have to listen to the White Wolf." Sam smiled.

"Stop calling me that."

Sam just shrugged and looked to his watch. "Ten minutes."

"I'm not dying, and I think we need to head back to the truck," Pandora stated, turning to Abby and Mason.

"We should go," Abby agreed.

"We need some real food anyways," Mason added. "All we've had today is donuts and trail mix."

"I can drive you to your truck," Sam stated. "There's a back road hidden in the trees that I found a few years back. That way there are no more rock-climbing incidents."

"I don't think I want to be near any of you in ten minutes," Pandora stated firmly. "So, how about you just point us to the road, and we'll walk it."

Mason groaned a little then gasped in pain as Abby hit him with her elbow.

"I'm not going to hurt you," Sam promised.

"And as much as I want to believe that, I can't," Pandora stated.

"No. I mean I actually can't."

"Why's that?"

"Descendants can't harm one another. Even when any of us are angry at each other or roughhousing, we can't injure one another. We physically stop ourselves."

"Sorry if I don't believe you at the moment, but I'm done with this conversation. I'm leaving."

Abby and Mason stood and followed Pandora to the door. The men followed the trio outside, Nature was the only one not asking Pandora to stay.

"It's your house," Sam called over everyone else. "We'll leave. I can go pick up food and bring it back to you after your birthday has passed. Will that work?"

Pandora stopped and turned to the men.

"You'll all leave?" she questioned them. "No sticking around in the dark where we can't see you?"

"And I'll be the only one to return," Sam promised to which Warren threw his hands up to him.

"Deal," Pandora agreed before an argument could begin.

Pandora, Abby, and Mason passed the five men and went back up the steps of the cottage. Pandora sat on one of the wooden rocking chairs and Abby and Mason took the porch swing. Pandora kept her eyes on the men as they went around the house. Once they were out of her sight, she stood and went to the end of the porch and watched Sam as they all went into a small opening in the trees that Pandora was sure led to the trail that Sam had mentioned earlier. Once they were out of her view, Pandora sat back down in her rocking chair and turned to her friends.

"So, this is really fucking weird," Abby stated.

"Yeah. Can we leave while they're gone?" Mason asked.

"Wait about ten minutes, and then we will. I want to make sure they aren't hiding somewhere," Pandora stated.

"Good deal," Abby agreed.

"Want to explore while we wait?" Mason asked.

"It's too dark to explore out here, so let's look around inside," Abby stated.

Abby and Mason led the way inside. Abby went into the kitchen and began going through all of the cabinets and the refrigerator. Mason went into the living room and checked under the couches. For what, Pandora did not know. Pandora ventured out of the main area and into the hallway.

In the hall, there were nine doors, the farthest one leading to a covered back porch. Pandora guessed that the rooms were all around 250 square feet. The door to her left and right were the only ones that were open. The one to the right was a master bathroom and seemed smaller than the room to her left, but not by much. She stepped into the bathroom and took a look around.

The countertop on the sink was reclaimed redwood with a his and hers sink in it. The shower alone took half of the bathroom and, instead of a curtain, had small, square plexiglass windows on the top half of one side of it. The other half was built up with white, black, and grey stones. The white toilet was in the corner with a small wall in front of it to make it less noticeable. The floor was white and silver marbled, making the bathroom seem bigger. The walls were made of the same stones from the shower.

Pandora stepped out of the bathroom and into the bedroom across from it. Instead of a wall, the accent wall was a huge window that took up the whole area, allowing the moonlight to drift in easily. The wall to the left was made of white stones and had a king bed leaning against it with fluffy white sheets and a dream catcher hanging above it. On the right wall were two doors. Pandora opened to closest one and realized it led to a walk-in closet. The second door led to another bathroom. This bathroom had his and hers sinks again but had a white clawfoot bathtub. The bathroom was all white, lighting up the small space that it took and had a small window with a white curtain in between the sink mirrors.

Pandora smiled as she looked around the bathroom before noticing that the bathroom connected to another room. She walked to the room and turned the handle but frowned when it refused to open.

"Must not be my room," Pandora said to herself.

"Pandora?" Abby's voice carried throughout the cottage that seemed much bigger than it should have been now that Pandora had counted all of the doors. "Where are you?"

"In the first bedroom," Pandora called back, heading back into the bedroom to meet her friends.

Abby and Mason were standing just inside the room, looking around it carefully.

"It's so pretty," Abby commented.

"Did you see that bathroom?" Mason asked, pointing behind him.

"This place is huge," Pandora agreed. "I didn't think it was this long."

"Have you tried the other doors?" Abby asked.

"I tried one of them, but it wouldn't open. I assume it's just not my room."

"Kind of like how the house was locked for the boys, but not for you?" Mason asked.

"I guess," Pandora shrugged. "I feel like they were lying to try to freak me out, and we're just wondering around some random person's home."

"Well, all of the kitchen appliances work, but nothing is stocked. I found linens, plates, and stuff, but no food," Abby said.

"All of the furniture looks brand new," Mason added. "A little bit of dust here and there, like no one has been around."

"It's so weird," Pandora stated. "Did you see the back door yet? I haven't gotten that far."

"Let's go together." Abby smiled.

They all went into the hall where Pandora noticed another door had opened at the end of the hall on the right.

"What the hell?" Pandora questioned out loud. "That was closed before I walked into that room."

"It was closed when we came looking for you," Abby stated, worry creeping into her voice.

"I'll go first," Mason stated, taking the initiative.

Pandora followed close behind him, leaving Abby in the back to keep her safest. They made their way to the open door quickly. Once there, Abby gasped at how beautiful the room was. The bedroom had slanted windows in the back of it and on the left wall. On the back wall was also a door leading outside to a small deck with an outside shower. There was a hanging chair with a quilt on it next to a long couch that was against the left wall. The wall to the right had a queen-sized bed in the center and two doors on the sides of it. Abby walked to the farther door and opened it to reveal a closet as Mason opened the closer door that led to a bathroom that looked like the white one in Pandora's room but with a waterfall shower in it instead of a tub.

"So, I'm guessing this is our room?" Abby asked excitedly.

"I don't know," Mason stated worriedly. "I don't trust this place. The door opened on its own and we don't know these people. We don't know this place at all."

"He's right," Pandora stated as Abby pouted. "We don't know these people. They're probably crazy. I mean, they think they're werewolves. That doesn't sound sane to me."

"It does not," Mason agreed. "Plus, they want Pandora to die and lead them in their fantasies."

"Yeah, that's fucked," Abby agreed. "Maybe we should go ahead and leave."

"Let's go," Pandora agreed, turning back towards the front door and froze.

"What is it?" Mason asked as he and Abby rushed to Pandora.

Pandora just pointed towards the front door. Mason and Abby looked at the door and Pandora in confusion.

"What are we looking at?" Abby asked. "It's just the door."

"You don't see it?" Pandora asked.

"See what?" Mason asked.

Pandora turned to her friends in disbelief.

"The wolf," she stated.

CHAPTER EIGHT

THE WHITE WOLF

Pandora stared at the Great White Wolf standing in the open doorway. It stood tall and proud, never removing its bright blue eyes from Pandora's green ones.

"There's nothing there," Abby stated.

The wolf turned and walked out of the door. Pandora immediately followed the wolf out of the front door. It waited for her at the bottom of the steps, watching to see if Pandora would continue to follow it. When she stepped to the stairs to follow it, it turned towards the pond on the side of the house. Abby and Mason followed close behind Pandora trying to get her attention.

"There's a huge ass white wolf right in front of us," Pandora pointed. "You're telling me you don't see it?"

"We don't see anything, Dora," Abby stated.

"Then maybe I've gone crazy too," Pandora whispered more to herself than to her friends.

She continued following the wolf. It led her to a small deck that reached out over the pond. It sat at the end of it, looking out at the water with grace. Pandora slowly approached it, stood next to it, and looked out towards the moon that hung in the sky. She stood with the wolf for a few moments, careful not to move too much as to not upset the wolf. Eventually she turned to the wolf, waiting for it to do something. It looked to her and seemed to smile.

"What do you want from me?" Pandora asked it.

Its smile seemed to warm towards her. It turned back to the water and laid down. Pandora took that as an invitation and sat next to the wolf, her legs hanging over deck just above the water. Pandora could hear Mason's watch alarm beeping behind her. She smiled when she realized the time.

"Happy birthday, Dora," Abby whispered from behind Pandora.

"Thank you." Pandora smiled, turning to her friend.

Pandora moved closer to the wolf and patted the empty spot next to her for Abby to sit. Mason sat behind Abby, his legs on either side of her. Abby rested her hand on Pandora's leg which Pandora took gently. Abby placed her empty hand on the wolf next to her, feeling its soft fur between her fingers.

"How do you not see her?" Pandora asked her friends. "I can literally touch her, but you can't see her."

"Is it the wolf from your dream?" Mason questioned.

"Yeah," Pandora stated. "White fur, glowing blue eyes. She's beautiful."

"So, she's a girl?" Abby asked. "You never said before."

"I'm just guess…" Pandora gasped in pain as her head fell backward.

"Pandora!" Abby screamed.

Abby's terrified face was the last thing Pandora saw before everything went black.

Pandora felt like she was floating. Everything around her was dark, pitch black. She looked around at her surroundings, trying to figure out where she was.

"Hello, child," a man's deep voice came from behind her.

She turned quickly, ready to defend herself. The man before her was half-man, half-jackal. His head was that of a black wolf with grey fur. From his neck down, he was a man dressed in gold armor with a bow on his back. He smiled at Pandora playfully.

"I have a mission for you," he stated.

"Who are you?" Pandora demanded.

"It is I, Wepwawet. The opener of ways," he stated simply.

"What do you want?" Pandora asked.

"I have a mission for you," he said again.

"I'm not dying for you," Pandora said strongly.

"I do not wish for you to."

"Well…what?" Pandora asked confused.

"The White Wolf bows to no man," Wepwawet stated. "I would never ask for you to die for me. You are to lead your pack so that they may survive what is to come."

"My pack?" Pandora asked.

"The five men who wish to accept you."

"Sam seems more like a leader than me," Pandora shrugged.

"Your mate will look out for you and assist you in any way you wish. It is up to you if he is a powerful leader beside you."

"Mate?" Pandora asked in shock. "You don't get to decide that."

"I have not. As I said, the White Wolf bows to no man. The White Wolf has always been a woman, and she chooses her own path. I know of the past and the future. Sam will be your mate in every future."

"So, there are multiple ways that this could go?" Pandora asked.

"There are infinite possibilities. I hope that you find your way to the most prosperous of them. You shall be a strong Alpha. The strongest that has ever lived."

"Has anyone ever told you that you're really vague?" Pandora questioned.

Wepwawet smiled.

"My wife has said this, yes."

"Smart woman."

"You are our decedent," Wepwawet stated.

"How?" Pandora questioned. "I'm not Egyptian. I'm Indian and white."

"Every living being is connected. You are many great generations away from my child but still one of mine nonetheless. I look forward to how you shall rule."

"I don't want to rule," Pandora stated. "I want to do whatever I want with my life without worrying about things that are out of my control. Let me go."

"I cannot. Unfortunately, the choice is not ours to make. You are in great danger, child."

"I am not a child!" Pandora yelled.

"You are my child." Wepwawet smiled. "You will grow in every stage of life, and what is a child besides a growing being? We are all children in our own ways. This danger will come soon. You must be ready. You have been running for a long time now. I think it is time that you return to your pack. Your mate demands your presence."

Wepwawet was upon Pandora in a moment. He pushed her head back with his hand, causing a blinding light. Pandora squeezed her eyes shut and tried to pull away from him.

"Pandora!"

Pandora opened her eyes to find Sam above her.

Pandora sat up quickly and looked around. Abby was crying in Mason's arms reaching for Pandora now. Abby threw her arms around Pandora, squeezing Pandora hard. Pandora held her quickly, trying to catch her breath.

"What happened?" Pandora asked Mason.

"You fell backwards and started screaming. Then, you just stopped moving. We thought you were dying, but you were still breathing and had a heartbeat," Mason explained.

"I was so scared," Abby whispered, still crying. "I thought you were gone."

"I'm alright," Pandora told Abby, holding her tighter and looking to Sam. "When did you get here?"

"I got here just a second before you woke up," Sam stated, staring into Pandora's eyes in confusion. "I was about to get some food to bring back, but I felt like I needed to be here."

"I saw him," Pandora whispered, causing Abby to pull away. "I saw Wepwawet. He talked to me. He told me he didn't want me to die and that I was in danger."

"What kind of danger?" Mason asked as Sam puffed out his chest and looked around as if someone was going to jump out at them any moment.

"He didn't say. He said I was in danger, and I needed to lead my pack so that they would survive. Then, he told me my mate needed me, and he touched my head, and I was back here," Pandora rushed.

"Your mate?" Abby asked as Sam turned back to Pandora.

"Yeah," Pandora said, looking at her hands, refusing to make eye contact with anyone. "He said my mate was demanding I return."

After a few beats of silence, Pandora looked to Sam, catching his eye immediately. Sam looked at her in fascination before looking at her hands. He took her left hand quickly, examining her finger.

"What are you doing?" Pandora asked.

"When did you get this?" Sam asked, holding Pandora's hand up to show her a tattoo that had appeared on her ring finger.

"What the hell?" Pandora yelled, pulling her hand away from Sam and looking at her hand angrily.

"There's one on your arm, too," Abby stated, lifting Pandora's sleeve.

Pandora looked at her arm and gasped. She immediately stood and took off her overshirt to reveal tattoos climbing around her body.

On her upper arm, Pandora had a tattoo of a wolf with trees behind it, its snout raised as if in a howl, in all black. Connected to that tattoo was a woman's face, her hair hanging down around the wolf and trees below it with what looked like a wolf's face as a winter hat on top of her head, a red streak across her face being the only color. Under her arm, along her ribs, was the side view of a naked woman floating, a red wolf erupting from her chest. Pandora could see that there were tattoos on her back, but she couldn't see them, so she looked to left side of her body. On the inner crook of her elbow, there was a wolf's face with a crescent moon overlapping it, and on her shoulder, there was a wolf running sideways, the full moon behind it.

Pandora looked at her chest and noticed ink over her heart. She pulled her shirt down a bit and saw the small pup looking up to her. Pandora smiled gently at that one before looking at her hand again. The tattoo on her finger was a simple black circle. She looked to Sam and saw a white circle around his finger before looking back into his eyes again.

"When did you get yours?" Pandora asked.

"When I died," Sam stated. "But you didn't die."

"No," Pandora answered even though it wasn't a question. "Let's go inside."

Sam immediately grabbed Pandora's shirt from where she had dropped it and dipped his head to her in a small bow as he handed it to her. Pandora walked next to Abby towards the cabin, Mason on Abby's other side. Once to the door, Pandora noticed that a new wolf had been added to the collection before her. Above the door, a painted white wolf stood tall. Pandora smiled and continued inside. She looked down the hall and saw that the door next to hers had opened once Sam stepped inside.

"I think that's going to be your room," Pandora stated, pointing to the open door. "Guess I know where the other bathroom door goes to."

Pandora took a seat on the couch and crossed her legs under her. Abby sat next to Pandora as her stomach growled.

"Maybe we should go get food instead," Pandora suggested.

"I can still leave?" Sam said, asking Pandora if that was what she wanted with his eyes.

"No," Pandora rushed out before correcting her speed. "I mean, I want to talk to you."

"Alone?" Mason asked with a smirk.

"Shut up," Pandora rolled her eyes.

Sam smiled and passed his car keys to Mason.

"She sticks in fourth gear sometimes, but other than that, it's a smooth ride if you know how to drive stick," Sam informed him. "She's parked about five minutes into the path if you want to go pick up some food for everyone. My wallet is in the center console."

"I can buy the food, man. You're letting me drive your car." Mason smiled, helping Abby to her feet.

Mason kissed Pandora's forehead before leading Abby out of the door. Sam sat on the coffee table across from Pandora. Pandora shivered a bit which caused Sam to grab the blanket that was across the back of the couch and wrap it around her. Pandora thanked him with a small smile as he sat back down across from her.

"Are you okay?" Sam asked.

"Yeah," Pandora stated. "I just feel weird. And cold."

"I felt that too." Sam smiled. "I was shivering in the middle of July for no reason. It was crazy."

"That sounds terrible." Pandora laughed. "I can just imagine you wrapped in coats and blankets trying to stay warm but ending up with heatstroke."

Sam smiled a crooked grin before nodding.

"I stayed cold until I transformed for the first time," he stated.

"Transformed?" Pandora asked. "Into your wolf?"

"Yeah."

"How do you do that?"

"It was the first full moon after my birthday." Sam laughed at the irony. "I can transform whenever I want now, but before that I didn't know what was wrong with me. I thought it was PTSD from everyone thinking I was dead and from waking up in a morgue."

"I'm sorry," Pandora stated, putting her hand on Sam's.

She felt a spark again when their skin touched. Instead of pulling away, she looked into Sam's eyes. He stared back at her, his eyes wide and intense.

He let out a ragged breath, trying to control himself in a way. Pandora felt herself wanting to reach for him, to hold him in her hands. Her breathing was coming out harder than she wanted it to, giving away the fact that something was happening inside of her.

"Wepwawet said that you are my mate in every future," Pandora stated, licking her lips that had suddenly gone dry.

The flick of her tongue caught his attention, and he stared at her lips as if he was drowning.

"Is that why I haven't been able to stop thinking about you since I saw you walk into that bar?" Sam questioned.

"You noticed me when I walked in?" Pandora asked, causing Sam to look into her eyes again.

"I couldn't take my eyes off of you. When that man grabbed you and you started yelling for help, I don't know what happened. It was like I blacked out when I saw you in danger. If the guys hadn't been there, I think I would've killed him."

"That's insane." Pandora breathed.

"I know," Sam stated.

Pandora realized that she was only a few inches from Sam's face now. She took a deep breath and sat back, shaking her head to try to release herself from the spell she seemed to be under.

"What's happening to me?" she asked herself, taking her hand from Sam's and holding her own face.

"It's a full moon tonight," Sam stated.

"Why haven't I transformed?" Pandora asked, looking to Sam again.

"Maybe you aren't letting yourself," Sam shrugged.

"Wepwawet said I didn't bow to anyone. Maybe that includes myself," Pandora stated. "I might be trying to block it out."

"Why though?" Sam asked.

"I'm afraid of losing control," Pandora stated simply. "I'm a control freak in every sense of the term. If I can't control the situation, I lose my grip on reality."

"Understandable," Sam stated. "You've lost a lot in your life. Having some stability and control is how you keep yourself from losing again."

"But, how do I give in to something if I don't want to?" Pandora asked.

"Let's go outside," Sam stated, standing and holding out his hand for Pandora to take.

Pandora stood on her own, eyeing his hand like it was the enemy. She walked past him and out the front door. Sam followed close behind, careful not to reach out and touch Pandora like he wanted to. Once outside, Sam led Pandora to the middle of the clearing.

"Just breath," he told her. "Slow, deep breaths."

Pandora closed her eyes and listened to Sam's voice.

"In through your nose. Out through your mouth. Nice and slow. There is something inside of you that you have never felt before. It's creeping just under your skin, trying to break through."

"This sounds like a horror movie," Pandora stated.

She heard Sam's deep laugh and smiled.

"Let me try something?" he asked, causing Pandora's eyes to open.

Sam stepped towards her and reached for her, stopping just before making contact with her skin. Pandora nodded her acceptance of his touch. Gently, he laid his hands on her arms. Pandora shivered at the contact and took a deep breath, forcing herself to not lean into him. She could see Sam fighting his urges as well but holding back nonetheless.

"Keep breathing," Sam demanded. "You feel that spark?"

Pandora nodded.

"Give into it," Sam said.

"I don't know if that's a good idea," Pandora stated.

"It's part of the transformation. It's part of giving in. If you give in to one thing at a time, it might help," Sam stated.

Pandora nodded, but waited a moment before closing her eyes again. She felt Sam's finger sliding up and down her arms as he tried to keep her warm. She put her hand on his chest where his heart rested and felt it rushing at her touch. She opened her eyes and looked into Sam's deep brown eyes with her own green ones, seeing the specks of honey that reflected there. Finally, Pandora gave into her feelings.

Quickly she leaned forward and wrapped her arms around his neck. Sam lifted her easily as Pandora wrapped her legs around his waist. He held her up with one arm under her and the other around her back. Their lips crashed together, and Sam let out a small growl at the contact.

Pandora could feel something inside of her rising and gasped. Sam set her down quickly and took a few steps back as Pandora fell to the ground on all fours. She could feel something inside of her, clawing its way out, causing a pain she had never felt before. She let herself go, knowing it was the only way to survive what was happening to her. She felt hot, hotter than she had ever felt before. She pulled at her shirt, lifting it over her head as she kicked off her shoes.

Pandora turned onto her back and scratched at the ground, letting a scream rip through her. The scream turned into a howl as her spine cracked forwards and then back again. Pandora rolled to her stomach and looked at her hands. Her nails had grown and turned into black claws. She gasped as white fur broke out across her body where previously there had been skin. She looked for Sam, wanting him to save her.

"Just let it happen!" Sam called over her screaming. "It won't hurt if you give in!"

Pandora groaned and put her forehead to the ground. Her breathing was erratic as she closed her eyes.

"This is how I die," Pandora thought to herself, finally giving in to all of the pain.

The pain stopped immediately, and she gasped at the reprieve. She looked up to Sam to see him standing close to her with a huge smile on his face. His eyes were wide with amazement as he gazed upon her. He reached towards her and Pandora reached for him. That was when she noticed that her hand was not a hand anymore, but a paw. She stood immediately and noticed that her arms had turned into legs covered with white fur. She turned to Sam and tried to talk, but all that came out was a small yelp like a dog.

"It's okay." Sam smiled. "You're okay. I'm right here."

Pandora stepped towards him and rubbed her head against his hand. He patted her head gently and let out a small laugh.

"May I join you?" he asked Pandora.

Pandora nodded her head quickly and stepped back to watch Sam transform. He lifted his shirt off of himself and then turned away from Pandora as he stripped off his pants and boxers. Pandora watched as the skin across Sam's back rippled. Sam bent down onto his hands and knees and let out a low growl as black fur broke out across his skin. Pandora blinked and, when she opened her eyes again, a black wolf stood facing her.

CHAPTER NINE

TRANSFORMATION

Sam yelped at Pandora, jumping towards her. Pandora barked back and spun around in a circle, feeling a breeze lifting her fur. Pandora lifted her head to the moon and howled. Sam joined her until she lowered her head again and looked to him, smiling. Sam ran towards the woods, challenging her. Pandora chased after him, matching his strides easily.

Sam turned and snipped at her legs with his teeth, causing Pandora to laugh and jump over him without incident. Sam followed behind her, trying to keep up. Pandora picked up her pace and ran as fast as her new legs could carry her. She heard Sam bark from behind her, but Pandora continued her run, feeling the wind whip through her fur as she easily avoided trees and rocks. She stopped once she reached her rock from her dream. Pandora climbed onto her rock and waited for Sam to catch up to her.

Once he did, he seemed to frown at her. Pandora raised her ears and cocked her head to the side to poke fun at Sam for losing their race. Sam barked at her again and pounced at her. Pandora let him knock her off her rock and onto the ground. She felt a warmth rise in her stomach as they wrapped around one another in a play fight. Pandora nibbled at Sam's front leg. Sam hopped out of the way quickly and pinned Pandora to the ground. Pandora yelped and poked her nose into Sam's. His eyes widened, and he smiled at Pandora.

Pandora knocked Sam off her easily with strength she hadn't had before that night. She turned and ran back towards the cottage, running slow enough for Sam to keep up this time. Sam barked at her and tried pulling ahead. Pandora picked up her pace, easily reaching the clearing before Sam. She stopped in front of her clothes and sat down. Looking to Sam, she tilted her head, asking how to change back. Sam changed quickly; Pandora averted her eyes so she wouldn't see Sam naked.

Once Sam had his pants back on, he turned to Pandora.

"All you have to do to turn back, is will it to happen. It only hurts the first time you turn. After that, it's effortless. Like the wolf is a part of you now," Sam explained, kneeling down in front of her. "Take your time. I'll turn around, and here are my boxers that way you have something to wear. Your pants kind of shredded when you turned. I should've warned you. I'm sorry."

Sam turned away from Pandora as she sat patiently. Pandora concentrated, trying to will herself as Sam had stated. She pushed the wolf back down as she painlessly turned back into her human form. Once she had turned, she pulled on her tank top and Sam's boxers quickly, noticing another tattoo, this one covering her upper left thigh. This one was the face of a wolf with glowing blue eyes. Surrounding its outer fur were the colors blue, pink, red, and orange, as if its fur had been painted.

"You can look now," Pandora stated.

Sam turned to her and smiled as he looked into her eyes.

"Want to go back inside?" Sam asked her.

Pandora smiled, walking with Sam into the cottage. She made her way to the door that would lead to Sam's room. Sam followed her closely. She stopped in the doorway and stepped aside to allow Sam to look into his room. Sam whistled low as he looked around the room. His room almost completely matched Pandora's, but there was a grey quilt at the end of his bed instead of the fluffy white sheets that decorated Pandora's. Pandora passed Sam and headed to the window that took up the whole wall.

"I think that opens," Sam stated, walking over to the side of the window wall and pulling a chain.

As he pulled the chain, the window began to lift like a garage door. Pandora wondered briefly if hers opened as well before realizing that the window led to a covered porch that connected to hers. On the small porch, there were twinkle lights and a small cot just big enough for two people. There were candles lining the banister and a small outdoor table. Pandora smiled at the simple yet romantic setting before her. Sam just smiled at Pandora as she sat on the small cot and looked into the woods.

Sam sat next to her, careful not to touch Pandora in the process. Pandora smiled at his consideration and continued to watch the woods. She could see lights and figured Mason and Abby had returned with food.

"They didn't take long." Sam smiled.

"How long were we out there?" Pandora questioned.

"About half an hour," Sam stated.

"Really?" Pandora asked in surprise. When Sam smiled, she continued, "It felt so much faster than that."

"It always does." Sam smiled. "Time flies when you're having fun."

Pandora smiled to him and waited for her friends to come through the trees.

"So, I think we should talk," Sam stated nervously.

"About?" Pandora asked, knowing Sam meant the kiss and what Wepwawet had said about them being mates.

"Well, firstly, that kiss was the best moment of my life," Sam let out.

Pandora smiled and felt a blush creep into her cheeks. She looked down at her hands for a moment to try to get her face to go back to its normal color before finally making eye contact with Sam who had a goofy grin on his face.

"It was pretty amazing," Pandora agreed. "I've never kissed anyone like that before."

"Well, you did say you've never had a boyfriend," Sam stated.

"I've had a few flings before," Pandora stated and let out a laugh when Sam seemed jealous. "Nothing ever meant anything serious, Sam. You can breathe."

Sam let out a shaky breath and looked towards the woods as Abby and Mason came out of the trees.

"I think they have suitcases," Sam stated.

"They probably stopped at the hotel and grabbed our stuff," Pandora nodded. "I'll go help them. I need to eat and see if the hot water works."

"I'll come with," Sam stated, hoping over the banister easily and then holding out a hand to help Pandora.

Pandora took his hand and allowed him to help her over, feeling the spark, but ignoring it the best that the two of them could. They walked to Abby and Mason, reaching them easily, still standing close enough to each other to feel the warmth radiating from one another. Abby gave Pandora a weird smile as she approached, noticing the closeness of the two.

"So, what happened?" Mason asked. "Did you turn into a hairy, little creature?"

"And why are you wearing boxers?" Abby asked, demanding the answer to her question.

"About that." Pandora laughed, looking down at the boxers she had forgotten about. She looked back to her friends and let out a breath. "There's something that I need to show you guys."

CHAPTER TEN

GRANDFATHER'S SECRETS

"Holy shit!" Abby yelled out, staring at the wolf that was now facing her where Pandora had just been. Mason turned and looked at the wolf, having had adverted his eyes when Pandora had begun undressing suddenly.

"What the fuck?" Mason breathed, stepping in front of Abby and covering her with his body.

"It's okay," Sam told Pandora's friends. "It's Pandora."

"That is a wolf," Mason stated, obviously trying to come to some sort of reasonable explanation.

"The wolf is Pandora," Abby stated, looking to Mason. "I saw her change. Holy shit."

"What?" Mason asked. "What do you mean you saw her change."

Mason looked to the white wolf and gasped as it shifted back into Pandora's naked form. Mason stared at her for a moment before he fainted.

"Shit," Pandora stated, racing to catch Mason before he hit his head.

Sam caught him easily though.

"I've got him," Sam stated, not looking at Pandora. "Go ahead and get dressed."

Pandora dressed quickly and followed Sam and Abby into the cottage, Sam carrying Mason. Sam set Mason on one of the couches and tried shaking him awake. When it didn't work, he looked to the girls.

"Maybe we should toss him into the pond? Water might wake him up," Sam shrugged.

"Or we could pour some water on him instead of almost drowning him," Pandora stated.

Abby ran to the kitchen and grabbed a glass from a cabinet, filling it with water before returning.

"Stand back," Abby stated.

Sam stood next to Pandora as Abby poured water onto Mason's face. Mason woke with a start and swung his arms out, as if fighting an invisible force. Mason looked around wildly, looking from Abby to Sam and, finally, resting his eyes on Pandora.

"You...you..."

"Yeah," Pandora stated, raising her arms and taking a step towards Mason.

"But...how?" Mason asked, standing from the couch.

"Magick, I guess?" Pandora shrugged. "Sam taught me how to turn while you guys were gone. We had just changed back not too long before you got here. Unfortunately, my clothes ripped up when I turned."

"You can turn into a wolf too?" Mason asked Sam.

"Yeah." Sam shrugged. "It's pretty awesome. I would definitely suggest you try it sometime if you, ya'know, could."

Pandora and Abby rolled their eyes at Sam.

"Are you alright?" Pandora asked Mason.

"Are you?" Mason questioned back, worry wearing down on his face.

"I've never felt better honestly." Pandora smiled.

"What's it like?" Abby asked, sitting on the arm of the couch.

"Freeing." Pandora smiled widely. "It's like when I run, but more."

Abby nodded, smiling at her friend.

"I feel like I need to be put in a mental hospital," Mason stated. "This shouldn't be possible."

"It shouldn't," Pandora agreed. "It is happening though."

Mason just nodded, not sure what to do with himself.

"We should eat," Pandora stated. "After that, I need to shower. I smell like woods and sweat."

"You kind of smell like dog." Abby laughed.

"Shut up." Pandora laughed.

Sam and Mason went outside to retrieve the luggage and food as Abby and Pandora waited at the kitchen island.

"So, did something happen while we were gone?" Abby asked Pandora.

"Yeah. I turned into a wolf. Were you not listening?" Pandora laughed.

"I meant with you and Sammy boy." Abby rolled her eyes.

"We may have kissed a bit," Pandora mumbled.

"What was that?" Abby asked.

"We kissed!" Pandora yelled. "We kissed, and it was amazing, and oh my goodness, I don't know what to do when he touches me! It's as if every nerve in my body wants to jump on him! It's crazy!"

Abby laughed as Pandora put her head down, making whining noises in the process.

"This is going to be great. Pandora finally has feelings for someone, and it happens to be with someone who can understand everything that she's going through," Abby said to herself.

"Stop that," Pandora frowned, knowing Abby felt like she was going to be pushed aside with everything that was happening to Pandora. "You are the most important person in my life and that will not change because some deity has turned me into some Alpha, warrior creature."

"I know you would never push me away, Dora." Abby smiled sadly. "I also know that, when Mason and I first got together, I didn't make as much time for you as I should have. You have even more going on with yourself now than I've ever dealt with in my life. I'm just curious how I'll fit into your new life."

"You'll fit." Pandora smiled, taking Abby's hand. "You will always fit. You're my puzzle piece, remember?"

Abby smiled at the memory from kindergarten. Pandora had been frustrated in class because a piece to the puzzle she had been working on had gone missing. Abby had appeared with the piece a few minutes after Pandora had begun throwing a fit, helping Pandora set the piece into its rightful place. Ever since, Pandora had called Abby her puzzle piece whenever Abby needed reassurance.

The boys finally came back into the house, setting the luggage by the hall and the food on the bar.

"How does this place exist?" Sam asked, looking around the kitchen.

"I have no clue, but I feel like all of this stuff is brand new," Pandora stated, taking fries from the bag in front of her.

"It looks brand new. Just look at the fridge. I've wanted one like this for years now," Sam stated, opening the grab-and-go door that only opened part of the fridge.

"Yeah, that's actually awesome." Pandora laughed.

"All of this stuff is awesome." Mason smiled. "I mean, the rooms alone are amazing. The kitchen is all brand new. Somehow there's electricity and running water. I don't understand how it got here."

"Have you ever tried looking for information about this place?" Abby asked Sam.

"Yeah," Sam commented. "This land is owned by some guy named Robert Williams."

"What?!" Abby and Pandora yelled at the same time.

"Robert Williams?" Sam shrugged. "You know him or something? I couldn't find anything about him in the state except that he owned the clearing land and some of the woods, including the trail."

"Robert Williams is dead," Pandora stated clearly.

"How do you know?" Sam asked.

"He was my grandfather," Pandora stated, feeling tears fill her eyes.

Abby squeezed Pandora's hand hard, trying to help Pandora hold herself together.

"He never told you about this place?" Abby asked.

"No," Pandora stated, shaking her head. "He never said anything about Pennsylvania or the wolves. Grandma is the one who told me the legend. Do you think she knows about this place?"

"She must," Abby stated, feeling just as confused as Pandora.

"Why didn't she tell you about the trail then?" Sam asked.

"Well, it took her ten years to even tell me about the legend, so I don't honestly know," Pandora stated, feeling herself become angry.

"Hey, hey," Sam said, sitting next to Pandora and taking her free hand in his. "It's okay. I'm right here."

"I'm fine," Pandora stated, standing and taking her hands back from the two people around her. "I just need some time."

With that, Pandora dropped her fries back into the bag of food that she had been given. Grabbing her food bag and suitcase, she went to her room, shutting the door behind her. She flipped a switch next to the door and looked around as the room lit up with fairy lights that wrapped around the ceiling in a canopy effect, drooping down the walls in various places. Pandora sat in a small white chair that looked towards the window and absentmindedly continued eating.

She felt lost and confused, trying to figure out who she was now. She knew that she was still Pandora, but now she felt like she needed to be more than that. She was angry with her grandmother for not having spoken in so many years, choosing to speak only when it benefitted herself rather than helping Pandora. Pandora knew in her heart that her grandmother was probably just looking out for her and wanted her to discover to cottage in her own time, but it still threw Pandora how unhelpful her grandmother had actually been.

What if Abby or Mason had fallen during the climb? What if one of them had been bitten by a rattle snake? They could have been hurt and no one would have been able to help them. Her grandmother had put her and her friends into unnecessary danger. Pandora couldn't forgive her grandmother for that, not at the moment anyways.

Pandora finished her food and grabbed her shower bag out of her suitcase. She went into the bathroom across the hall from her room, wanting a shower more than a bath. She could hear Abby, Mason, and Sam talking quietly in the kitchen still but ignored them as she shut the bathroom door. Pandora felt relief when she found towels in a cabinet next to the sinks and began the shower, sighing as she stepped under the spray of the hot water. She scrubbed at her skin with her soap and washed her hair three times before she felt that she was clean again. When she finally laid in her bed, under the softest blankets she'd ever had, she felt sleep enter her mind immediately.

CHAPTER ELEVEN

TENSION

Pandora woke to the sun shining into her window. She opened her eyes slowly, adjusting to the light. She smiled and cuddled into her blankets further, wishing to never leave them. A small knock at her door caused her to groan as she covered her face with her pillow, hoping it would stop the knocking.

"Dora?" Abby asked, opening the door slightly.

"No one's home," Pandora called, still hiding under her mountain of blankets.

Pandora felt her bed shift and the covers beside her lift a bit before feeling Abby wrap her arm around Pandora's back. Pandora rolled to face Abby, smiling at her in the process.

"Are we going to hide under here all day?" Abby asked.

"That sounds nice." Pandora smiled, closing her eyes and cuddling up to Abby. Abby let out a small laugh, holding Pandora to her.

"You're a mess," Abby stated.

"Always." Pandora laughed.

Pandora's stomach growled, causing Pandora to groan again.

"We should go get food," Abby said.

"Nooooo!" Pandora yelled, digging her head under her pillow again.

Pandora could hear laughing coming from the door and popped her head up to glare at Mason and Sam in the doorway. They both just smiled at her, knowing her heart wasn't in the glare. Pandora laid her head down again to stare at Abby.

"Pancakes sound really good," Pandora stated.

"And bacon," Abby added.

"Hash browns," Mason added.

"Scrambled eggs," Sam added.

"Damn it," Pandora whispered, sitting up.

"Have you seen the tattoo on your back yet?" Abby asked.

"No. Can't really stretch that far." Pandora smiled. "Take a picture of it for me."

Abby pulled her phone out of her pocket and took a picture for Pandora. Pandora took the phone and smiled. Her left shoulder had what looked like a potion bottle with a wolf on it howling at the moon. Her right shoulder had what was meant to be a yin-yang symbol, but with a white wolf and a woman. In between her shoulder blades was a large wolf with its head tilted back, orange, purple, and black swirls bleeding out of it.

"How many tattoos did you get?" Pandora asked Sam.

"A few." Sam smiled. "I don't think any of us have as many as you though. You're also the only one that has more than one with color on it."

"I'm a rainbow." Pandora smiled, standing a stretching. "I'm going to change and meet y'all in the living room."

"Yes, ma'am." Sam smiled, exiting the room with Mason.

Abby stayed behind, shutting the door behind the boys.

"So, Sam is nice." Abby smiled.

"Yeah?" Pandora asked. "How long were y'all up talking to him last night?"

"Not too late. I was pretty tired."

"Same."

"Have you called your grandma?"

"No," Pandora shrugged. "I don't know what to say to her right now. I'll probably just text her and tell her I found the cottage and nothing else. See if she responds with something other than emojis for once."

Abby smiled and leaned on the door behind her. She watched Pandora carefully as Pandora tried to pick something to wear.

"Are you looking for something cute?" Abby asked as Pandora threw another shirt to the side.

"Yes," Pandora whined. "I don't know why though."

Abby laughed. "I'll be right back with something."

With that, Abby left Pandora alone for a moment. Pandora changed out of Sam's boxers that she had kept on last night, finding comfort in wearing them. She quickly pulled on her own underwear and a pair of dark jeans, tossing on her real bra in the process as her sports bra had been destroyed the night before. She sighed as she sat in her chair, waiting for Abby to return. She didn't have to wait long as Abby entered the room almost as soon as Pandora sat down.

"That didn't take long," Pandora commented.

"I had a feeling this was going to happen this morning." Abby smiled, tossing a shirt into Pandora's waiting hands.

Pandora smiled at the see-through Rolling Stones shirt in her hand.

"Really?" Pandora asked.

"Really." Abby smiled. "Wear your mom's leather jacket with it. Don't pretend you didn't bring it with you. You take it everywhere."

Abby left the room again, giving Pandora privacy to pull the shirt over her head and take her mother's jacket out of her suitcase. Pandora smelled the leather and could swear she could still smell her mother's shampoo on it, like roses and honey. Pandora sighed, slipping her arms into the jacket and pulling her hair out of it. She brushed her hair and teeth quickly, ready for the day to start.

She zipped the jacket halfway up and stepped out of her room and into the living room. Sam's attention immediately left Abby and Mason's conversation when he felt Pandora enter the room. His eyes locked on hers for a moment, a warm smile lighting his face before he saw what she was wearing. His eyes went wide and his mouth opened slightly. He gaped at her, trying to find words to say.

"Should we get going?" Pandora asked, breaking the tension that had been building in her stomach as Sam had stared at her hungrily. "I'd like to get my truck today."

"You might have a ticket," Abby stated.

"That sucks," Pandora groaned, covering her face with her hands for a moment before grabbing her keys from the kitchen island and leading everyone out of the door. "Are the boys meeting us for breakfast?"

"Yeah." Sam smiled, following close behind Pandora. "They're at the IHOP already. Just waiting on us."

"Well, let's go." Pandora smiled to him, taking his hand easily and pulling him next to her.

She smiled when Sam let out a shaky breath. Pandora felt the small spark between them, but kept her grip, determined to get past the feeling every time they touched. Sam let go of her hand suddenly and wrapped his arm around her shoulders. It cut off skin-to-skin contact, but they were still touching. Pandora rolled her eyes and smiled to herself.

Once they reached Sam's car, Sam held the passenger door open for Pandora. She climbed in gracefully, feeling more confident than she had in a while. Mason helped Abby into the backseat before climbing in after her. Sam started his car and turned it around, leading them away from the cottage and towards town. Pandora looked out the window and watched the trees go by as Sam drove, his music low to allow conversation.

"It's beautiful out here." Pandora smiled.

"It is." Sam smiled. "Wait until fall."

"You wait until fall." Abby laughed. "Pandora will have that cottage decked out in Halloween decorations like it's no one's business."

"True." Mason smiled.

"Is Halloween your favorite holiday?" Sam asked curiously.

"Yes." Pandora smiled. "What's yours?"

"Fourth of July." Sam smiled.

"You just want to blow stuff up, don't you?"

"Yes."

Everyone laughed as Sam finally pulled out of the trees and onto a deserted road. The road led to the parking lot where Pandora's truck sat untouched except for a note on the windshield wiper.

"Let's grab the ticket, and when we come back, we can grab the truck," Sam stated.

"Okay." Pandora sighed, stepping out of the car once Sam had stopped. She grabbed the ticket and climbed back into the car.

"Only forty dollars." Pandora smiled. "I can afford to park anywhere I want here."

"How much would that ticket be back home?" Sam asked.

"Well, we live in a college town near the beach, so around $150 on a day where the cops are feeling generous," Pandora rolled her eyes.

"I've never been to the beach," Sam stated. "I've always wanted to go."

"Pandora was basically a fish growing up." Abby smiled. "We went to the beach every day after school when we didn't have track practice."

"So, swimming and track?" Sam asked.

"Yes." Pandora smiled. "The swimming was for fun though, not sport."

"Ah." Sam smiled, pulling into the IHOP parking lot.

Sam opened Pandora's door before she could climb out herself. Abby and Mason smiled at how quickly he had moved to let Pandora out.

"I can open my own doors." Pandora smiled.

"I'm aware." Sam smiled. "Again though, my momma raised me right."

"I noticed." Pandora smiled, pulling Sam's arm over her shoulder again.

"Don't forget to text Grandma," Abby stated before they got to the door. Pandora let out a low growl, causing Sam to jump.

"Sorry," she whispered her apology to him.

Sam just let out a small laugh and allowed Pandora to walk into the restaurant ahead of him. Once inside, Jordan waved them over to the tables that they had pushed together to occupy. Pandora sat across from Nature, allowing Sam to sit at her left and Abby to sit to her right, Mason on Abby's other side.

"Morning." Warren smiled, sipping his coffee with his eyebrow raised. "How was your night?"

"We can talk about it later," Sam demanded, making the men drop the subject automatically.

Pandora smiled as Sam had taken control of the situation, happy to know he would be looking out for her. A waitress came over and got Pandora, Mason, and Abby's drink orders, dropping off a coffee in front of Sam. He smiled his thanks to her, causing her to blush. Pandora set her hand on Sam's knee, causing Sam to rest his arm behind her chair with ease, making it known to the waitress that he was with someone. The waitress pouted for a moment before smiling again, returning with their drinks a moment later.

"The usual boys?" the waitress asked the group, causing all of the men to nod. "And for you?"

Pandora let Abby and Mason order before her and then handed the menus back to the waitress gently. Once the waitress left, Warren and Loren began laughing.

"What?" Sam asked.

"So, are you two together now?" Jordan asked, a twinkle in his eye.

"Shut up," Sam rolled his eyes, throwing a straw at Jordan.

Abby let out a small laugh and the table broke into different conversations. Pandora smiled to Nature before pulling out her phone to text her grandmother.

"Found the cottage. Mad at you."

She sent the text and put her phone under her leg, listening to everyone around her as she waited patiently for her phone to vibrate. Pandora had expected the smile emoji that she received and tucked her phone back under her leg instead of responding. She smiled as Abby laughed at whatever Jordan had just said. Sam squeezed Pandora's shoulder to get her attention. She turned to him and saw him holding his phone out to her.

She took it, realizing he had made a contact in his phone for her to fill out. She put her information in and sent herself a text, ignoring her phone this time before handing his back to him. He smiled and sent her another text. She pulled out her phone and looked at the two messages.

"Sam

Dinner tonight?"

Pandora smiled and nodded to him.

"I'm cooking though. I promised Abby. We can eat on the back porch so that we're alone."

"Should we invite the guys to see their rooms today?"

"Yes"

"So, we need to go grocery shopping and then we should all head to the cottage?" Sam asked Abby out loud to get everyone's attention.

"Sounds like a plan." Pandora smiled. "You guys want to see your rooms, right?"

"Our rooms?" Warren asked curiously.

"You each have a room in the cottage," Pandora nodded, sipping her drink. "Ours all opened last night once everyone left. I figure yours will open when you go back."

"Grocery shopping and then the cottage." Jordan smiled. "Sounds like a good day."

"Are you going to cook for me?" Abby asked.

"I already told you I would." Pandora smiled.

"You can cook?" Loren asked rudely.

"Can you not?" Pandora asked, just as rude.

Loren rolled his eyes, saying nothing as the waitress appeared with their food, two people helping her carry all of their meals. Sam glared at Loren as Loren stabbed his eggs aggressively.

"Your food isn't going to run away from you," Jordan stated.

Loren ignored Jordan and continued eating, more careful of his strength this time though.

"We should get the truck before shopping," Abby stated, trying to break the tension. "It'll hold more than Sam's car."

"Can we use your truck, Nature?" Jordan asked his silent neighbor.

Nature nodded, smiling. Everyone ate silently, collectively ignoring the glares between Sam and Loren. Once finished, Sam paid before Pandora could argue.

"Can you ride with Nature?" Sam whispered to Pandora. "I need to talk to Loren."

"Yeah," Pandora nodded. "What about Abby and Mason?"

"I'll ask Warren to take them. Loren and I will meet you guys in a bit," Sam kissed Pandora's forehead before standing and walking to Warren.

Pandora saw Warren nod and turned to Abby.

"You guys are going to ride with Warren and I'm going to ride with Nature. Is that okay?" she asked.

"Yeah," Mason nodded, glaring at Loren who was giving Pandora a dirty look.

"What's his problem?" Abby asked quietly.

"Probably doesn't like that I'm new, but supposed to be in charge over Sam," Pandora whispered back as Nature and Jordan appeared at Pandora's side.

"Ready?" Jordan asked. "I'll let you ride shotgun."

"It's okay." Pandora laughed. "You can ride up front."

Everyone headed to their respective rides, the tension fading once the car doors were shut.

Sam got behind his driver's seat, waiting for Loren to finish his cigarette before getting in with him. Once in the car, Loren sat silently, avoiding Sam's eye.

"What's your problem?" Sam asked bluntly.

"I don't have a problem," Loren countered.

"Yeah, you do. Everyone can tell something's up. So, you can either tell me now, or I can beat the shit out of you," Sam stated, causing Loren to scoff.

"You know it doesn't work that way. We can't hurt each other."

"I can try," Sam grunted.

"Can we go?" Loren asked.

"No."

"Why not?"

"Why don't you like Pandora?"

"Why do you?"

"She's my mate."

"What?!" Loren asked, turning to Sam quickly.

Sam lifted his white tattoo.

"She has the black one. Appeared last night."

"This is fucking bullshit!" Loren spat out. "She just showed up and she's supposed to be our leader? You've been leading us just fine without her. We don't need her."

"Well, she's here and you need to respect her!" Sam commanded. "She's the Alpha!"

"She can fuck off!"

"She's also my mate, and if you continue acting like a fucking child, I will put you in your place!"

Loren and Sam stared at each other hard, both breathing heavily, daring the other to move. Loren gave in first, turning towards his window and looking out of it. Sam let out a breath and put the car in reverse.

"She doesn't want to be the Alpha," Sam stated, turning onto the road towards Walmart.

"She doesn't?" Loren questioned.

"No," Sam answered. "She thinks it's ridiculous that suddenly she's supposed to lead the pack. She feels the same way that you do. There's nothing any of us can do about it though. She's happy that I'm here to help her with everything. You need to stop acting like you're the only one this is affecting. You think I like it? You guys are my brothers. I don't want someone else bossing you around either."

"She can't step down? If she didn't want this, then why did she die?" Loren asked.

"Pandora didn't die last night," Sam stated. "I haven't told anyone else yet. We were waiting until we were all at the cabin. Wepwawet told her she didn't need to die, because she'll bow to no man or something like that. She's pissed about everything being thrown at her. The cabin belongs to her dead grandfather. She's pissed at her grandmother for not telling her about it sooner."

"The cabin belongs to her family?" Loren asked.

"The cabin and the land. I'm guessing it's technically hers now. Well, all of ours. She's been making sure to include all of us."

"How kind," Loren spat.

"Knock it off," Sam commanded, parking his car next to Jordan's truck, noticing that everyone was already inside except for Pandora, who sat on the tailgate of Jordan's truck.

"Why's she waiting?" Loren asked curiously.

"I think she's waiting for me." Sam smiled.

Loren rolled his eyes at his lovesick brother.

"I don't like this man," Loren stated.

"I know you don't. You need to get over it though," Sam stated. "It's going to be hard. Warren told me last night he wasn't thrilled either, but he's moving past it better than you."

"I'll try, man. I really will. It's just going to take time."

"Try talking to her," Sam suggested. "It might make you feel a bit better."

"Yeah, whatever," Loren stated.

The two men climbed out of the Impala. Sam smiled as Pandora hopped off the tailgate and walked to him.

"Hey." she smiled to him, taking his hand in hers again.

Sam let out a small gasp and smirked down at her.

"Stop doing that," Sam growled quietly.

"Get a room," Loren called over his shoulder, heading into the store.

Pandora laughed and turned to Sam.

"Is he going to be okay?" Pandora asked.

"With time," Sam answered, pulling Pandora towards the store gently. "He just needs to get used to things."

"Same here," Pandora stated.

"I told him to try talking to you. Might make him feel better." Sam shrugged.

"I hope so." Pandora breathed. "I don't want anyone pissed at me. Or at you for that matter."

"Why would anyone be pissed at me?" Sam smiled. "You're the big, bad wolf that blew into town out of nowhere."

"Shush you." Pandora smiled as they reached the pack and her friends. "What's on the list, Abby?"

"So much." Abby sighed, leading the way with a cart.

Pandora let out a small laugh at Abby's dramatics and at the fact that Abby wasn't the only one with a cart.

"How are we going to pay for all of the groceries?" Sam asked. "We're feeding a small army."

"Well," Pandora let out slowly. "I got my inheritance about ten minutes ago."

"Inheritance?" Sam asked. "From your parents or grandfather?"

Loren turned his head upon hearing that Pandora's parents were dead.

"Both," Pandora stated. "Groceries are on me. Also, the electricity bill and water bill have a very big payment already on them. I don't think we ever need to worry about bills again."

"Now you know how I feel around Mom," Mason joked.

"Oh, yes. Please remind us how wonderful your mother is." Abby rolled her eyes.

Pandora laughed at her friends' antics and turned to Sam.

"You okay?" she asked.

"Are you?" he asked.

"I will be," Pandora stated, cuddling into Sam's side.

Sam smiled at her as they followed their pack through the store. Everyone was grabbing whatever Abby pointed to, keeping the groceries organized for easier unpacking later. Once they had finished, Pandora paid as Nature, Warren, and Sam brought their vehicles to the front. The boys all carried the groceries out, Sam and Mason not allowing Pandora or Abby to carry anything. The girls rolled their eyes but didn't argue. Sam dropped Pandora and Abby off at Pandora's truck, allowing the girls to go pay the ticket while the guys unloaded the groceries.

Once they returned to the cottage, Pandora smiled at the open bedroom doors.

"Does everyone know which room is theirs?" Pandora asked.

"It was pretty easy to figure out." Sam smiled. "The doors only opened for whoever the room was meant for. Loren is next to me and Warren is across. Jordan is next to Abby and Mason. Nature is at the end of the hall, next to the back patio. We can't get in there by the way."

"I'll try." Pandora smiled, stepping past the pack and to the porch door, glancing into the rooms as she went.

Loren's room was all grey, kind of like him, with skylights. Warren's room had oak paneling and a slanted window like Abby's and Mason's with a chandelier made from deer horns. A small fireplace was in the corner with a small stack of wood next to it. Jordan's was red and white, looking a bit polished and with two windows that would let in the sunset light once the time came at night. Nature's room caused Pandora to stop and gasp.

"Wow." She breathed. "This is gorgeous, Nature."

Nature's bedroom had plants surrounding it, true to Nature's own name. A small bed sat next to a white panel window that had twelve squares in it and opened at the middle. Nature's room was the only other one with its own bathroom.

"May I?" Pandora asked, pointing towards the bathroom door.

Nature nodded for her to go ahead. The bathroom had a claw foot tub in one corner and a small shower stall across from it. The sink sat on the same wall as the door with the toilet adjacent to it. The bathroom had plants hanging in it, draping over the bathtub to create a canopy. The tiles and walls were white marbled.

"How?" Pandora questioned. "How did all of this stuff get here, and how are these plants alive?"

"How was there a fire in the living room and my bedroom?" Warren questioned.

"How are all of the appliances brand new?" Jordan asked as well.

"Some one knew we were coming, obviously," Loren stated, looking to Pandora. "But you were going to tell us about that after we saw the back patio."

"So, Sam told you the cottage and land belonged to my grandfather before he died?" Pandora smiled. "I already told everyone else while we were waiting for y'all."

Loren rolled his eyes and turned towards the back-patio door, annoyed that he couldn't get under Pandora's skin. Pandora rolled her eyes with a smile, reminding herself it would take time. The pack followed Pandora to the patio door. She turned the handles on the black, double French doors and pushed them open, stepping down the seven steps inside to get a look around. Sam let out his low whistle again as he stepped next to her.

"Holy shit." Loren breathed from her other side.

The back patio was enclosed with slanted windows. There was a stocked bar to the left of the steps with eight bar stools. A white, round couch was in front of them, a small fire pit in the middle. A wooden dining room table was next to that with enough room for twenty-five people. A long, green couch sat against the back wall, cornered against the windows to the right. A door opened inward to allow people to go outside to the pond, stairs leading up to it. There were lights surrounding the whole room, causing it to glow on the cloudy day they were having. Plants were scattered along the room like in Nature's bathroom. Pandora went to the door that led outside, opening it slowly to reveal that there was also a vegetable and herb garden.

Pandora smiled, looking to Sam as he followed her to the door.

"It's perfect." Sam smiled, wrapping his arms around Pandora's waist.

"I don't know how any of this is real," Pandora whispered.

"Me, either. I'm so happy that it is though." Sam smiled.

Sam leaned down and kissed Pandora slowly and gently. They both fought the urge inside of them to go further than just a kiss as they pulled away from each other. Jordan catcalled as they had kissed, causing Pandora to blush.

"Shut up," Sam called to him, leading Pandora back to the pack. "Anyone want to go for a run before it rains?"

# CHAPTER TWELVE

The Pack

Pandora and Sam were in front of the cottage, already having shifted into their wolf forms, chasing each other in circles as they waited for their pack to join them. Nature's red wolf bounded towards them, tackling Sam off Pandora to join in their fun, silent but smiling. Jordan appeared next, grey and white fur flashing pass Pandora as she watched Sam easily knock Nature off him. Warren's spots seemed to bounce on his fur as he chased Jordan. Loren sat next to Pandora, grey fur that almost had a blue tint.

Pandora studied him as he watched the pack, unmoving as he sat tall and proud. Finally realizing that Pandora was watching him, he turned to her, raising his head a bit to make eye contact as Pandora was taller than him in wolf form. She smiled at him, careful to not show teeth so she wouldn't seem threatening. Loren nodded to her, accepting her smile before looking back to the pack. Pandora turned as well, watching as the boys chased and nipped at one another, never harming each other. Pandora laid down, content to watch for a bit.

Loren remained next to her. He seemed to be trying to get used to her being there, which Pandora was thankful for. In wolf form, it was harder to say the wrong thing to set him off. As a wolf, all Pandora had to do was sit with him and everything would be fine. Loren and Pandora sat together for a few more minutes before Pandora rose, Loren following her as she walked to the pack. Sam, seeing them approach together, smiled a goofy grin, tongue hanging over his mouth. Loren made a coughing sound that Pandora guessed was a laugh.

"Be careful," Abby called from the porch swing where she sat with Mason, both drinking sweet iced tea.

Pandora barked back before nodding to Sam to lead the way. Sam took off towards the woods, the pack and Pandora following just behind him. Pandora ran in the back, able to see any threats as they may come to the pack best from her vantage point. Sam led the pack, running hard, but less than last night. Loren matched his strides easily, Warren and Nature behind him. Jordan was in front of Pandora, keeping pace, but breathing harder than he should be. After a while of watching him struggle, Jordan stopped and sat. Pandora slowed a bit as to not pass him, barking to Sam.

Sam stopped and turned, tilting his head to her as he saw that Jordan and she had stopped. Jordan took deep shallow breaths, trying to control himself. Sam came to them. Pandora ran her head under Sam's neck as he passed her to get to Jordan. He tilted his head to Jordan, asking if he was alright. Jordan yelped quietly, showing he just needed a moment. Pandora nodded to Sam, telling him and the others to go as she stayed with Jordan.

Once the rest of the pack was out of sight, Jordan shifted back to human form, sitting behind a rock to not embarrass Pandora with his nudity.

"I'm sorry," he stated. "I don't run often. I had muscular dystrophy growing up. I couldn't walk until I died. Running wears me out."

Pandora shifted, covering herself with the same rock as Jordan.

"I'm sorry," Pandora stated.

"It's not your fault." Jordan smiled. "At least I can walk now. That alone is a miracle."

"I'm happy that you can walk." Pandora smiled. "If you don't want to run, we can go back to the cottage? I need to start dinner anyways."

"I don't want you to not run because of me," Jordan said, looking sad.

"I can run with Sam later." Pandora smiled. "I don't mind waiting."

Jordan gave her a sad smile before morphing back into his wolf. Pandora followed suit, turning and jogging with him as they headed back to the cottage. They reached the cottage easily, Jordan breathing easier than before. Abby had left the front door open for them to enter, a mat at the door reading "Wipe Your Paws" for the wolves to use.

Pandora could hear Jordan laughing at the mat in his wolf form, causing Pandora to laugh as well. Pandora and Jordan both went to their rooms in wolf form and returned to the kitchen once they were dressed. Jordan nodded to Pandora as he took a spot at the island, causing his brown hair to dip in front of his face a bit.

"What's for dinner that takes so long to get ready?" Jordan asked.

"Jambalaya." Pandora smiled. "Anyone have any allergies I should know about?"

"Nope." Jordan smiled.

"Good." Pandora smiled.

"So, should we all live here?" Jordan asked.

"What do you mean?" Pandora asked as she began cutting sausage, chicken, and shrimp.

"Like, I have a lease that's almost up. Warren lives with his mom. Sam and Loren share an apartment."

"It's up to each of you," Pandora stated. "I don't want anyone to move just because anyone else is. I don't even know how long I'm going to stay here. I need to be near my grandmother."

"Why not bring her here?" Jordan suggested.

"I hadn't thought about it yet," Pandora answered honestly. "I also don't know if Abby and Mason are going to stay either. Plus, I just graduated college. There are things that I want to do, and I don't know how to do them here."

"Things like what?" Jordan asked curiously.

"Well, I want to open a shop," Pandora shrugged. "Just knick-knacks and stuff like that. Maybe some food."

"You can do that in Somerset. There are open shops all over town for lease. I thought you didn't have to work though."

"I don't have to, but it would be boring not to. I'm sure you guys have jobs."

"True," Jordan stated. "We all made it where we have off the same two days though."

"That's smart," Pandora nodded. "I just don't know what to do yet. If Abby wants to stay, then I definitely will. If not, then I don't know."

"So, I just have to convince Abby?" Jordan smiled.

"And Mason. But he'll follow her anywhere."

"Have you talked to Sam about this stuff yet?"

"No," Pandora stated. "We haven't really gotten into anything serious yet. You're just easy to talk to."

"So I've been told." Jordan smiled.

"Can I ask you something?" Pandora asked.

"Of course."

"Why can't Nature talk?"

Jordan seemed to struggle for a moment, not sure if he should answer or not.

"Well, Nature was abused when he was younger. I only know because he texted it all to me. He hasn't told everyone how bad it was, but I know that he doesn't have a tongue."

"What do you mean he doesn't have a tongue?" Pandora questioned.

"His father cut it out of him."

Pandora stopped what she was doing and turned to Jordan in shock. She couldn't speak as she imagined a small Nature, hiding in a corner as his father attacked him. Pandora could feel anger rising inside of her that she had never felt before. She stalked past Jordan and onto the front porch, breathing in the fresh air to try to calm herself. Jordan followed behind her, keeping his distance to not set her off.

"I was angry too," Jordan stated. "It took everything in me not to track the man down and kill him."

Pandora tried listening to Jordan's words, but all she could see was red. How? How could someone do that to a child? Parents were supposed to love their children, not harm them. Pandora was shaking with anger as she walked down the steps of the cottage, falling to her knees to feel the earth beneath her. She could hear Sam howling close by, seeming to call to her.

Sam's wolf appeared beside her a few moments later, the pack close behind. Sam rubbed his nose on Pandora's cheek to get her attention. She wiped the angry tears from her eyes before meeting Sam's. He yelped at her, obviously worried.

"I'm fine," Pandora told him, scratching behind his ears. "I didn't mean to worry you."

Sam ran inside and came out a moment later in jeans.

"What happened?" Sam asked Pandora sitting beside her.

Pandora had her hands covering her face, trying to hide herself. Sam took her hands in one of his and tilted her chin up with his other.

"Not here," Pandora stated.

Sam nodded and lifted Pandora to her feet gently, leading her back inside. The pack followed, shifting as they entered the cottage behind Pandora.

"That's a whole lot of naked," Abby called from the kitchen, causing the boys to blush and head to their rooms.

Pandora turned into her room, pulling Sam with her and shutting the door for privacy.

"Jordan told me about Nature," Pandora whispered.

"Oh," Sam said, understanding crossed his face.

"I didn't mean to worry you," Pandora stated. "How did you know I needed you?"

"I could feel your anger," Sam stated. "At first, I thought it was me. I was really confused considering I had been fine right before. Then I realized it wasn't my emotions."

"So, we can feel each other's emotions?" Pandora asked.

"I guess," Sam shrugged.

Pandora nodded, looking at her feet to avoid eye contact again. She thought about Nature again and began shaking, sobbing loudly. Sam took her in his arms quickly.

"It's okay." He held her tightly. "I've got you. It's okay. He can't hurt him again."

"I want him dead," Pandora stated. "He hurt Nature and I want him dead. How dare he! How dare he hurt my pack!"

Pandora's voice rose as her anger grew again. She pulled away from Sam and walked past him, looking out the window and trying to control her breathing. Sam kept his distance this time, letting her emotions roll off of her.

"I understand," Sam stated. "For you, the anger is stronger, because you're the Alpha and it's new. Emotions are hard to control when you first change. Being Alpha, it'll probably be harder. Any time someone in your pack gets hurt, you're going to see red. You have to learn to control it though. Not for you, but for them."

Pandora listened to Sam's words carefully. She knew she needed to calm down, but the idea of someone in her pack being harmed caused a surge of protection she had never felt before.

"How do you deal with this?" Pandora asked, turning to Sam. "I don't even know Nature, but because he's in my pack, I want to protect him from dangers that aren't even around anymore."

"It's hard," Sam stated, walking to Pandora's side. "It'll take time. A lot of patience, too. But it'll get easier."

Pandora leaned her forehead against Sam's chest, causing the spark between them as their skin met. They both took deep breaths, ignoring the feelings inside of them as Pandora calmed herself. She relished in the warmth of Sam's skin, opening her eyes to study the tattoo on his chest. The tattoo over his heart was a wolf standing on a cliff, howling at the full moon behind it. Pandora smiled, tracing the lines with her finger, causing Sam to shiver at her touch.

"We really need to figure out why this keeps happening," Sam commented.

Pandora let out a slow breath as she removed herself from Sam.

"It'll probably feel like that for a while," Pandora commented. "New mates and all that."

"Do you think it'll be like that if we ever… ya'know?"

"If you can't say the word sex, then we shouldn't have it," Pandora laughed.

Sam smiled mischievously.

"What?" Pandora asked.

Instead of answering, Sam grabbed Pandora, lifting her up and pulling her against him. He pulled her legs around his waist, holding her ass in one hand and wrapping the other hand in her hair before kissing her hard. Pandora gasped at the contact, wrapping her arms around his neck and kissing him passionately. Sam pressed Pandora's back into the window, trapping her against him as his hand unwound from her hair. He ran his hand down her side, reaching under her shirt and stroking her breast. Pandora moaned into Sam's mouth, giving Sam access to her mouth. He happily dove his tongue into her mouth, tasting her as much as he could.

Just as quickly as Sam had started, he stopped, setting Pandora down gently and stepping back from her, smirking at her like the cat that caught the canary.

"What the hell?" Pandora questioned, trying to catch her breath.

"I may not want to use the word sex, but we should definitely be having it. I'll see you in the kitchen."

Sam turned and left the room quickly, shutting the door behind himself and leaving Pandora to catch her breath. She let out a small, surprised laugh before going into the bathroom to check herself. She brushed out her hair and fixed her bra and shirt. She shook her head, a stupid smile on her face.

She felt her lips which looked red from kissing. She could still feel Sam's mouth taking hers. She shook her head again, leaving the room and heading to the kitchen.

Pandora smiled when she entered the kitchen and saw the scene before her. Jordan, Pandora and Nature were throwing tomatoes at Warren, Mason and Loren as the three boys threw sliced bell peppers back. Sam was standing at the end of the hallway, laughing. Pandora wrapped her arms around Sam's waist from behind. Sam held her arms and leaned his head back to rest slightly on Pandora's.

"This is perfect." Pandora smiled.

CHAPTER THIRTEEN

Conflict

Three nights after her twenty-fifth birthday, Pandora called her grandmother. The breathing on the other end told Pandora that she had answered.

"I know you can talk to me," Pandora stated.

Silence.

"Fine." Pandora breathed. "I don't know why I'm calling you. I know you aren't going to talk to me. I should just hang up…"

"Pandora." Her grandmother breathed.

Pandora let in a sharp breath, feeling all the emotions from the past few days. She let her shoulders rock as she began to cry. She wished her grandmother was there to hold her. All she wanted was her last parental figure with her.

"I'm on my way," Pandora heard her grandmother say.

"Okay," Pandora sobbed. "Okay."

"I'll be there tomorrow," her grandmother stated. "Go to your mate."

"How do you know about Sam?" Pandora asked.

"Every Alpha receives a mate," her grandmother answered.

"Okay," Pandora stated. "I love you."

"I love you."

Her grandmother hung up, leaving Pandora feeling alone. She let herself cry for a bit longer before seeking out Sam. She went into their bathroom and looked in the mirror, realizing how much of a mess she looked. She splashed water on her face from the sink closest to her, trying to take away the redness on her face. She dried her face gently as to not make her face puffier. She let herself breathe for a few minutes before turning to Sam's door.

Sam was leaning against his closed door. He could hear when Pandora had entered the bathroom behind the door. He wanted to go to her. Every fiber in his being was pushing him to her, to hold her as she had broken down. He could feel her pain as it had been building up inside of her, all of the anger that she had felt had sent every nerve in his body on fire. When she had first started crying, it had brought him to his knees. Once he had found the strength to stand again, he took his spot against the door, waiting for her to come to him. She finally knocked on his door, softly, three times.

Sam turned to face the door and slowly opened it. Pandora stood in the doorway, looking into Sam's eyes. Sam stared back intensely, waiting for Pandora to decide what she wanted. She bit her bottom lip, drawing Sam's attention to it. He licked his lips, anticipating what was to come.

Pandora jumped to him quickly. Sam lifted her easily, holding her up as he had done twice before now. She wrapped her legs around his waist, and he slammed her to the wall, finally letting the spark between them catch fire. They groaned into each other's mouths, both demanding the other's submission. Sam carried her to his bed, throwing her into the center of it and lifting his shirt over his head in a quick motion. Pandora climbed to the top of the bed so that her head was against the pillows. She sat up and pulled her shirt over her head, Sam crawling on top of her as she tossed it to the floor. He took her mouth again, pressing his skin to hers, feeling her warmth against him.

Sam kissed down to Pandora's neck, then sucked at her collarbone, causing her to gasp his name. Sam growled at the sound of her wanting him. She pushed her hips into him, wanting to feel some sort of friction. He pushed back into her, cursing his pants for being in the way. Pandora ran her nails down his chest, reaching the button on his jeans and opening them. She pushed his pants down, and he kicked them off, his boxers flying with his pants at the same time, lost in the sea of blankets at the end of the bed.

He kissed down Pandora's body, nibbling on her sides as he went down. He pulled her pants down her legs slowly, climbing back on top of her, pulling a blanket up to his waist in the process. He held himself above her, kissing her hungrily, but waiting until she told him it was okay for him to continue. She pulled his waist towards her own. They both let out satisfied moans as Sam finally gave in. Pandora scratched Sam's back, her nails turning to claws momentarily. Sam bit into his pillow to keep from calling out her name.

In the morning, Pandora woke to Sam kissing across her shoulders, the rain keeping the sunlight from entering Sam's room. She snuggled into him and he wrapped his arms around her. She could still feel the spark when their skin touched, but not pushing her to jump him every time they touched.

Pandora turned in his arms, facing him. Sam smiled as he stared into her eyes.

"Where have you been all my life?" he asked, more to himself than Pandora.

Pandora just smiled, leaning forward and kissing his lips gently. He deepened the kiss, causing Pandora to push herself against him. He pulled her leg over his waist and rolled so that Pandora was straddling him. They made love slowly to each other, learning where the other liked being touch, whereas the night before had been a rush of passion. They stayed in bed for hours as everyone else slept, only stopping when they could hear movement outside of the door.

"Time to get up." Pandora smiled.

"I already am," Sam joked, causing them both to laugh.

"I'll see you in the kitchen," Pandora promised, finally leaving Sam's bed.

Sam groaned at her absence from his bed. Pandora giggled as she shut the door that separated her room from their bathroom. She leaned against the door for a minute, taking a minute to realize how happy she felt. She walked to her suitcase and dressed quickly, brushing out her hair before throwing it into a messy bun. She walked out of her bedroom and to the kitchen where Abby was sitting, drinking a fresh cup of coffee.

"Sex hair, don't care?" Abby asked Pandora, eyebrows raised.

"Shut up," Pandora demanded, walking to the kitchen cabinet and pulling down ingredients for blueberry pancakes.

As Pandora began cooking, Mason joined them.

"Blueberry pancakes?" Mason asked. "Did someone get laid?"

"Shut up," Pandora stated again, ignoring Abby and Mason's laughter from behind her.

Her pack slowly trickled into the kitchen as the smell of Pandora's cooking wafted through the cottage like a drug. Sam joined them last, looking a bit too happy for Loren's liking.

"Why are you smiling like that?" Loren questioned.

"Leave me alone," Sam demanded, taking the cup of coffee that Pandora offered him.

He kissed her forehead before sitting at the closest stool to her. Loren rolled his eyes as Warren let out a groan.

"They're going to be like bunny rabbits now," Warren complained.

"Remember Lindsey?" Loren asked, trying to annoy Pandora. "When they first got together, I couldn't even stay in the apartment it was so loud."

Pandora let out a small growl, silencing Loren quickly. Sam stood and grabbed Loren by the back of his neck, dragging him out the front door easily. Sam threw Loren down the steps, following close behind.

"The fuck, dude?" Loren questioned.

"The fuck is wrong with you?" Sam questioned. "I thought you were dealing with your shit."

"What the hell are you talking about?" Loren yelled back. "I was just comparing…"

"Well, don't! Don't compare anyone to her! In fact, you say one more fucking thing to upset Pandora, and you're cut! Do you understand me?"

Loren remained silent for a moment, not sure what to do. His brother had just threatened to kick him out of the pack. Over a girl.

"You're going to throw me out of the pack over some bitch!" Loren yelled, anger vibrating from him.

"Say one more fucking thing," Sam whispered threateningly. "I fucking dare you."

Loren remained silent, looking behind Sam to see the rest of the pack. Pandora stared at Loren silently, no emotion in her eyes as she watched the scene in front of her. Loren looked to Warren for help. Warren shrugged his shoulders to Loren, showing that he was on his own.

"Whatever, dude," Loren stated, walking away from Sam and towards the path. "I'm done."

"Loren!" Jordan called.

Loren kept walking, ignoring the calls from the pack as he left. He got into his car and drove away, leaving his brothers behind, waiting until he was on the main road before finally breaking down.

CHAPTER FOURTEEN

LOREN'S RETURN

A few hours after Loren had left, Pandora's grandmother arrived. No one noticed her at first; her silence keeping her presence a secret. Nature noticed her first, being the only other mute around. He smiled to her kindly, curiosity in his eyes. Her warm smile calmed him as she raised a finger to her lips. Nature nodded, turning back to his book as he sat in front of the fire in the living room. Pandora's grandmother wandered through the cottage, glancing into the rooms as she went, searching for her lost granddaughter. She saw the pack, each in their rooms. She admired the men that would stand by her Pandora, how strong they must be. She passed Abby and Mason's room, smiling at the sight of the two best friends Pandora could ever had asked for. They were lying in bed together, cuddling and speaking in hushed voices.

Her grandmother continued to the back patio where she found Pandora's mate at the bar, drinking from a bottle of gin. She sat beside him silently. Sam looked over to her, his eyes widening at the sight of her.

"Are you her grandmother?" Sam asked.

Her grandmother nodded, taking the bottle from him and putting the lid on it. "She's outside," Sam stated. "She's been looking for Loren for a few hours now."

Pandora's grandmother took Sam's hand and squeezed it gently. Sam felt himself relax at her touch. He didn't understand the power the woman in Pandora's family had over him, but he never wanted to be on the receiving end of one of their bad days. He gave her a weak smile before standing.

"I'll go find her for you," Sam promised, walking out of the back door and into the pouring rain.

He returned twenty minutes later, Pandora behind him, both soaking wet. Pandora's grandmother passed them both towels.

"When did you get here?" Pandora asked.

Her grandmother just smiled.

"Not talking again, I see?" Abby questioned, walking into the enclosed patio.

Her grandmother nodded to Abby as the rest of the pack and Mason joined them. Nature and Pandora's grandmother shared a fond smile with one another before Pandora's grandmother turned to Pandora again.

"Okay. Guys, this is my grandmother, Dot," Pandora introduced her grandmother to them, pointing to each man and telling her the names.

Dot simply smiled to them before looking to Pandora again.

"And he is?" Dot asked, pointing to the still open patio door.

Everyone turned quickly to see Loren standing in the threshold. Loren watched as the pack's eyes all filled with shock at his appearance. Instead of focusing on everyone else, Loren looked to Pandora.

"I heard you looking for me," Loren stated.

"I was," Pandora whispered.

"Why?" he asked.

"Because you are a part of this pack," she shrugged.

"Sam kicked me out."

"Sam can't kick you out."

"Yeah, 'cause you're the Alpha."

"I can't kick you out, either. We are all bound to one another through our ancestors and the magick that they performed on this land. You didn't come back because I was searching for you. You came back because, no matter how much you think you despise me, we are a family now. And I protect my family."

Loren remained silent, letting Pandora's words sink into his mind. He grabbed to her calling him family. He had been nothing but an ass towards her, but she had been the only one to chase after him when he had run. Not Warren. Not Nature. Not Sam. Pandora. Maybe she couldn't be the worst thing to happen to them. Maybe she really would be the one to lead them one day.

Loren lowered his eyes for a moment before looking back into Pandora's. He walked to Pandora quickly, both of them ignoring Sam's protective growl. Loren held out his hand for Pandora to shake. She took quickly.

"I'm Loren," he introduced himself, allowing a small smile.

"Pandora." she smiled back.

They stared at each other for a moment before Pandora pulled Loren into a tight hug. He hugged her back, more in surprise than anything else. She pulled away quickly and punched his arm, hard.

"Ow," Loren joked.

"Don't ever do that again." She pointed into his face.

"Yes, ma'am," Loren laughed, holding his hands up in surrender.

Pandora hugged him again. This time Loren embraced her gently, knowing she wouldn't hit him again. She pulled away from him and passed him her towel, taking Sam's in the process.

"Are there any pancakes left?" Loren asked.

CHAPTER FIFTEEN

Home

The pack sat around the fire pit in the patio, all laughing and talking with one another. Nature and Dot sat next to each other, silently smiling around them. Sam was lying down, his head in Pandora's lap as he looked into the fire as Pandora talked to Abby across from her. Sam's head was still buzzing a bit from the gin but had calmed quite a bit once Loren had returned to them. Loren sat next to Pandora, seeming to accept his new position better than he had earlier that very day; his arm draped across the back of Pandora's spot. Jordan, Warren, and Mason were talking about all of the places that they had been to, having been the only three to travel outside of the country. The weather outside was moody and grey, the rain still pouring from the sky without mercy. Being inside the patio with the warmth and homey feeling surrounding her, Pandora didn't even notice.

"So, Dora?" Abby asked. "We have a week left."

"Do we?" Pandora questioned, noticing that the pack had turned to listen to the conversation suddenly.

"I'm almost out of clothes," Abby stated.

"We can go to a laundry mat," Pandora shrugged.

"And my mom called me this morning." Abby smiled.

"Yeah, well..."

"Don't do it."

"I'm going to do it."

"Don't..."

"It's up to you, Abby." Pandora smiled as Abby glared at her.

"What's going on?" Sam asked, sitting up.

Abby let out a frustrated sigh, turning to Mason. Abby took Mason's hand and led him into the cottage and to their room. Jordan let out a soft chuckle as he looked to Pandora. Jordan was still the only one to know that the final decision on if Pandora stayed was down to Abby.

"Let me know what you want to do!" Pandora called to her friend.

"Yeah, yeah!" Abby's voice called back before Pandora heard the bedroom door close.

"What was that about?" Sam asked.

"I'll tell you after Abby and Mason talk," Pandora promised.

"What did she mean that you only have a week left?"

"That's how much vacation time I had saved at work," Pandora admitted.

"What do you mean?" Sam questioned again.

"I'll talk to everyone after Abby and Mason have spoken," Pandora stated, rising from her seat and heading into the cottage, knowing Sam would follow her.

Jordan told everyone else to stay in the patio so as to not interrupt the argument that was bound to follow and pulled the doors closed when Sam and Pandora had passed them. Sam followed Pandora into the kitchen where she began to pull out food for dinner. Sam watched her cautiously for a few minutes, waiting to see if she would explain herself. When she didn't, he took initiative.

"Pandora…"

"Don't," Pandora cut him off. "Don't ask me what I mean again. I love being here, Sam. I have never felt so at home before. This place is perfect. I do have a life outside of here, though. There are things that I still want to do with my life. Don't try to convince me to stay longer if Abby doesn't."

Sam just stared at Pandora, confused. He didn't understand how she could still think about leaving the pack, about leaving him, in a week's time. She had just called them her family. She had just told him she felt home. Why would she leave that behind?

"I don't understand," Sam admitted.

"I know you don't," Pandora nodded. "We don't know much about each other, Sam. There are things that I've been through that I don't want to share with you. There are things that you probably don't want to talk about with me yet either…"

"I'll tell you anything you want," Sam shrugged.

"And I appreciate the openness. I truly do. I'm not ready for that though. I have issues that I don't want to dump on anyone."

"Like the medications in your bag?" Sam asked.

"Excuse me?" Pandora questioned, feeling anger rising in her.

"I saw the pill bottles."

"You went through my bag?!"

"Like you said, we don't know one another that well. You were supposed to lead this pack. I had to make sure it was safe."

"So, everything you've said to me is bullshit? You never thought I could do this initially. You lied to me and went through my stuff without my permission."

"I have to protect my brothers."

"Yeah, just fuck me and then break my privacy. No big deal."

"It wasn't like that, Pandora," Sam stated.

"When did you look?"

"What?" Sam asked.

"When did you go through my stuff?" Pandora questioned.

"I don't think you want me to say," Sam admitted.

"When?" Pandora questioned.

Sam remained silent, not taking his dark eyes from Pandora's green ones that lit up every time she wanted to punch something.

"This morning," he finally admitted. "After."

"Fuck you," Pandora stated. "Get out."

"You're kicking me out of the cottage?" Sam asked.

"Get out!" Pandora screamed.

Abby and Mason entered the kitchen quickly.

"What's going on?" Abby asked.

"I'm not leaving," Sam stood his ground.

"Then I am," Pandora stated, leaving the kitchen and heading to her room.

The pack and Dot had come into the cottage at some point, waiting at the end of the hall. Pandora ignored them and went into her room, leaving the door open. Sam followed her quickly, Abby and Mason right behind him.

"You can't leave," Sam stated.

"Oh, I can't?" Pandora laughed. "Are you going to stop me?"

"Pandora," Sam growled.

"Don't fucking growl at me!" Pandora yelled. "Get out of my room!"

"No," Sam stated.

"Did you even look up what the medicines are?" Pandora questioned.

"No," Sam stated.

"Didn't have the time, I guess. You were too busy drinking while I was out looking for Loren! I'm good enough to fuck but not to trust, yet I was the one calling out for him for hours at end! You claim him as your brother but acted like a child when he was angry! His anger was completely justified! I'd be pissed if I was him too!" Pandora yelled.

"Pandora, I didn't look them up, because I knew it didn't matter!" Sam yelled back.

"Obviously it fucking did!" Pandora countered. "If it didn't matter, you wouldn't have brought it up! Hell, if it didn't matter, you wouldn't have waited until you had my trust before breaking it!"

Pandora went to her bag and pulled out her medicine bottles. She walked up to Sam, getting in his face.

"Celexa is for the anger issues, depression, and anxiety. Buspirone is a serotonin enhancer, also for depression. Mirtazapine is for depression, anxiety, and insomnia. I've been taking these medicines since I was seven years old. Olanzapine is an antipsychotic that helps with anorexia, which I've been dealing with since I was ten. I tried killing myself four years ago, Sam. Abby was the one that found me. That's why I depend on her so much. Because I owe her my life. I may be Alpha, but she is my pack more than you ever will be."

Pandora turned back to her suitcase, throwing her medicine inside of it and gathering all of her clothes. She went into the bathroom, collecting her shower supplies before tossing them into her suitcase as well. She moved past Sam easily, heading towards the front door. Abby and Mason had grabbed their things as Pandora had been yelling at Sam about her medicine. They met her at the door with Dot, Mason holding her keys for her to take.

"I'll drive your grandmother home. You and Abby go in the truck," Mason commanded as they went down the cottage steps. "Let me know if we need to stop for sleep. I'll call my mom, so you don't have to spend any money."

"Thank you," Abby told Mason, kissing his cheek for Pandora since she was too angry to speak.

Mason held Abby's door open for her as Pandora put their bags into Dot's '74 VW Beetle. Pandora hugged her grandmother tightly before opening the passenger door for her.

"I love you, Grandma," Pandora told her before shutting her door for her.

She walked over to the truck and got behind the wheel. Mason patted the top of the truck before getting into the Beetle, looking a little out of place behind the wheel of it. Pandora started the truck and forced herself not to look back at Loren trying to chase her truck down as she drove away, heading south back towards her hometown.

CHAPTER SIXTEEN

Issues

They drove all the way through, Abby taking over for Mason about halfway through the trip at one of the gas stops. Pandora pulled her truck into its spot along the road, Abby taking the spot in the garage with Dot's small car. Pandora woke Mason gently, letting him know that they had made it. Mason nodded in acknowledgement, opening his door and climbing out.

"Y'all can crash in the guest room," Pandora told Abby and Mason. "Your parents are probably asleep."

Abby nodded, following Pandora and Dot up the steps of their home. Mason followed closely, still half asleep. Abby led him to the guest room easily, laying him in bed and removing his shoes from his feet. She kissed his head and covered him with a blanket before heading to Pandora's room. She found Pandora on the floor, crying as she hugged the picture of her parents to her chest. Abby went to her, sitting beside her on the floor and holding her tightly, knowing Pandora just needed to cry for a bit.

They ended up falling asleep there. Abby was leaning her head back against the wall for support, Pandora's head in her lap and still clutching the picture for dear life. Mason woke them, careful not to startle them. Pandora rubbed her eyes groggily, finally letting go of the photo in her hands to do so. She sat up carefully, feeling her head pounding from all of the crying she had done. Mason passed her a glass of water and a bottle of Tylenol. Pandora thanked him before taking a few and drinking half the water, passing the rest to Abby, sure that she probably had a kink in her neck.

"Shannon saw the truck out front this morning," Mason informed them. "He took the day off work. Wants to know why we're home early."

"That's Dad." Abby smiled weakly. "Nosey."

"He's not nosey," Pandora stated. "Just curious."

"What do we tell him?" Mason asked.

"That I didn't feel good," Pandora stated. "He won't question it."

"Okay," Abby nodded.

The trio stood up and headed towards the living room. Shannon and Candace were in the living room with Dot, sipping on iced tea as they waited for the three young adults to join them. Once in the room, Candace and Shannon stood, hugging the girls individually before Shannon shook Mason's hand.

"When did you get back?" Candace asked.

"It was either early this morning or late last night," Abby admitted.

"What happened?" Shannon asked.

"I didn't feel good," Pandora stated, not wanting Abby to have to lie to her parents, not that it was much of a lie considering she probably looked like hell. "I just needed to be home."

"Did Dot go looking for you?" Candace smiled. "We noticed she was gone all of yesterday."

"Yeah." Pandora smiled sadly.

"Want to go get some breakfast?" Shannon asked. "You can tell us about your adventure."

"Sure." Abby smiled. "There wasn't much to see though. Just a few hiking trails and a small town."

"Still." Shannon smiled.

"And obviously you were up to something," Candace stated, rolling her eyes. "Pandora got tattoos while you were gone. Why the wedding band?"

Pandora looked down her arm to the tattoo on her ring finger, trying to come up with a reason for it.

"It's not a wedding band, Mom." Abby sighed. "It's a metaphor."

"A metaphor for what?" Shannon asked.

"The patriarchy trying to hold women down through marriage," Mason filled in quickly. "Damn government."

Abby let out a small laugh as Dot tried not to choke on her tea. Pandora went to her grandmother immediately, patting her back to help. Dot held up her hand to signal she was okay, shaking a bit as she tried not to laugh. Pandora smiled to her before standing again.

"Where to?" Pandora smiled to Shannon.

"If you're up for another drive we can go to Tupelo Honey?" Shannon suggested. "If not, we can just go down the street to Annie's."

"Please no more driving," Abby begged Pandora.

"Annie's it is," Pandora stated, her smile still not quite reaching her eyes.

"Do you feel up to going out?" Candace asked seriously. "You look pretty worn out."

"I need to eat, or I'll end up grouchy." Pandora sighed. "Can someone else drive the truck though?"

"I'll drive." Mason smiled to Pandora before turning to Shannon. "We'll meet y'all there."

Shannon, Candace, and Dot went to Shannon's car next door as Mason led the girls to Pandora's truck. Pandora sighed as she shut the passenger door, Abby between herself and Mason.

"Are you okay?" Abby asked her seriously.

"No," Pandora answered. "I will be though. I just need to calm down and think."

"Sam called me this morning," Mason blurted. "He said you haven't been answering."

"I turned my phone off." Pandora shrugged. "I don't want to talk to him any time soon."

"Understandable," Abby stated. "I'm pissed, too. Don't ignore the rest of the pack because of him though."

"I won't," Pandora promised. "I just need distance from him. I'll text the rest of the guys after breakfast."

"Good," Abby nodded. "I let Jordan know to calm down."

"Is he freaking out?" Pandora asked.

"They all are," Abby admitted. "Loren was the first one to call me, weird as that is. I told them we made it home and that you would talk when you were ready. They're all pissed at Sam."

"Same," Pandora coughed out.

Mason grunted, nodding his head as they turned into the parking lot. They sat at their normal corner booth. Pandora sat between Abby and Dot, facing the doorway. As they received their drinks, Shannon began asking Abby questions about the hiking trail. Candace began asking Mason questions about what he wanted to do for the rest of the summer before he was supposed to start his job with his mother. Pandora just listened to the conversations around her, holding her grandmother's hand under the table. Dot rubbed her thumb over the back of Pandora's hand, calming her just enough that Pandora didn't fidget in her seat.

"Are you alright, Pandora?" Candace asked, concerned at how little Pandora had eaten.

"Yeah." Pandora smiled. "Just not too hungry right now."

Mason and Abby shared a look that Pandora missed. Abby packed Pandora's food to go, knowing Pandora would end up forcing herself to eat it later. They rode back to the house in silence, Pandora with her head leaning against the window. Once home, Pandora went into her room, locking the door behind her to be left alone. She finally turned her phone on, watching as it lit up with new messages and missed phone calls. Pandora sighed, ignoring the tones as they flooded her phone, waiting for it to stop.

Once it finally had, Pandora picked the phone up from her bedside table and scrolled through it. She had seventeen missed calls from Sam alone, about five from each of the other men. There were too many text messages for Pandora to count, so she clicked the conversation between herself and Sam and scrolled to the top.

"Pandora"

"Answer me please"

"Please"

"I'm sorry"

"I'm an idiot"

"I fucked up"

"Damn it, Pandora! ANSWER ME!"

"I'm so sorry Pandora. Please come back. Please."

There were more, but the one that caught her attention was the most recent and longest one she had received.

"I know I fucked up. Everyone is pissed at me which they should be. I shouldn't have hurt you the way that I did. I should have trusted you. I know that you're an amazing Alpha. You're probably the best thing to ever happen to the pack. Not probably. You are. I betrayed your trust after we spent the night together. You were so vulnerable, and I took advantage of that and for that I will forever be sorry. I know you'll probably never trust me again, but please, just come back. Come home.

"Hit me, beat me, kick me out if you need to. I promise I'll leave if you tell me to. I don't know what to do Pandora. I miss you. I can feel how far you are from me and it's killing me. I want to go to you, everything in me is telling me that you need me there, but I can't go to you without your permission. It's up to you Pandora. I will wait for you for the rest of my life if I have to, but I will make it up to you. I will fight for you every day of my life. I will stride to be better for you and only you. You are my life now.

"I don't understand everything that has happened since the moment I saw you, but I know that I'm already in love with you. I am terrified of these feelings. We haven't known each other long enough for this to be real and I know that you may not feel this strongly about me yet, but I do love you. It may be the mate bond talking, but it's true. I need you Pandora. Forever. I'll wait for you until my last breath if I have to.

"Please, just let me know that you're okay."

Pandora let out a long breath, rereading the message a few times before checking her other messages and calling Jordan back.

"Shut up!" she heard Jordan's accent when he answered the phone directed towards someone else. "Pandora, are you okay?"

"I'm okay," Pandora whispered.

"Is that Pandora?" Loren's voice was in the background.

"I'm going to put you on speaker," Jordan said before Pandora could argue. "You're on speaker."

"Don't really want to be," Pandora stated.

"Sam isn't here," Warren's southern draw sounded so far away.

"Oh," Pandora whispered.

"Are you okay?" Jordan asked again.

"Yeah." Pandora sighed. "I just needed to check on you guys and wanted y'all to know that we made it home."

"No," Loren stated. "You left home."

"Ha-ha," Pandora rolled her eyes. "You know what I mean."

"I'm sorry, Pandora," Jordan interrupted. "Sam fucked up big time. He's been gone all day now. I hope he doesn't go looking for you."

"He won't," Pandora stated. "He sent me a long text saying he couldn't come to me without my permission."

"Oh," Jordan said. "Well, I guess that'll work then."

"Yeah," Pandora whispered. "I'm sorry for leaving you guys. I didn't want to."

"You don't have to explain yourself to us, Pandora," Warren stated. "Sam shouldn't have done what he did."

"No, he shouldn't have. However, I would have done the same thing. If Sam and I were reversed, I would've gone through his stuff too. I wouldn't have waited until he trusted me to do it, but still."

"But he did wait until you trusted him. That's the whole point," Loren stated. "He waited until you trusted him and then hurt you. We all tried to kick his ass after you left, but pack bond and all that."

"Don't push him away guys. He was just worried about y'all. He wants y'all safe, and I completely understand that…"

"You are our family, Pandora," Loren interrupted. "Not just Sam. We protect family, remember?"

Pandora smiled before whispering okay again. A knock on her door brought Pandora back to her old life.

"I should go guys. I'm going to take some time to figure out what I want, but I'll probably be back sooner than you think," Pandora promised.

The boys called their goodbyes as Pandora walked to her door. She hung up her phone and unlocked her door. She opened it wide and found Abby waiting for her.

"Hey." Abby smiled.

"I don't really want to talk right now," Pandora admitted.

"I know," Abby said. "I was just letting you know that Sam called again. I told him to stop calling and that we were fine."

"Thank you," Pandora nodded. "I just got off the phone with the rest of the pack. He isn't with them."

"So, when are we going back?" Abby asked.

"What?" Pandora asked.

"You heard me. You aren't going to leave those boys to their own devices, and you know it."

Pandora sighed and smiled.

"You're right," she nodded. "You don't have to go with me if you don't want to. I know you had a plan for after the trip."

"Nonsense." Abby smiled. "Mason and I had already wanted to stay before you said it was up to me. I just wanted to make you sweat a bit."

"Rude." Pandora laughed.

Abby and she shared a look before Pandora sighed again, sagging against the door a bit.

"Want to read the message Sam sent me?"

CHAPTER SEVENTEEN

Returning

Mason, Abby, and Pandora sat facing Candace, Shannon, and Dot. They were all gathered on Dot's back porch, all staring at each other.

"So, nothing happened in Pennsylvania?" Candace asked.

"Correct," Pandora stated.

"But you're moving there?" Shannon asked.

"Also, correct," Pandora stated.

"And you want to go with her?" Candace asked Abby.

"Yes, ma'am," Abby answered.

Candace leaned back in her seat.

"And you're going with them?" Shannon asked Mason.

"And Dot," Mason added.

"You're leaving too?" Candace asked Dot.

Dot just nodded, a smile lighting her face. Candace seemed a bit defeated. Shannon's face was red, but Pandora couldn't tell if he was going to blow up on them or cry. Shannon let out a long, slow breath before leaning back in his seat.

"What are you going to do about a place to live?" Shannon asked.

"I already have a place there," Pandora stated honestly. "Grandpa left it to me. It's a gorgeous wooden cottage. We saw it while we were there."

"So, you knew it was there?" Candace asked.

"No," Pandora stated. "We found it on accident honestly. I didn't know it belonged to Grandpa until after. The bills for it are paid and everything. We won't have to buy anything except for groceries for a long time."

"How do you plan to buy those groceries?" Shannon asked.

"My inheritance will cover all living cost that are not covered already," Pandora stated. "I plan on opening a shop there, too. That way it's not just us sitting around, blowing money that was left to me for fun. I'll be working and Abby already said she'd help me with the shop. Mason too."

"What about the job with your mom?" Shannon asked Mason. "You made a commitment to her a long time ago. Are you just going to break your word?"

"No, sir," Mason stated. "I already spoke to her earlier today. The work she needs from me can all be done on a computer. If she needs me in person, then I'll drive to her."

"You only have one vehicle between the three of you," Candace stated.

"Two if we count Dot's Beetle," Shannon added.

"How do you plan to drive to her? Pandora can't let you take the truck for long periods of time. She'll need it for the shop," Candace argued.

"I have a car," Mason stated. "Pandora just likes to use her truck, so I haven't driven it in a while. A friend of mine has been keeping an eye on it for me."

"Why?" Candace asked.

"Because he…"

"No," Candace interrupted Mason, looking to Abby. "Why are you really leaving? There's something you three aren't telling us, and I want to know what it is."

"I have a boyfriend," Pandora blurted.

"What?" Candace asked.

"I have a boyfriend. He lives in Somerset. We've been seeing each other for a while now, but it's been long distance this whole time. We met in person while we were there. He and I want to live near each other though." Pandora breathed evenly.

"So, you're leaving to shack up with some guy that you've met once?" Candace asked.

"No," Pandora argued. "He won't be living with us. He has his own place."

"Why not visit each other a few more times first?" Candace asked.

"Because we don't want to," Pandora stated before continuing. "We are adults you know. We can make these decisions without your consent. We understand that it's a shock and that you're angry. I know that Abby leaving is going to hurt…"

"Not just Abby!" Shannon yelled before calming himself again. "You're a daughter to us too, Pandora. I know we aren't your real parents, but we've done our best to help you every step of your life. We just wish you would have spoken to us when you were still thinking about the move, rather than waiting until after your minds were set to just tell us you were going to be leaving. If you had told us from the beginning, this conversation would be going differently. We might be going with you had we had notice. Had you told us just a week ago, I wouldn't have signed another five-year contract at work."

"We didn't know a week ago," Pandora said honestly. "We didn't know about the cottage or that Sam and I would feel so strongly about each other."

"So, he has a name?" Candace grumbled.

Pandora smiled at her for a moment before she continued.

"Yes, his name is Sam. He's a complete gentleman so you have nothing to worry about."

"That's not how that works," Shannon stated. "I want to meet him before you leave."

Pandora let out a small breath, not sure she wanted to even see Sam anytime soon. She nodded anyway, knowing it would help Shannon and Candace feel better.

"And you knew about this?" Candace asked, turning to Dot.

Dot just smiled, saying nothing again.

A week after the conversation with Shannon and Candace, Pandora called Sam. He answered on the first ring.

"Pandora?" he asked.

"Sam," she answered.

"Are you okay?" he asked quickly.

"Yes," Pandora stated. "I need you to come to South Carolina though. Can you get the time off of work?"

"I can be there tomorrow," he stated.

"Don't rush it. Shannon and Candace want to meet you."

"Who?"

"Abby's parents. My kind of parents."

"Oh."

"I told them you were my boyfriend."

"Oh?"

Pandora could hear the smile in his voice.

"Shut up. They kept asking why Mason, Abby, and I are moving to Pennsylvania and I needed a reason, so I said that you and I have been in a long-distance relationship for a while…"

"Wait!" Sam interrupted Pandora's rant. "You're moving here?"

"Yes," Pandora stated. "And if they ask, we are not going to be living together, which you need to trade rooms with someone because I do not want to be next to you right now. Also, we've been seeing each other for a while."

"I'll trade Warren. How long is a while?" Sam asked.

"I don't know. I didn't say an actual amount of time."

"Maybe we should talk for a bit, then. Figure out a story and get to know each other more. I don't even know what you graduated with for college."

"I graduated from Coastal Carolina College, just like my parents. I have a master's in management and business. Also, I got a 34 on my ACT. You?"

"Damn, you're smart," Sam stated. "I started at Penn State, but dropped out because I couldn't keep up like I did in high school. I was studying photography."

"You told me you were into photography," Pandora stated.

"Yeah," Sam stated. "I moved here from…"

"Ohio."

"Yeah."

Pandora and Sam remained quiet for a few minutes. Sam thought that Pandora had hung up at one point, but then she took a deep breath to signal she was still there.

"I'm still angry at you," Pandora stated.

"I know," Sam said. "You and everyone else."

"I don't trust you."

"I don't blame you."

"Four years."

"Four years?" Sam asked.

"We'll tell them we've been seeing each other long distance for four years. That's the last time they heard Abby talk about me having a fling, so it'll be believable."

"Fling?" Sam asked.

"Nothing serious."

"Okay." Sam sighed. "What about the little things?"

"What little things?" Pandora asked.

"You've really never been in a relationship before, have you?"

"We've already discussed that."

"Well, in a relationship, there are little things that people know about each other. Like, favorite color, movies, books. Things like that."

"Yellow. *Breakfast Club*. *Harry Potter* series."

"Of course, you're a Harry Potter girl."

"Shut up. What are your little things?"

"Well, my favorite color is grey which people think is weird. I don't have a favorite movie, but my favorite thing to binge is *Stranger Things*. I don't read a lot of books. I have comics."

"DC or Marvel?" Pandora asked.

"DC. Can't beat Batman."

"Iron Man could."

"Shut up."

Pandora let out a small laugh. Sam smiled into his phone, happy to hear the sound again. Her laugh was his new favorite song, and he wanted it on repeat. They talked for a few hours, getting to know the "little things" as Sam called them. The whole concept was completely foreign to Pandora, but she felt like she was in an actual relationship suddenly.

"So, tomorrow?" Pandora asked.

"Tomorrow," Sam promised. "Goodnight, Pandora."

"Goodnight, Sam," Pandora hung up the phone and set it on the charger, falling asleep as soon as she closed her eyes.

She woke up to the sound of car doors outside her window. She groaned and rolled to her other side, covering her head with her pillow and cursing whoever had woken her. A few minutes later she could hear Abby's laugh drifting down the hall and towards her room.

"No!" Pandora yelled when she heard her bedroom door open, not coming out from under her pillow and blankets. "I don't want any breakfast, Abby! Let me sleep!"

"I'm not Abby," a British accent reached her ears, causing Pandora to sit up.

"Jordan!" Pandora yelled, jumping out of bed and into Jordan's open arms. "What are you doing here?"

"You think we were going to let Sam be the only one to see your town?" Warren's drawl said from behind Jordan.

Pandora hugged Warren tightly after she had released Jordan. Loren and Nature were next.

"You didn't all have to come." Pandora smiled to her pack.

"They didn't really give me much choice."

Pandora turned at the sound of Sam's voice in her doorway. He was leaning against the frame, his eyes meeting hers easily. He gave her a small smile. She nodded to him, not smiling back.

"So, you two are going to have to act more couple-y than that," Abby stated, passing Sam to get to Pandora. "We're having dinner with mom and dad tonight in Myrtle Beach. They're gone for the day, so you have until then to figure some shit out. You two stay here; Mason and I will show the guys around."

Abby pulled the rest of the pack out of Pandora's room, leaving Sam and Pandora behind to fend for themselves. Sam looked around Pandora's room, eyeing everything a bit.

"Looking for more pills?" Pandora asked, crossing her arms over her chest.

"No," Sam stated. "I was just looking around. People's rooms say a lot about them."

"Or you could just ask the person standing in front of you," Pandora countered. "It would save a lot of time and effort."

"I could do that," Sam stated.

They both remained silent, keeping eye contact as they each tried to figure out what to do next.

"I'm sorry, Pandora," Sam finally said. "I know I fucked up. You have no reason to trust me ever again. I don't blame you for being angry at me. I'm angry at me, too."

"It wouldn't be so bad if you hadn't waited until the morning after to look through my stuff," Pandora stated. "You waited until I trusted you before you did it, Sam. Had you done it before that, I honestly wouldn't be near as mad. I'd still think you need to work on your shit a bit, but I wouldn't be so angry that I want to punch you right now."

"I know," Sam stated. "I'm sorry."

"So you keep saying."

"I don't know what else to say right now. I know I can't ask you to forgive me yet. I don't deserve it. I need to prove myself to you, and I'm willing to do that."

"Well, you can start tonight," Pandora stated. "All you're getting is me sitting at your side and holding your hand for Shannon and Candace's sake. When they aren't around, don't touch me."

"Yes, ma'am," Sam stated.

"Does your mom know about the legends?" Pandora asked.

"Yes," Sam answered.

"Does she know about me?"

"Yes."

"Does she know what you did?"

Sam hesitated before shaking his head no.

"Call her and tell her."

"You want me to tell my mom?" Sam asked.

"Yes. Every bit of it. That way she can bitch you out for your treatment of me. I know she raised you better than that."

Sam let out a low breath before pulling out his phone. He clicked his mom's contact and pressed call.

"Hey, baby," his momma answered. "How are you?"

"I'm okay, Momma," Sam said.

Pandora walked past Sam and out of the room, closing the door behind herself so Sam would have some privacy.

"What's wrong, baby?" his mom asked. "You sound upset?"

"I'm in South Carolina," Sam stated.

"Oh?" his mom asked. "Did you go to meet Pandora?"

"Yes, ma'am," he said. "She's angry at me right now."

"What happened?"

"I messed up," Sam admitted.

"What happened?" she asked again.

"So, remember when I told you that Pandora left Pennsylvania to help her grandmother?"

"Yes?"

"I lied to you. I'm sorry, Momma."

"So, why did she really leave?" his mom asked.

"Pandora and I slept together the night before she left," Sam blurted.

"Took you long enough. Mates typically don't last five minutes around each other." His mom laughed.

"Yeah, well, the very next morning, I went through Pandora's stuff," Sam stated.

"Why?" his mom asked.

"I didn't trust her," Sam stated.

"You slept with her but didn't trust her?" his mother asked.

"Yeah." Sam sighed. "Let me finish before you start yelling at me, please?"

"Okay," his mom's agitated voice came through the phone.

Sam told his mom the whole argument that had broken out between himself and Loren and then the one with Pandora that had followed. His mom listened patiently, absorbing his words as he spoke. He stopped talking after he explained why he was in South Carolina.

"Mom?" he asked when his mom didn't say anything.

"Boy, you are lucky that she is letting you be under the same roof as her right now. If I was there, I would slap the hell out of you," his mom stated angrily. "That poor girl sounds like she has been dealt a bad hand and somehow has made the most out of it, just for you to tear her trust down. She deserves better than that from her damn mate. I cannot believe you! I thought I had raised you better than that...."

"You did, Momma...."

"And then for you to treat Loren the way that you did. I mean, I'm going to call him as soon as I'm done with you. How could you not go looking for your brother, though? That girl was out there alone looking for him. She wasn't the one that should have been looking for him. You were, Sam!"

"I know," Sam whispered. "I messed up bad. Loren won't even look at me right now. The guys have all pushed me out. I don't know how Pandora is in the next room from me right now."

"Let me talk to her," his mom demanded.

"What?" he asked.

"You heard me! Put her on the phone."

Sam sighed as he headed out of Pandora's room. He found her in the kitchen, headphones in her ears as she danced around the kitchen cooking. Sam smiled at the sight before remembering why he had gone looking for her.

"Hold on, Momma," he said into his phone before putting it on speaker and setting it on the kitchen table.

He walked behind Pandora and placed his hand on her hip. Pandora jumped at his touch having been caught off guard.

"Shit!" she yelled. "You scared me."

"Sorry," Sam apologized. "My mom wants to talk to you."

"Okay," Pandora nodded.

Sam retrieved his phone and passed it to Pandora.

"Hello?" Pandora asked, leaving the phone on speaker so she could continue cooking.

"Hello, Pandora. This is Sam's mom, Zuri. Is Sam in the room with you?"

"Yes, ma'am, he is," Pandora stated.

"Go away, Sam!" Zuri called.

Sam groaned and left the room, going back to Pandora's and closing the door.

"He's gone." Pandora smiled.

"Wait a few minutes and then give him his phone back. I just want him to worry." Zuri laughed.

Pandora laughed quietly.

"How are you, dear?" Zuri asked.

"I don't know how to answer that," Pandora said honestly.

"Don't worry about Sam, Pandora. He's a man, and they're all stupid," Zuri assured her.

Pandora let out a light laugh.

"I have to go call Loren, but I wanted to make sure you were okay first," Zuri stated.

"I'll be okay," Pandora promised her.

"Good. I'm sorry for my son's behavior."

"You don't need to apologize. Like you said, men are stupid."

Zuri and Pandora hung up quickly. Pandora waited until she was almost done cooking to call Sam back into the room. Pandora passed Sam his phone and pulled two plates from the cabinet.

"Where's Dot?" Sam asked.

"Farmer's Market," Pandora stated. "She has a stand that she works throughout the week."

"That's cool," Sam stated.

"Yeah," Pandora agreed, passing a plate with eggs, roasted tomatoes, and ham to Sam.

"I feel like I should make a joke about your name rhyming with ham, but I'm still tired," Pandora stated.

"I heard a lot of green eggs and ham jokes growing up," Sam admitted.

"Hmm," Pandora hummed, pulling orange juice from the fridge and pouring Sam a glass.

Sam gave Pandora a strange look as she passed him his orange juice and then joined him at the table.

"What?" Pandora asked as she sat down.

"Do you always serve everyone else before you eat?" Sam asked.

"Yes," Pandora stated, waiting for Sam to take a bite.

"Why?" Sam asked.

"Always have," Pandora shrugged.

"Okay," Sam said, taking a quick bite.

Pandora followed his lead and began to eat. They ate in silence, neither really having anything to say. Once done, Sam took the plates from Pandora and began washing them.

"I can do that," Pandora stated.

"You cooked. I can clean," Sam shrugged.

Pandora just sighed, leaning against the back of her chair while facing Sam.

"We need to find a way to be around each other," Pandora stated.

"I'll do whatever you need me to," Sam stated, facing Pandora as he finished the dishes.

"I don't know what to do," Pandora stated. "I've never had to deal with something like this before. I know I'm going to have to forgive you eventually...."

"You don't need to forgive me any time soon," Sam interrupted. "Take as much time as you need. We won't even think about it tonight. Tonight will be all fake smiles to help Abby's parents feel better. I'll act like everything is finally perfect and that I'm grateful that you're moving to be closer to me, because I am. The only thing I won't be faking is that you're angry with me."

Pandora gave Sam a leveled gaze. She studied him for a moment before nodding.

"Tonight, I won't be mad at you. Tonight, I'll pretend that we never fought about anything serious before."

Pandora said the mantra more to herself than to Sam. Sam just leaned against the kitchen counter, watching Pandora.

"We need to do more than hold hands," Pandora stated. "We're going to have to cuddle against each other at the table and act like we're in love."

"I mean…"

"Don't tell me that you love me," Pandora stated. "It's already shitty enough that you said it over a text message when I wasn't speaking to you. I'm trying to be angry with you for one thing at a time right now though, so I'm focusing on the thing that I can handle."

Sam closed his mouth and stared at Pandora.

"Should we practice pretending to be in love?" he finally asked.

"I don't know how we can do that," Pandora stated.

"We can sit on the couch and watch TV," Sam suggested.

"That's all?" Pandora asked.

"Yes," Sam stated. "We'll cuddle up on the couch and watch whatever you want to. I won't even complain if it's something girly and cheesy."

"You're going to regret that." Pandora laughed as she headed towards the living room.

CHAPTER EIGHTEEN

Dinner

"Those were the cheesiest movies I have ever seen in my life." Sam smiled.

"Oh, just wait. We haven't even gotten to the good stuff yet." Pandora laughed.

"There are cheesier movies than that?" Sam asked.

"Of course." Pandora smiled. "*Sweet Home Alabama* and *Fried Green Tomato*es are amazing, and if you continue to call them cheesy, I may have to kick you out."

Sam held up his hands in mock surrender. Pandora smiled and stood from the couch, stretching in the process.

"I'm going to go take a shower before we head to Myrtle Beach," Pandora stated. "If you want to, I can put in another movie for you."

"Please don't." Sam laughed.

"Just wait." Pandora smiled. "Soon, you'll be quoting those movies to get on my good side."

"I never pegged you for a chick flick kind of girl," Sam admitted.

"All girls are. We just don't like to admit it."

"Fair point." Sam smiled.

"I'll see you in a bit." Pandora smiled, leaving Sam alone in the living room.

Sam looked around as Pandora showered, smiling at the pictures of his mate growing up. He started at the picture of Pandora her senior year of high school, the rest of the pictures going down in age as he went. There were pictures with

Abby and her grandmother and some of Pandora alone. He reached a picture of Pandora with what had to be her grandfather and smiled. Pandora was sitting on the man's knee, smiling and reaching for the camera, her grandfather holding her small body as he sat in a rocking chair. She couldn't be more than ten.

The next photo made him pause. The picture was a small family of four. He recognized Pandora easily as he had seen all of the pictures aging her down. The adults were, if he had to guess, her parents. Sam didn't recognize the baby in the photo though. Pandora had never mentioned having a younger sibling and he didn't see pictures of any other children. Maybe she hadn't mentioned it because it was too hard to talk about?

Pandora returned to the living room as Sam was still looking at the photo. Her hair was still wet as she stood beside him. She looked at the photo too, barely breathing. Sam turned to her, waiting for an answer.

"His name was Apollo," Pandora whispered, still looking at the photo. "He was with my parents in the car accident. I don't talk about him, because the police reports say that they couldn't identify his body. Mom and dad had taken him to the doctor because he had a temperature. Grandma and Grandpa were watching me so that mom and dad didn't have to deal with two crying babies. I guess they lost control of the vehicle. Mom was thrown from the vehicle and dad died on impact. The car caught fire though. The police don't think Apollo died right away."

Sam let out a ragged breath as Pandora still stared at the photo. She shook a bit and held in the tears that she always had for Apollo. She hadn't said his name in so many years that her heart ached. Sam wrapped his arms around her quickly, holding her to his chest. She sank into his body, accepting his support.

"Mason and Abby don't even know that story. I'm sure if they looked at the pictures, they would have questions. Abby's never needed to look at the photos though, and Mason is always so focused on Abby. It's really weird to think about him now," Pandora stated.

"Do you remember him at all?" Sam asked.

"Sometimes, when I'm sleeping, I remember his laugh. I mean, all babies sound the same when they laugh. It's a high pitch, precious sound, but still. I feel like I could pick his laugh out of any other babies."

Sam smiled and kissed the top of Pandora's head. She sniffled a bit before pulling back from Sam.

"I got your shirt wet with my hair," Pandora stated.

"I have another one with me," Sam shrugged. "I'll go change real quick."

"I'll go dry my hair." Pandora smiled. "I'll be in my room if you want to join me."

Sam nodded to her and watched her walk back to her room. He went out to his car and opened the truck of his car, pulling a shirt out of his overnight bag quickly and changing in the driveway. He rushed back inside to meet Pandora in her room, glancing at the picture once more before entering her room. Sam smirked as he saw her drying her hair. She was bent at her waist, brunette hair falling in front of her in waves, spiral curls longer than he had realized. He couldn't see her face from how she was standing, but he was sure it was red from being upside down.

She turned the blow dryer off a few minutes later and flipped her hair. Sam's eyes grew as he watched her hair fall into place. Pandora's green eyes met Sam's and she raised an eyebrow at him.

"I've only ever seen that happen in movies where the hot girl flips her hair in slow motion," Sam stated.

"You're so weird." Pandora laughed, running her brush through her hair before pulling it into a messy bun on top of her head.

"Why do you always put your hair up?" Sam asked.

"It keeps it out of the way," Pandora shrugged. "If you had thick hair, you would understand."

Sam just shrugged and watched as a few curls fell from Pandora's bun, making her look like a cute librarian. Car doors alerted Sam and Pandora that the pack had returned. Pandora smiled as she headed to the front door, opening it wide to let everyone in. The pack each gave her a hug as they entered the house, most of them ignoring Sam along the way. Loren gave Sam a curt nod as he passed him. Pandora let out a small breath, not sure if she should be thankful that the pack was standing with her, or upset that they were standing against Sam.

"So, the boys are going to meet us on the boardwalk after we have dinner with mom and dad," Abby told Pandora as she and Mason entered the house. "Mom and dad are going to head home afterwards, so it'll just be a fun night, and they won't ask a bunch of questions about a bunch of random guys showing up."

"Sounds good." Pandora laughed. "What sort of trouble will the guys be getting into while we're gone?"

"I'm sure we can find something to do." Jordan smiled.

"Don't make me bail you out of jail," Pandora stated.

"None of us have ever been to jail," Warren stated.

"Well, look at that!" Abby laughed. "We're technically the bad influences!"

Pandora laughed at the confused expressions on her packs faces. Mason filled them in as Pandora and Abby headed to Pandora's room to change. Once they had finished changing, they joined the pack on the back deck, finding that Dot had finally returned home. Dot and Nature were sitting next to one another again, both observing the pack around them. Abby plopped into Mason's lap as Pandora took the seat in between Sam and Loren with ease, feeling like it was her designated spot.

"Zuri is a character, huh?" Loren asked Pandora as she got comfortable.

"She's sweet." Pandora smiled. "We had a really good talk."

"Did you?" Sam asked curiously.

"And I won't be telling you any of it," Pandora commented, smirking to herself.

Sam groaned a bit, feeling like he had been discussed at more length than he actually had. Loren just smiled.

"She got onto me a bit," Loren admitted.

"I'm sorry," Pandora said.

"Don't be. I deserved it."

Pandora squeezed Loren's hand for a moment before releasing him to steal Sam's tea from him. Sam just gave her a look as she drank from his glass. She smiled as she passed it back to him.

"So, are you two good?" Loren asked quietly, trying not to draw attention to them.

"No," Pandora stated. "We need to try to be though, so for tonight, I won't be mad. After tonight? He's fair game again."

Loren laughed as Sam leaned his head back, not sure if he wanted to know what Pandora had in mind. Once it was about an hour before they were supposed to meet Abby's parents for dinner, the small group consisting of Abby, Mason, Pandora, Dot, and Sam piled into Sam's car, Dot riding up front as Sam drove. With the traffic, they made it to the restaurant with five minutes to spare.

"That was terrible," Sam commented as they finally parked the car.

"I hate people," Mason moaned.

"We almost died, like, seven times," Abby said.

"You guys are dramatic." Pandora laughed as Sam opened her door for her.

"You're crazy," Abby stated.

"No. Grandma had me tested," Pandora joked.

Mason held the door as the group entered the restaurant, Abby taking the lead when asked for a name by the host. They were led to a semi-private table where Shannon and Candace were already waiting, a bottle of wine opened for the table.

Shannon stood when he saw them walking towards the table, trying to seem taller than Sam. Sam took his hand and introduced himself. Shannon looked Sam over before introducing Candace. Sam pulled out Pandora's chair for her before sitting next to her. Candace smiled at the gesture before taking Shannon's hand. Pandora took Sam's under the table and leaned her body towards him, surprised at how easy it felt. Sam smiled to her before looking around the table.

"We've already ordered for everyone," Shannon stated. "I hope you don't mind. Thought it would save some time. Plus, Pandora told us you weren't allergic to anything, but that you don't like mushrooms."

"Not at all." Sam smiled, trying to figure out when in his head Pandora had figured out that he didn't like mushrooms.

Pandora smiled and squeezed Sam's hand, reassuring him that she was still there before the questions would begin.

"So, Sam," Candace finally began. "Tell us about yourself. Pandora hasn't told us much. You're quite the mystery."

"Not much to tell, ma'am." Sam smiled. "I'm from Ohio. I moved to Pennsylvania for college and ended up staying there even though I ended up dropping out."

"Why'd you drop out?" Shannon asked.

"Dad," Abby warned.

"It's okay," Sam assured Abby before turning to Shannon again. "I didn't feel like the things I wanted to learn could be taught to me. I felt that I needed to go figure things out on my own."

"Makes sense," Candace nodded.

"Pandora was valedictorian in high school," Shannon stated. "Did she tell you that?"

"She didn't, but I knew she must've been in the higher percentage of her class when she told me her ACT score." Sam smiled.

"I wasn't even trying that hard." Pandora smiled.

"Which makes it scarier." Sam smiled to her.

"What do you want to do with your life, Sam?" Shannon asked, interrupting the moment.

"I want to be a photographer," Sam answered.

"That's not steady work," Shannon commented.

"It isn't, but my mother tells me that I should do what makes me happy. Photography makes me happy."

"How can you be happy without stability?" Shannon asked.

"Shannon," Candace whispered, trying to rain her husband in.

"Well, I've already done two art shows this year. I sold every photograph at each show for one thousand dollars. Each showcase contained thirteen photos. I have three more shows this year. It's pretty stable for me at the moment. However, if I ever don't sell my photographs, I have a job as an assistant librarian at Penn State."

Pandora did her best to not looked shocked at Sam's answer. Instead, she smiled, letting herself feel proud of Sam for the things that he had accomplished.

"Would I know any of your work?" Candace asked curiously.

"I'm not sure," Sam answered honestly. "Not a lot of people have seen my work. It's mostly private showings."

"Well, we'll have to come to one of your next shows." Candace smiled excitedly.

"The next one is at the end of summer in New York. I can give Pandora the details to give to you."

Pandora smiled to Sam as Shannon cleared his throat.

"How did the two of you meet?" Joseph asked, catching Pandora and Sam both off guard.

"Oh, well..." Pandora turned to Sam.

"Facebook," Sam suggested.

"Facebook," Pandora nodded.

"Facebook?" Shannon asked. "You don't seem too sure about that."

"Well, we aren't friends on Facebook," Pandora stated. "We both are on a few of the same Facebook pages and began messaging each other at some point."

"Why not be friends on Facebook?" Shannon asked.

"I don't really use it that much," Sam answered. "I only kept it for my art page honestly. Now, I have it for that page and for messenger, which I use to talk to fans. I can send you the fan page if you like."

"That sounds great." Candace smiled.

Pandora squeezed Sam's hand again, causing Sam to look to her and smile. Their food was brought to them and the conversation died down a bit. Sam watched as Pandora waited for everyone to take a bite before her. She looked to Sam last, noticing that he hadn't eaten yet. Shannon watched the interaction carefully. He noticed that Sam gave Pandora a challenging look when she refused to eat before him. He saw how Pandora cocked her eyebrow to him, accepting the challenge without hesitation. Sam gave Pandora a small look that caused Pandora to nod. At the same time, the couple each took a bite of their own food. Shannon nodded his head, liking that Sam was trying to help Pandora break a few of her eating habits. Maybe Sam wasn't so bad after all.

Candace asked Sam a few more questions about his photographs as everyone finished dinner. He answered the questions proudly, causing Pandora to smile fondly. Shannon wasn't sure he liked the man that was stealing his daughters away to a new state, but he liked how Sam looked at Pandora when she wasn't looking. He liked how Sam and Pandora would share looks with one another, silently communicating. He liked that Pandora and Sam never let go of one another and that they seemed to drift towards each other like magnets.

Once dinner had ended, Shannon, Candace, and Dot left the two couples and headed home. Pandora and Sam walked slowly behind Mason and Abby, still holding each other's hands as they went to meet up with the pack.

CHAPTER NINETEEN

BOARDWALK

"This is so cool!" Jordan yelled as they waited in line for the Ferris wheel.

"I don't think Warren agrees with you." Pandora laughed.

"He'll be okay." Jordan smiled.

"If I puke on you, it's your own fault," Warren stated.

"So, the bull rider is afraid of heights?" Abby asked.

"Bull rider?" Pandora asked Sam quietly.

"Yeah," Sam stated.

"Shut up," Warren said to Abby, climbing carefully into his seat on the ride that he was sure was to kill him.

Being that the Ferris wheel was enclosed, Jordan sat next to Warren. Abby and Mason sat across from the two boys and waved to Pandora as their door closed and they were pulled away. The next set of seats stopped in front of Loren, Nature, Sam, and Pandora and they climbed in, Sam keeping his spot next to Pandora.

"Twenty says he pukes," Loren held his hand out to Nature who took it without a second thought.

"So, what are we doing after this?" Sam asked Pandora.

"Well, there's a bunch of souvenir shops with really expensive seashells," Pandora stated. "Or, I know a secluded beach that has parties every night."

"I vote party," Loren stated.

"I second his vote," Sam stated.

Nature held up three fingers.

"And Alpha rules: party." Pandora smiled.

Loren and Sam cheered as Nature lifted his arms in celebration. Pandora smiled at her boys, loving how happy they looked. Pandora looked out at the ocean, a content feeling in her heart.

"Wow," Sam stated, looking at the ocean for the first time.

"This is why I wanted us to do this," Pandora told him. "You said you never saw the ocean before. I wanted to get you up here before the sun went down."

Sam smiled brightly to Pandora, kissing her forehead before looking at the ocean again. Pandora watched Sam instead. She watched how his eyes had grown when he saw the ocean. She watched as he gazed out to it, probably wondering how far it went. Pandora snuck out her phone and took a picture of Sam, making sure he didn't see her. She took a picture of the boys across from her as well, just as sneaky as before.

Once they were back on the ground again and Loren had paid Nature, everyone piled into Sam's car and Nature's truck. Mason drove Sam's car so that they wouldn't get lost on the way to the private beach, Abby in the passenger seat. Pandora laid across the backseat, taking a small nap on Sam's lap, knowing it would be an hour before they reached their destination.

Sam shook Pandora's shoulder gently. Her eyes fluttered open, and she looked up to Sam.

"Are we there?" Pandora asked.

"Yeah." Sam smiled.

Pandora sat up and Sam helped her climb out of the car. Pandora let her hair down after she got out of the car, letting the ocean breeze lightly kiss her skin. She hummed at the feeling and took Sam's hand again. Mason and Abby led the way down the long path from the full parking lot to the beach ahead.

"Seems like someone got started without us," Abby joked.

"How rude of them," Pandora stated, rolling her eyes.

Once they reached the end of the path, the beach opened up. It was filled with locals and college kids. There were kegs all over the place and two huge bonfires burning. In the water, Pandora could see a few skinny dippers that disappeared behind the rocks for privacy.

"Did I just see naked people in the water?" Jordan asked Pandora.

"Yup." Pandora smiled. "Congrats, boys. You are now in Lover's Cove. Bathing suits are optional from this point forward."

Pandora let go of Sam's hand and walked forward, meeting Abby and Mason at the closest keg. The pack all looked to one another, some with shock, some with excitement. Warren was the first to strip and run to the water, not bashful in the least, Loren following him right after. Jordan and Sam joined the trio at the keg as Nature wondered towards the bonfire, eyes set on a pretty girl dancing in the wind.

"How do you find a place like this?" Jordan asked Pandora.

"It was shown to us," Pandora stated. "Some guy wanted to see Abby naked."

"I thought it was the easiest way to get her out of her clothes at the time!" Mason yelled.

Pandora, Abby, Sam, and Jordan all laughed loudly. Mason just smiled at his two girls, knowing they wouldn't admit that they had been the ones to show him.

"I thought you were the good kid." Jordan pointed to Mason. "You're just as bad as them."

"No, no. We're worse," Pandora argued with a smile.

"How so?" Sam asked, low in Pandora's ear so only she could hear him.

"I think I'll go swimming now," Pandora stated, moving from Sam with a suggestive grin. "See y'all in a bit."

Pandora walked away from her friends and towards the rocks, not taking any of her clothes off in the process. Pandora walked around the rocks, avoiding the water in general. Sam followed her, not too closely as he was curious to what she was doing. She wandered down the beach a bit, stopping at the mouth of a cave. She kicked off her shoes and stripped to just her bra and underwear, folding her clothes neatly before entering the cave's mouth.

"Pandora?" Sam called.

"Come on!" Pandora called back, laughter in her voice.

Sam striped to his boxers and followed Pandora's lead, careful of where he stepped. He wandered for a bit before he heard a splash ahead of him.

"Pandora?" he called again.

When she didn't answer, he rushed forward too quickly. He lost his footing as he stepped over a cliff and fell towards water. He turned his stumble into a dive, easily breaking water. He opened his eyes under the water to search for Pandora. Once he opened his eyes though, he gasped and had to swim back to the top. He had fallen into a freshwater pond somehow. It was glowing blue from bioluminescent algae. Pandora was sitting on a rock along the wall, watching Sam's reaction.

"Holy shit." Sam breathed.

"Yeah." Pandora smiled. "I should've warned you about the fall, but it's funnier when people aren't expecting it."

"Thanks," Sam said sarcastically, pulling himself out of the water to sit next to Pandora. "How is it glowing like this?"

"Well, it's a type of plankton," Pandora stated. "How it survives in fresh water, I have no clue considering there are barely any that can. It gets in through a tunnel over there though."

"How do we get out of here?" Sam asked.

"Why would you want to leave?" Pandora asked.

"Just curious." Sam smiled.

Pandora pointed towards a path along the rocks that led back to the beach where their clothes sat. Sam smiled and looked to Pandora.

"Why'd you tell me to come with you?" he asked.

"I told you, you get one night where I'm not mad at you." Pandora smiled. "Maybe if I pretend that I'm not mad at you tonight, it'll make me less mad tomorrow."

Sam nodded, kind of understanding what she meant.

"So, tonight, I am yours." Pandora smiled.

"All mine?" Sam asked.

"I'm giving you an inch. Don't take a mile."

"Yes, ma'am." Sam smiled before looking around again. "How did you find this place?"

"I didn't," Pandora stated. "Again, I was shown. Not exactly the best memories here, but I figured I'd make a good one with you."

"What happened here?" Sam asked.

"Well…" Pandora breathed. "It's a long story. Sure you have time?"

"I have all of my life." Sam smiled.

Pandora returned his smile before looking around the glowing cave.

"So, I told you that I tried to kill myself a few years back." Pandora waited until Sam nodded to continue. "There was this guy named Mark. He showed Abby and I this beach five years ago, not Mason. Abby and I showed Mason two years ago.

"Mark had a bit of a thing for me. By thing, I mean he was obsessed. He stalked me and broke into my grandmother's house at one point. I took out a restraining order against him and didn't hear from him again for a year. One night, I was having a rough time and wanted to be alone. I came here not really thinking about him since it had been so long. I didn't realize that he had just been waiting until I was alone.

"He waited a whole year. He kept just enough distance that I didn't notice him for that long. When I came here though, he saw it as his chance, I guess. He approached me and, when I told him I didn't want anything to do with him, he tried to kill me."

Pandora pointed to a jagged corner on the rock Sam was sitting on.

"He hit my head right there. I lost a lot of blood and it scared him, so he ran and left me here to die. I don't know everything that happened, but the doctors said that he raped me, and later I found out that I was pregnant. I got an abortion immediately. I didn't want a child to come from violence. He's in prison right now."

Sam remained silent, anger rising inside of him as he stared at the jagged rock under him. He pulled Pandora into his lap and scooted to her rock instead. He held her closely, not wanting to let her go ever again.

"I'm okay," Pandora whispered to him. "I'm okay."

"I'm sorry," Sam said. "I'm sorry for hurting you. I'm sorry for betraying your trust. I will never do it again, I swear."

"I forgive you," Pandora stated, pulling away from Sam so that she could look into his eyes.

"Why?" he questioned.

"Because I can." Pandora shrugged, not really sure of the reason herself.

Pandora pulled Sam to her, taking his mouth with her own. They kissed deeply, losing themselves in the kiss. The spark they felt was quickly growing into a fire, and Pandora knew if they kept kissing, she would find herself lost to Sam again. She straddled his lap, deciding that she didn't give a damn anymore and grinding against him. Sam moaned and kissed Pandora's chest. He undid her bra and threw it towards the path before taking her left breast in his mouth.

Pandora gasped at the feeling and held his head to her chest. Sam bit her gently, causing Pandora to squirm. He lifted Pandora and set her on the rocks so that she was laying down. He pulled her underwear from her and let them join her bra. He kissed up her leg until he reached her center, diving in to taste her. Once Sam had rocked Pandora with his mouth twice, he kicked off his boxers and lifted Pandora to his lap. He lowered them into the water, finding a ledge that he could stand on that kept them just over waist deep. He plunged into her, pushing her back against the rocks. She begged him for more, and he gave it to her willingly. Once they were through, they swam for a bit in their private cave, teasing each other the whole time.

They rejoined their pack about an hour later, finding everyone except for Nature drunk by one of the bonfires with dripping hair from the water.

"Where's Nature?" Pandora asked Jordan.

Jordan just giggled and pointed towards a kissing couple. Pandora laughed when she realized that Nature was kissing the girl that had been dancing earlier, and it seemed to be getting heated.

"Damn, Nature." Sam smiled.

Pandora just laughed and turned to see Abby making out with Mason in the sand. She walked to them, wondering if they were drunk too. Hearing Abby giggle louder than normal answered the question itself.

"Looks like we're driving home," Pandora told Sam.

"Us and Nature." Sam smiled. "He doesn't drink."

"If he isn't busy." Pandora laughed.

"Well, I think that girl is leaving."

Pandora turned to see Nature walking towards her and Sam, a big smile on his face. His kissing buddy had disappeared.

"Should we collect our people?" Pandora asked the two sober men.

"Nature and I will get the pack. You get the love birds and we'll meet at the cars."

Sam passed Pandora his keys and headed towards the fire. Pandora walked to Mason and Abby, calling their names in the process to get their attention.

"Time to go y'all." Pandora smiled.

"Dora!" Abby yelled, pulling Pandora down to the sand with them, causing Pandora to let out a small "whoa." "I missed you!"

Abby kissed Pandora's cheek sloppily. Mason hugged both of the girls to him tightly.

"My girls!" Mason stated loudly.

Pandora just laughed and stood back up.

"Time to go." Pandora smiled.

Mason stood with Pandora and lifted Abby to her feet. Pandora led her friends to the parking lot, having to chase Abby down a few times in the process. Once they reached the pack, Sam laughed at Pandora's expression.

"Children," Pandora told him. "They're both children. One runs off, and the other acts like it's the end of the world, I swear."

"Can we get food?!" Abby asked loudly.

"Food!" Jordan yelled excitedly.

"I would like one hamburgular, please!" Warren called.

"And some fries!" Loren yelled.

Pandora laughed as Sam groaned.

"Pancakes!" Abby yelled.

"Pancakes!" the pack and Mason yelled back.

"You guys are too drunk for pancakes," Pandora commented.

"We'll be good, Dora! I promise!" Abby yelled.

"You're too loud," Pandora told her.

"I promise," Abby said, trying to whisper.

"Well, we have a bit of a drive. If you've all calmed down in about half an hour, I promise we'll stop for pancakes," Pandora stated.

"Yay!" Abby yelled excitedly. "I wanna ride in the truck!"

Mason and Abby climbed into the backseat of the truck. Jordan got into the passenger seat and Nature went to drive. Loren and Warren were laying down in the bed of the truck and refusing to move, so Sam shut the tailgate and held his passenger's side door open for Pandora.

"Follow us, I guess." Pandora shrugged to Nature before getting into Sam's car.

"I'm surprised they all got drunk so fast." Sam laughed as they pulled out of the parking lot and onto the main road.

"I'm not." Pandora smiled. "Honestly, a couple of them probably aren't drunk. When people are happy and have a bit of alcohol, they copy the interactions around them, mimicking drunk behaviors."

"What?" Sam asked, surprised.

"It was a thesis paper I did." Pandora smiled. "I watched a lot of drunk people for a month before writing it. I think Jordan and Loren aren't actually drunk, just happy."

Sam nodded, a smile gracing his lips. Pandora turned up the radio before taking Sam's hand again. They road silently, both content as they headed down the road.

"I feel bad for Nature. Poor guy has to deal with them all at once."

"I don't think he minds after his little make out session." Sam laughed. "He's probably not even paying attention to them."

Pandora just laughed and rested her head on Sam's shoulder comfortably. They remained silent for another twenty minutes as they drove before Pandora texted Jordan.

"Still want pancakes?"

"YES!!"

Pandora smiled, shaking her head a bit before directing Sam to an IHOP. Sam and Nature parked near the door before everyone piled out of the vehicles. Loren let out a howl towards the sky, Warren and Jordan following behind. Pandora sighed as Sam told the boys to calm down. They entered the restaurant and asked for a booth for eight. They were sat quickly, and Pandora ordered coffee and water for everyone. They all sat around the booth, laughing and eating together. Pandora smiled, cuddling into Sam's side, feeling content again. Sam and Pandora waited until everyone else had started eating before taking a bite of food at the same time.

CHAPTER TWENTY

Packing

The pack had passed out in the living room that night, spread out across each other and the floor with Nature's truck parked down the street. Sam had slept in Pandora's bed, holding her close to him as they slept. They left the next evening while Abby's parents were still at work so they wouldn't see all of the men that piled out of the house like clowns in a car. Pandora, Abby, Mason, and Dot made plans to move at the end of the month, Abby's parents finally holding back their arguments as long as they were allowed to see the cottage when they got there.

The pack made sure to keep the cottage clean, making sure it didn't look lived in. Pandora left her job after she had received her vacation pay so that she would have time to help Dot pack the house. The days went quickly, everything they didn't need packed in little square boxes with labels. Pandora had donated quite a bit of her stuff before college, so her room had been fairly easy, and Dot never kept anything that she didn't need. The hardest part had been when Pandora had gone into the attic while Dot was at the farmer's market.

The attic contained everything that had belonged to her parents and grandfather. Pandora let out a long breath, knowing this would be the hardest thing she had to do. She began going through the boxes and, before she knew it, five hours had passed with her going through her parents' stuff. A knock at the front door had been what alerted her to the time.

She climbed down the attic ladder carefully before going to the door, wondering who was on the other side. Sam stood in the doorway, his warm smile making her feel better.

"Hey." She smiled, surprised.

"You needed me?" Sam asked curiously.

Pandora let out a breath before holding the door open so that he could enter Pandora's almost empty childhood home. After she shut the door behind him, Sam pulled her into a tight hug, kissing the top of her head. Pandora took a deep breath, taking in the familiar scent of him.

"Thank you," Pandora whispered.

Sam just smiled into her hair in response. Pandora pulled away and headed back towards the attic.

"Will you help me with everything in the attic?" she asked him.

"Yeah." Sam nodded. "What's up there?"

"Stuff that belonged to my parents and grandpa," Pandora stated, climbing the ladder easily, Sam behind her.

They worked together silently, creating a system with one another on how to decide what to keep. Pandora kept all of the jewelry and important documents, one of which was the deed to the cottage with her name on it. Pandora had laughed when Sam had showed it to her. She put almost all of the clothes into a donation pile, keeping her father's old-school sweatshirt and two of her mother's dresses, one of which was her wedding dress. The only other thing she kept was a small cradle that had belonged to Apollo, a dull, yellow blanket inside of it with his name stitched in.

Sam held Pandora as she had cried, holding the blanket against her chest and feeling her losses weighing on her. Once they had finished the attic, Sam took all of the donation boxes to Goodwill for Pandora, so she could have some time to herself. Pandora threw the sweatshirt and the blue sundress into the washer with her clothes before unzipping the wedding dress bag. She smiled at the dress, imagining how her mother had probably looked in it. She zipped the dress back up and placed it in her closet with her boxes. She sighed and laid on her bed, cuddling Apollo's blanket and letting her eyes drift closed.

Sam woke her a few hours later.

"Hey, beautiful." He smiled.

Pandora smiled to him, pulling him close to her and kissing him deeply. Sam crawled into the bed next to her, wrapping his arms around her and holding her close.

"I missed you," Pandora admitted.

"I missed you too," Sam stated. "It's weird when you aren't around. Like I'm missing a piece of myself."

"Yeah." Pandora smiled. "I feel it, too."

Sam smiled and kissed her head as it laid on his chest.

"Want me to take some boxes with me when I leave tomorrow?" Sam asked.

"It's up to you," Pandora stated. "I don't want you to do anything extra. You showing up today was enough."

"I don't mind." Sam smiled. "I'll put them in your room for you. The pack has been waiting for you to get back before moving in. They don't want to freak out Abby's parents."

Pandora smiled at how considerate the boys were being.

"Did Jordan's lease end yet?" Pandora asked.

"Yeah. He's crashing with Nature for now."

"Why doesn't he stay at the cottage and just clean up after himself?" Pandora asked. "I know he's the clean one out of all y'all boys."

Sam shrugged his response, not really sure why.

"Maybe he just doesn't want to feel lonely." Pandora sighed. "It's a pretty big cottage for only one person."

"I have so many questions that I know we'll never get the answer to when it comes to that place."

"Like what?"

"How did your grandpa know how many rooms we would need? And there's just enough bar stools in the kitchen and in the patio for the eight of us. Is your grandma moving into the cottage with us?"

Pandora shook her head no, knowing her grandmother planned on living in a trailer park in Somerset.

"So, somehow he knew how many people were going to be living there."

"Maybe he kept track of the descendants."

"So, there are only six descendants left in the world total?" Sam asked. "I don't think that's right. Plus, he knew that Abby and Mason would be there. You didn't even meet Mason until college. Your grandfather never met him."

"I don't know. Everything surrounding my grandfather is a mystery at this point."

Sam and Pandora sat quietly for a while, both drifting in and out of sleep as the day wore on, comfortable enough to just lay together all day.

When Dot got home, she went to Pandora's room to check on her. She found Pandora and Sam asleep and smiled. She went to the kitchen and began preparing dinner for the three of them. Sam woke first, the smell of food bringing him back to consciousness. He sleepily sat at the dining room table, smiling to Dot as she gave him a glass of tea. She sat with him at the table and they ate together, deciding not to wait for Pandora to get up since she hadn't been sleeping well lately.

Sam went to ask Dot a question when Pandora began screaming. Sam and Dot both raced to Pandora's room, throwing the door open to find Pandora sitting up and clinging to Apollo's blanket like an anchor. Her face had tears streaming down it but was pale as a ghost.

"What happened?" Sam asked, going to Pandora immediately.

Pandora just stared into Sam's eyes, not speaking. She sat quietly, barely moving as she caught her breath.

"What happened?" Sam asked again. "Did you have a nightmare?"

Pandora just nodded yes and leaned into Sam. Sam held her tightly as he whispered into her ear that everything was okay. Dot left the couple alone, going to the kitchen instead. She made Pandora a plate and put it into the microwave. Dot then wrote a note telling Pandora she would be back the next morning before grabbing her keys and heading out the door. Dot remained silent as always as she sped away from her house. She knew what was about to start happening to Pandora now that she was the Alpha. She had seen her husband go through much similar feelings, his wolf gene wanting to activate, but being unable to.

No descendants had changed in over a hundred and fifty years. There was a reason that they had started changing again. Dot just hoped that they would survive whatever was coming to them. She drove for an hour, heading further and further into the swamplands of South Carolina. She knew where she needed to go to get her answers. She needed to know how to help Pandora and her pack. She was already withholding more information than she wanted to, but Wepwawet had forbidden her from speaking. She could only speak when it was truly needed, like to tell Pandora the legend or to comfort her recently.

Finally reaching the grounds where the church she had married her late husband at had once stood, Dot parked her Beetle. She walked onto the bit of concrete that remained after the fire with a small bag with supplies. She set her candles in a circle around her, forming a moon big enough for Dot to lie in. She laid down her wooden figurines of wolves at each directional point before lighting her candles and stripping off her clothes. Once bare, Dot lay in the middle of her moon and closed her eyes, leaving her wrist facing the sky.

She called to Wepwawet and her ancestors, demanding they speak to her. At first, no one answered. She was about to give up when she felt an unnatural breeze dance across her skin. She opened her eyes and was face to face with Wepwawet.

"Child," he stated.

"Why are the descendants shifting?" Dot questioned.

"Danger," Wepwawet answered.

"What danger?"

"Close."

"What is the danger?" Dot commanded.

Wepwawet did not answer. Instead he looked to his right, searching through the bog. Dot turned her head, wondering what she was missing. Wepwawet let out a low growl, and Dot sat up. She squinted in the dark, trying to see what he saw. Finally, she saw what Wepwawet had been trying to warn her of. She gasped, but it was too late.

The police sirens outside the front door caught Pandora's attention. She went to the front door and opened it wide, not caring that she seemed nosey. There were two police cruisers in front of her house. A policeman had been walking up her driveway but had stopped when he saw her open her door. Pandora recognized the officer as Joseph, a man who had graduated two years before her in high school.

"Joseph?" Pandora asked. "What's going on?"

"Pandora." Joseph nodded. "Can we go inside?"

Pandora froze. She knew what that meant. She had seen it twice in her life already. She looked towards Abby's house quickly, noticing Abby, Mason, and Abby's parents walking towards her. Pandora was confused for a moment. Everyone that she cared about was either with her or in Pennsylvania. Then Pandora realized who was missing. She looked back to Joseph.

"Where's my grandmother?" Pandora asked him.

"Pandora," Joseph said softly, trying to lead her into the house.

"No!" Pandora yelled. "Where is she?!"

Pandora sped to the police station, ignoring the cars that followed behind her. She pulled in front of the station doors, parking illegally and running inside. The police chief, Richard, was waiting for her there. He gave her a sad look before leading her to the morgue. Sam had somehow caught up to them right before they entered the room. The room was silver and cold. There were four tables, but only one of them occupied, a white sheet covering the body on the table. Pandora went straight to the table with the chief, not taking her eyes off of the sheet.

"This may be hard to see, Pandora," Richard stated.

"Show me," Pandora demanded.

Richard hesitated for a moment before slowly moving the sheet back. On the table, pale and unmoving, Dot laid. Pandora didn't even flinch as she looked at her grandmother. She let out a low breath before nodding to Richard to replace the sheet. They left the room and went back to the main area of the station.

"She was an hour away at the old church," Richard explained. "There are troopers looking for whatever animal did this to her. I'm so sorry, Pandora."

Pandora walked past Richard and back out the front door. Sam walked behind her, not wanting to leave her alone. Abby, Mason, and Abby's parents had just pulled up outside and met Pandora at her truck. Pandora ignored them, climbed into her truck and pulled away.

Sam followed Pandora in his car, calling Abby after forty minutes of driving and telling her what the cop had said.

"Do you think she's going to hunt it herself?" Abby asked.

"If there are troopers out there, they might shoot her," Mason stated in the background.

"I don't know," Sam said. "She shut me out. I can't even read her emotions right now. All I can feel is that something feels wrong."

"Well, yeah something feels wrong. Her grandmother is dead," Abby stated.

"No," Sam stated. "Not like pain. Like something isn't adding up."

Sam got off the phone as Pandora stopped her truck. He parked next to her and followed her as she walked along a muddy path. The path led to a taped off scene that Sam guessed was where Dot had died. The concrete slab in the middle was covered in dark stains that smelled of copper. There were no cops around, so Pandora dived under the tape and came out on the other side. She walked up to the concrete, inspecting everything around her carefully.

Pandora remembered her nightmare from earlier that day. It had taken place where she stood. She had felt the hair on the back of her neck stand up as if alerting her that something was behind her in the dream. When she'd turned around, she'd seen her pack, dead. Every person she cared about had been covered in sticky, red blood, Sam reaching for her. Then, she had turned again. This time she had found Mason dead and pointing behind her. When she'd turned the third time, she saw a golden wolf eating from Abby's stomach with what had looked like a baby lying next to her.

Pandora shook off the dream as she searched for clues. She felt like her nightmare was somehow connected to what had happened to her grandmother. All she had to do was figure out why her grandmother had been there, and maybe she would learn more. Pandora reached the middle of the concrete and did a slow circle. She was about to turn to Sam when she noticed a few broken branches covering a path.

Pandora headed straight to the path that had been hidden, not saying a word. Sam followed her closely, trying to see what Pandora did. Pandora followed the path for about a minute before she saw tracks running along it. She kneeled by the track and studied it, realizing immediately that it was a wolf track.

"Is that…"

Sam didn't finish his question. He didn't need to. Pandora nodded yes and followed the tracks slowly, watching as they morphed from wolf tracks to human. After about a mile, the tracks turned into a tire track that Pandora guessed belonged to a motorcycle. Pandora turned around and went back to the place her grandmother had been killed.

"A werewolf did this," Pandora told Sam. "I need to figure out why."

She looked around the area for a bit longer, only finding six small, wooden wolves. Pandora took them back with her to the truck and headed home. Sam followed closely in his car. Pandora was grateful that he wasn't pushing Pandora to talk to him at the moment. He hadn't asked her about her nightmare either, which Pandora was also grateful for. Pandora stopped halfway home for gas, Sam parking behind her so he could pump the gas for her.

Pandora walked up to Sam after he put the gas nozzle away. She wrapped her arms around his waist and hugged him. He held her back, kissing her head.

"Thank you," Pandora whispered.

"I haven't done anything," Sam said.

"You're here and you aren't pushing me to talk yet," Pandora stated.

Sam kissed her head again.

"Let's get you home," Sam told her, opening her door for her and helping her climb inside.

They got back to the house and Pandora wasn't surprised when she found Abby, Mason, Shannon, and Candace waiting inside.

"Hi," Pandora said to them.

"Where have you been?" Candace asked, standing and engulfing Pandora in a hug.

"Driving," Pandora stated. "I just needed a few hours to clear my head."

"I'm so sorry, Dora," Abby said, wrapping her arms around Pandora once Candace had let go.

Shannon said nothing. He just pulled Pandora into his arms and held her like a father should. Mason gave her a quick hug before returning her to Sam.

"Do you want to stay with us tonight?" Candace asked.

"No." Pandora shook her head. "I'm kind of tired though. I think it's bedtime."

Everyone left except for Sam. Pandora walked to her grandmother's room and opened the door. The walls were already bare from packing, everything except for the bed and a small amount of clothes in boxes. Pandora took a deep breath and walked into the room slowly.

"We should search for clues," Pandora stated.

"We don't have to do that tonight," Sam told her.

"I need to know who killed her," Pandora stated.

"We don't know that a werewolf did this," Sam stated.

"Yes, we do."

"Us thinking it was a wolf and it actually being a wolf are different things."

"Sam," Pandora warned.

Sam let out a sigh. He walked over to Pandora slowly and wrapped an arm around her waist. She leaned back into his chest.

"Don't break yourself," Sam whispered. "You're allowed to cry and scream and throw punches, Pandora. Do whatever you need to do in order to begin dealing with the emotions that you're pushing down right now. I'm here for you."

Pandora took another deep breath, letting it out slowly.

"Not yet," she told Sam. "I need to plan the funeral and figure out what happened to her first. After I figure everything out, then I can deal."

Sam nodded and kissed her forehead.

"If you want to look for clues tonight, then I'll go pick up some food for us and help you. I'll stay as long as you need me to. I just need to make a few calls."

"Okay," Pandora answered him.

Sam kissed her once more time before leaving the house, his keys in hand as he went. Pandora waited until she heard his car door close before she began looking through her grandmother's boxes. She would unpack one, look through everything in it, and then repack it to not make a mess. She had gone through seven boxes by the time Sam returned to her.

"Anything yet?" Sam asked.

"No," Pandora answered. "Mostly just photo albums and clothes. I've gone through the boxes on that side of the room already."

Sam passed Pandora a bag of food and grabbed a box.

"Eat," he told her as he opened the box and began rifling through it.

Pandora did as she was told, stopping her search until she forced herself to finish her food. Once done, she grabbed a new box. They didn't realize how long they'd been going through Dot's things until Abby cleared her throat in the doorway. Pandora jumped and turned to her.

"I knocked, but no one answered," Abby stated. "What are we doing?"

"Trying to figure out why Grandma was at the old church," Pandora stated.

"Did you find the animal that attacked her?" Abby asked.

"We found…something," Sam stated.

"Something?" Abby asked.

"I think it was a werewolf," Pandora said bluntly. "We found wolf tracks that turned into human tracks. Then there were motorcycle tracks, but I lost that trail once it reached the main road."

"Oh," Abby stated. "Shit. How is that possible?"

"Well, we don't know how many wolves there are. It's possible that there are hundreds that we haven't met yet."

"But, why would one attack Dot? And I thought wolves couldn't hurt each other?"

"Grandma wasn't a wolf. In fact, I don't think there have been wolves in a while. So, technically, a wolf could have killed her," Pandora stated. "So, now I'm trying to figure out the why."

Abby nodded for a moment.

"Dora?"

"Yeah?"

"We need to plan the funeral."

Pandora froze for a moment before turning to Abby.

"I can do it later today. We're almost done in here and the only other boxes are from the garage. I can get to a certain point in the garage and then start the funeral planning after that. Once I have that done, I can go back to the boxes."

Pandora organized everything in her head. She knew exactly where she needed to stop in the garage to have enough time to get things rolling for the funeral. She felt the need to control the situation around her grow a bit stronger as Abby geared up to argue with the plan.

"Don't," Pandora told Abby firmly. "I know what I'm doing. It's not my first funeral."

Abby remained quiet, staring at Pandora. After a minute of holding each other's gazes, Abby turned and left the house. Pandora went back to the box that she had been searching as if Abby had never appeared. Sam had watched the interaction from the chair he had brought into the room last night, saying nothing as the two friends seemed to have a silent battle. Sam continued going through his box, waiting to see if Pandora found anything before him.

An hour and a half after Abby had visited, Pandora and Sam had finished the boxes in the bedroom. Pandora relabeled the boxes, sending most of them to donation centers instead of Pennsylvania. She remained expressionless as she did it, as if nothing was wrong with her actions. They went into the garage, set on beginning the boxes in there, but found that someone had already beat them to it.

"What are you doing in here?" Pandora asked Abby and Mason.

"Helping." Abby shrugged. "If all four of us do this, we'll cover more ground. That pile over there is done. Where's your stopping point?"

Pandora looked to the finished pile, impressed with Abby's progress.

"Two more boxes." Pandora shrugged.

"Make it one more," Mason commented, walking over and setting his box down.

"And done." Abby added her box as well.

"Oh," Pandora stated.

"Want me to relabel them?" Sam asked Pandora.

"I've already done it," Abby stated, pointing to the new labels written in Sharpie.

Pandora just stared at Abby, taking a long moment to think. Suddenly Pandora grabbed Abby and pulled her into a fierce hug. Abby hugged her back, knowing that all Pandora really needed was for the people to be there for her when she wasn't thinking straight. Sam smiled sadly at the interaction, not sure what to do with himself. Mason patted Sam's shoulder and headed inside. Sam followed, giving the girls privacy.

"So, how often does Pandora get like that?" Sam asked Mason.

"Not often," Mason answered. "It's only when she's dealing with too much stress. Once she gets some sleep, she'll let herself start to feel things again, and she'll deal with her emotions. Might want to stay out of the way when that happens though. She breaks things."

"Good to know," Sam stated. "What do we do now?"

"Give them a few minutes. They'll be back in here soon. I think Dot's lawyer should be here soon, too. The chief said something about the will being important."

"Fun," Sam joked.

The boys waited for ten minutes until the girls returned. Abby went to Mason and sat beside him. Pandora stood behind Sam, wrapping her arms around him. She was about to whisper something to him when a knock at the door caught her attention. She answered the door quickly, revealing Dot's lawyer, Gregory.

"Come in," Pandora told him, holding the door wide.

Gregory gave her a sad smile as he entered the house.

"Can I get you some tea?" Pandora asked, leading him to the kitchen.

"Yes, ma'am," Gregory answered. "That would be very kind."

Gregory sat at the dining room table where Abby and Mason had previously been sitting. Pandora set a glass of tea in front of the lawyer, smiling politely in the process.

"Should we leave?" Abby asked Pandora.

"No," Pandora insisted. "Please, stay."

Abby nodded and sat at the table with Pandora. They were across from Gregory, the boys standing behind them.

"I'm so sorry about your grandmother, Pandora," Gregory stated. "How are you holding up?"

"I'm fine," Pandora stated. "I was about to begin funeral arrangements, actually."

"Of course." Gregory nodded. "I'll get right to it, then."

Gregory opened the briefcase he had brought in with him, pulling a manila folder from it gently.

"Your grandmother updated her will the day before your birthday," Gregory explained. "She wrote that she wanted to make sure you knew the truth about things just in case she passed. Do you know what she meant?"

"No," Pandora lied, assuming she had meant the legends.

"Hmm..." Gregory nodded. "Well, I'm sorry to say that I did not understand, either. Here is your copy."

"Wait. You aren't going to read it to her?" Sam asked.

"That only happens in the movies," Pandora explained. "It's just a document given to the beneficiary stating what they receive after the death of someone. That's all."

Gregory stood, Pandora standing with him. She led him out of the house, thanking him at the door. She went back into the kitchen and gingerly picked up the folder given to her. She opened it slowly and began to read aloud for everyone.

CHAPTER TWENTY-ONE

THE WILL

LAST WILL AND TESTAMENT OF Dorothy Lyra Williams

I, Dorothy Lyra Williams, an adult residing at 403 Virginia Street, Conway, South Carolina, being of sound mind, declare this to be my Last Will and Testament. I revoke all wills and codicils previously.

ARTICLE 1
I appoint Gregory Dungeons as my Personal Representative to administer this Will and ask that he/she be permitted to serve without Court supervision and without posting bond.

ARTICLE 2
I direct my Personal Representative to pay out of my residual estate all of the expenses of my last illness, administration expenses, all legally enforceable creditor claims, all federal estate taxes, state inheritance taxes, and all other governmental charges imposed by reason of my death without seeking reimbursement from or charging any person for any part of the taxes and charges paid, and if necessary, reasonable funeral expenses, including the cost of any suitable marker for my grave, without the necessity of an order of court approving said expenses.

ARTICLE 3

I devise, bequeath, and give my properties in South Carolina and Pennsylvania to Pandora Evelyn Williams-Anput.

I devise, bequeath, and give my personal items and family heirlooms to Pandora Evelyn Williams-Anput.

I devise, bequeath, and give my Beetle to Pandora Evelyn Williams-Anput.

ARTICLE 4

I devise, bequeath, and give all of the rest and remainder of my residuary estate as follows:

- $40,000 to Mason Weatherly for his future travels
- $40,000 to Sam Anubis for his art
- $40,000 to Shannon and Candace Michaels for everything they have done for my granddaughter

The remaining balance to Pandora Evelyn Williams-Anput with love (see attached letter)

Dearest Pandora,

If you're reading this, then I'm afraid of what is to come. Wepwawet warned your grandfather with visions of death; that danger was coming in his dreams. I fear you may get these visions as well. There is so much about our people that you do not know, and I wish that I could have told you the truth. Wepwawet forbid me from speaking, afraid I would tell you too much. My loophole is death. It is time that I answered your questions.

There have been no wolves in 150 years. Your grandfather was psychic and knew the troubles you would face. When he tried to interfere, Wepwawet took him from us. He is not a trustworthy God but will still protect you in your journey. Your grandfather built the cottage for you and your pack, having seen them in visions. He used a magick to preserve everything inside and had me buy all of the newest appliances before you got there. I set the magick to make sure no one could enter until you did.

I am so sorry for not being able to help you more Pandora. I do not know all of the dangers coming to you, just bits and pieces. Your grandfather used to whisper in his sleep, and I would memorize the things he would say.

"Beware the golden wolf"

"Trust in Sam"

"Cottage safe"

"Leave Conway"

"Hunters coming"

"Apollo alive"

I love you, Pandora. Give them Hell.

XOXO Grandma

Pandora fell to her knees as she read her grandmothers letter. Sam just barely caught her before she made impact. Abby and Mason were watching Pandora carefully, not sure what to say. Pandora suddenly felt every emotion she had been holding inside of her rush to the surface. For a second, she tried to hold it in, losing as it overtook her. The scream that broke through her rattled the house. Abby and Mason covered their ears defensively. Sam, still holding Pandora, endured all of the ringing. Pandora began sobbing, and Sam pulled her into his lap, rocking her back and forth and rubbing her back.

They sat like that for hours until Pandora fell asleep, exhausted from crying. Sam carried her to her bed and tucked her under the covers, setting Apollo's blanket next to her head. He returned to Abby and Mason in the kitchen, keeping their voices low as they spoke.

"A golden wolf?" Abby asked.

Sam just shook his head. He had never seen one.

"And hunters? Like werewolf hunters?" Mason asked.

"Maybe they're the ones that killed Dot," Abby stated.

"Or the golden wolf," Mason suggested.

"Who's Apollo though?" Abby asked. "We don't know anyone with that name."

Sam remained silent, knowing it wasn't his story to tell.

"How did she scream like that?" Sam asked suddenly.

"Maybe it's an Alpha thing?" Abby asked.

"Maybe," Sam said, not sure. "I'm surprised no one came running or called the cops."

"I mean, they probably think Pandora is finally freaking out," Mason commented.

"True," Abby said. "One thing is for sure though. We need to leave Conway."

"After the funeral," Mason stated.

"She didn't get to plan any of it," Abby said.

"I think we can handle it for now," Mason suggested before turning to Sam. "Have you told the pack what happened yet?"

"Yeah. They'll be here in a few hours."

"Good. If Pandora is still sleeping, send them next door. We'll all come over when she's recharged."

Sam walked Abby and Mason out before going back to Pandora's room. He sat in her chair, watching over her as she slept. Every so often she would whimper, and Sam would reach over, taking her hand for a moment until she calmed again. Once calm, he would lean back in the chair again, keeping a protective eye on his mate.

Pandora was still asleep when the pack arrived. Sam went outside to greet them, Abby and Mason joining them outside. Loren and Sam hugged for a moment before Sam sent everyone to Abby's. Abby followed Sam back to Pandora's, and they sat at the kitchen table.

"So, I called the funeral home. She's being buried in the same plot as Pandora's grandfather. The funeral will be in two days. I just need Pandora to sign off on the papers approving it."

"I can sign now," Pandora's voice came from the hall.

Sam and Abby turned quickly, seeing Pandora wrapped in a blanket and her hair thrown into its messy bun. Pandora took the pen from Abby and signed where she was told.

"How is the service going to go?" Pandora asked.

"Well, they want you to get pictures together so they can make a slideshow," Abby whispered.

Pandora nodded, already knowing which box had the pictures she would be using.

"Flowers?" Pandora asked.

"Prairie gentian," Abby answered.

"Her favorite." Pandora smiled. "Thank you."

"The funeral director needs you to go down there to pick a coffin," Abby whispered carefully.

"Okay. I'll get dressed."

Sam and Abby watched as Pandora left the room, both not sure what to do. They remained silent and waited for Pandora to return. When she did, she turned to Sam.

"Can it just be me and Abby?"

Sam nodded, standing.

"The guys are all next door. I'll go hang out with them for a bit."

Pandora nodded.

"I'll go buy stuff for dinner tonight. We can have a cookout. We should also say that they're cousins of mine or something. Shannon and Candace might be a little curious as to why a bunch of guys just showed up."

Sam walked Pandora and Abby to Pandora's truck, holding Pandora's door for her.

"Are you okay?" Sam asked her quietly.

"Yeah." Pandora nodded. "I'm just tired."

"Okay." Sam nodded. "I'll see you soon."

They kissed goodbye, and Sam went to Abby's. The pack and Mason were all sitting in the living room, the TV on as a background noise. Sam sat next to Mason with a huff.

"They went to the funeral home," Sam explained. "Had to pick a coffin."

"Ah." Mason nodded.

"So, Mason said it was a wolf?" Warren asked.

"Yeah," Sam nodded. "A golden one maybe. We have to leave for the cottage after the funeral, too."

"Yeah. Mason told us about the will," Jordan said. "Who's Apollo?"

"I don't know," Sam lied, catching Loren's eye.

"Well, we're all off for the week. We made sure to take the time off when you called. Said there was a death in the family," Jordan stated.

"If Abby's parents ask, you're all cousins of Pandora's. We can say you all came in from Pennsylvania so that no one has to actually lie." Sam sighed.

"Go get some sleep, Sam," Warren said. "You look like hell."

"I feel like it too," Sam stated. "Pandora said she'll pick stuff up for dinner on the way back, so don't go anywhere."

Sam stood and walked next door, Loren following him.

"Who's Apollo?" Loren asked Sam once they were inside.

Sam sighed, knowing he couldn't lie to Loren.

"I can't tell you," Sam said.

"Why not?"

"It's not my story to tell." Sam shrugged.

Loren nodded, knowing Sam wouldn't betray Pandora's trust again aloud. He looked to Sam, who was staring at a photograph on the living room mantel. Loren followed his gaze and went to the picture. The picture was of a young Pandora, her parents, and a baby. Loren picked up the picture and studied it.

"Did Pandora have a sibling?" Loren asked Sam.

Sam just shrugged, refusing to answer any real questions. Loren just nodded, knowing the answer must be yes. He guessed that the baby had died with Pandora's parents, but that wouldn't explain why Sam couldn't tell him anything. The thoughts in his head clicked as he put the pieces together.

"Apollo is the baby," Loren said to himself. "But Pandora was told he died with her parents. So, somehow, he isn't dead, and we're probably going to try to find him."

Sam just walked into the kitchen, not speaking as he poured himself something to drink.

"Okay," Loren nodded, putting the picture back on the mantel and following Sam. "Go get some sleep. I'll tell you when Pandora is back."

Sam thanked Loren and went to Pandora's room, falling asleep as soon as his head hit the pillow.

Pandora and Abby drove to the funeral home in silence, Pandora fidgeting a bit as she drove.

"You okay?" Abby asked as they parked.

"Yeah," Pandora lied.

"No, you aren't," Abby stated. "What's going on?"

Pandora took a deep breath, trying to figure out how to tell Abby about Apollo.

"There's something I need to tell you, but I'm worried that I waited too long to tell you and you're going to be mad at me," Pandora admitted.

"If you tell me that you're in love with me and want to run away together, I'm sorry, Dora, but I think Sam would find us," Abby joked.

Pandora cracked a smile for a second before getting serious again.

"What is it?' Abby asked.

"It's about Apollo," Pandora stated.

"The not-dead person?" Abby asked.

"Yes."

"Who is he?"

"Well, that's the hard part. My parents weren't the only ones in the car the night of the crash," Pandora stated. "Apollo was with them."

"So, was he a family friend or something?" Abby asked.

"No," Pandora said slowly. "He was my little brother."

"What?" Abby asked, shocked.

"Yeah. He was one, and the cops said that they couldn't identify his body because of how badly the fire had been."

"Fire?" Abby asked.

"The car caught fire after it crashed," Pandora stated, feeling herself shaking.

"Do you know how hard it is for a car to catch fire, Pandora?" Abby asked.

"No," Pandora admitted.

"Well, it takes a lot of damage. Not only that, but wouldn't your dad's body have been hard to identify too?"

"They used dental records for him," Pandora said.

"Oh," said Abby simply. "I didn't know."

"I don't talk about it." Pandora shrugged.

"Understandable," Pandora stated. "Why hide Apollo though?"

"I was already the girl who had lost her parents." Pandora shrugged. "I didn't want to admit that I had lost him too, and people act even weirder than they already did. You remember high school. People would always try to bully me for shit."

"I also remember you beating the shit out of anyone who said something bad about me," Abby stated.

"Yeah, because you're my best friend," Pandora stated. "You're like a sister to me. No one was going to talk about you in front of me."

"Why didn't you tell me about him?" Abby asked.

"It's hard to talk about," Pandora admitted. "He was so little, and he had probably been in pain when he died. I didn't want to think about it. But, after Grandma's will, I'm wishing I had told somebody. Maybe he is alive, and someone took him. My brother could be out there, and he could be in danger, and it's my fault for not digging into the wreck. I'm not even sure the accident was an accident anymore."

"What do you mean?" Abby asked.

"If Apollo is alive, that means someone saw the wreck and didn't help them, just took a baby and ran. Grandma was just killed. There are hunters apparently. Maybe the hunters killed my parents."

"Or the golden wolf did," Abby suggested.

"We can go to the police station. They have to give information to the next of kin. We'll go tomorrow morning and dig through everything about the wreck and see if we find anything," Abby promised. "Today, we need to pick a coffin and feed a pack of wolves."

Pandora nodded, knowing Abby was right. They got out of the truck and headed inside the funeral home, Pandora feeling thankful that she had Abby in her life. They spent about an hour at the funeral home, picking a red wooden coffin that reminded Pandora of the cottage that she longed for. After, they went to the grocery store and grabbed supplies for burgers, Abby texting her dad and giving him the heads up about the boys and dinner plans.

Once back to the house, Abby and Pandora found all of the boys in Pandora's backyard.

"Hey, guys," Abby greeted, kissing Mason quickly.

Pandora walked to Sam, wrapping her arms around him. He held her closely and kissed her head.

"I need a girlfriend," Jordan stated, causing everyone to laugh.

"I need a boyfriend," Warren added.

Loren just rolled his eyes and looked to Pandora.

"How're you doing?" he asked her.

"I'm okay." Pandora nodded. "I need to tell y'all something though."

Pandora waited until everyone was sitting before starting.

"So, Sam and Abby already know about this, but I need to tell everyone. My grandmother mentioned someone named Apollo in her will, saying that he was alive. Well, Apollo was my baby brother. He was in the car with my parents when they crashed. They couldn't identify his body, because the car caught fire, and everything was burned too badly. The only reason they identified my father was because of his dental records. My mother was thrown from the vehicle.

"Abby and I were talking in the truck and, since the funeral is taken care of, I'm going to go to the police tomorrow and get the records from the crash. With Grandma being killed, I feel like there might be more to the accident than I realize. Especially if Grandpa said that Apollo was alive. I need to investigate what happened to see if there's more to what happened or not. I need to see if there's any chance that Apollo is alive."

The pack and Mason listened to Pandora carefully. Once she finished explaining, they sat quietly, all thinking.

"Are you sure you aren't being paranoid?" Jordan asked, making everyone except for Pandora glare at him.

Pandora just smiled at him.

"I am being paranoid," she admitted. "I still need to check all my bases, though."

Jordan just nodded to her, understanding her need to know the truth about her family.

"What are we going to do about the hunters?" Loren asked.

"Well, hopefully, we won't have to do anything," Sam stated. "We don't know who they are or what they can do to us. We already know that it would be hard to kill us in general."

"It would?" Pandora asked, turning to Sam.

"Yeah, we all might have done some stupid stuff," Sam admitted. "We wanted to test our limits and see what being a wolf meant we could do. We can run faster and are stronger, so we can push our bodies a bit more. Loren survived a five-hundred-foot fall. Jordan didn't even get scratched by a bullet, some Superman shit there. Nature got bit by a rattlesnake and didn't even feel it."

Pandora looked around at her pack, impressed.

"So, how can we be killed?" Pandora joked. "I'm guessing silver?"

"Nope." Sam smiled.

"Did you stab yourself with a silver butter knife?" Pandora asked.

"No. We used a silver bullet to shoot at Jordan." Sam shrugged.

"You shot at Jordan?!" Pandora yelled angrily.

"He was fine!" Sam defended.

"You didn't know that he would be!" Pandora yelled back.

"It's okay, Pandora," Jordan said. "It was my idea."

"You're all idiots," Pandora groaned, rubbing her face.

"Men," Abby scoffed.

"What did I do?" Mason asked.

"You would've helped," Pandora accused.

"How am I in trouble?" Mason asked, more to himself than to anyone else. "I wasn't even there."

"I'm going to start dinner," Pandora stated, heading into the kitchen.

Sam and Loren followed her.

"So, we should get a picture of your brother and see if we can download one of those apps that show what someone would look like now," Loren suggested.

"And then what?" Pandora asked. "I can't exactly run his photo through a bunch of computers to see if anything pops up."

"Actually, you can look up pictures on Google," Loren said. "We can paste the picture in the search bar and see if anything pops up."

"Wait, really?" Pandora asked.

"Yeah," Loren stated.

"I did not know that," Pandora said, turning to the task of dinner.

Sam and Loren began talking as Pandora worked. She tuned them out as she worked, content. Shannon and Candace showed up as Pandora was finishing her prep. Shannon took over the grill and began cooking everything. Candace was talking to Jordan and Warren as Shannon talked to Mason. The small fire pit was lit, keeping away any bugs that tried to venture over. Pandora sat next to Nature, smiling at the scene around her. Nature held her hand, letting her know he was there for her.

The boys slept in the living room again, pillows and blankets scattered across the floor and all touching, like they needed to know that someone was there. Sam and Pandora slept soundlessly in her room. Sam woke when Pandora began screaming. The room flooded with light as the pack ran in.

"Pandora!" Sam shook her. "Wake up!"

"Move," Loren commanded Sam, pulling him out of the way.

Loren took Pandora in his arms and lifted her. He carried her to the bathroom, still screaming and trying to escape Loren's hold. Loren laid her in the shower and turned on the cold water. The water woke her as it shocked her body. She gasped and wiped the water from her face. Loren turned off the water and passed her a towel.

"Sorry," he stated. "You weren't waking up."

"Sorry," Pandora stated, noticing the pack around her.

"Another nightmare?" Sam asked.

"Same one," Pandora stated.

"What was it?" Loren asked.

Pandora took a few deep breaths, not wanting to tell them. She shook her head, trying to convince herself to speak. She knew she should tell them, but she didn't want them to worry about her more than they already did.

"I need to eat first," Pandora told them, standing from the shower and heading out the bathroom door.

The pack followed her, Sam not taking his hand from her waist as she walked. She pulled the milk from the fridge and prepared cereal. The pack did the same, all knowing it was about time to start moving around anyways. Sam started the coffee maker before turning to Pandora.

"What was it?" he asked.

Pandora sighed and ate a few more bites of cereal first. She turned to him and patted the chair next to her. He sat willingly, waiting for her to speak.

"So, in the dream, I'm at the old church where Grandma was killed. I turn around, and you're all dead. When I turn again, Mason's dead. When I turn again, Abby is on the ground and a golden wolf is eating her."

"I'm not hungry anymore," Jordan stated, pushing his cereal away.

"Me, either," Warren stated, copying Jordan.

"Have you told Abby?" Loren asked.

"No," Pandora stated. "I've been trying to not scare everyone."

"Well, if Dot is right and these are visions, it means Abby is probably in danger," Loren stated.

"It means we're all in danger," Jordan stated.

"Obviously, but Abby was the only death in the dream that showed how she died," Loren said. "That has to mean something. Were there any other details?"

"Well, Sam was reaching for me and Mason was pointing to Abby," Pandora left out the detail of the child, thinking it too gruesome to share.

"So, you were shown this stuff for a reason," Loren stated.

"Why would the wolf go after Abby though?" Pandora asked.

"You're the Alpha. The wolf is probably trying to get to you. The quickest way to get to you is to hit your weak spots. Your grandma was alone and human. Abby is human. He can't get to us right now because we're always together and we're stronger than humans. Abby would be the next easiest target," Loren stated.

Pandora could feel herself beginning to shake. She stood from the table and went out the front door, heading straight to Abby's house. Shannon was at his car and waved to Pandora as she passed. She nodded back and let herself into the house. Candace was at the kitchen table, drinking her coffee before leaving for the day.

"Hi, Pandora," Candace smiled.

"Morning," Pandora smiled politely. "Is Abby up?"

"No," Candace said. "She's still asleep. I'm sure Mason will be here soon."

"He didn't stay last night?" Pandora asked.

"No. He said he needed to finish packing. Are you leaving after the funeral?"

"Yeah," Pandora whispered. "It's just hard being in the house without Grandma."

"I'm sorry, Pandora," Candace said, rising from the table and hugging Pandora close.

"I'll be okay," Pandora assured her.

Candace left for work and Pandora headed to Abby's room. The room had bare, white walls and three boxes in the corner. Pandora went to Abby, who was sound asleep on her bed. Pandora climbed under the covers, joining Abby. Abby stirred and opened her eyes. She smiled to Pandora and took her hand, closing her eyes again. Abby fell back to sleep quickly, leaving Pandora to her thoughts. Mason showed up ten minutes later and smiled at his girls. He climbed into the bed on Abby's other side and cuddled close to her, placing his hand over Pandora's, which still held Abby's.

They stayed there for a while, letting time pass until Abby's alarm woke her. Abby smiled to Pandora and kissed Mason as she rose from her bed. She dressed quickly and brushed her hair before turning to Pandora.

"You ready to go to the police station?" she asked.

"I'm not even dressed yet." Pandora smiled.

"I noticed." Abby smiled, tossing Pandora a pair of jeans.

"I'll wait in the living room." Mason smiled, leaving the room.

"I need to tell you something," Pandora said to Abby once the door closed.

"You have another long-lost sibling?" Abby joked.

"No," Pandora said seriously. "I've been having a nightmare."

"Like your grandpa?" Abby asked.

"Yeah." Pandora nodded.

"What happens in it?" Abby asked.

Pandora told Abby the dream, making sure to not leave out any details. She then told Abby that Loren thought it meant Abby was in danger. Abby nodded along, listening carefully.

"So, I'm just going to stick with you or one of the guys from now on," Abby stated. "Once we get to the cottage, we'll be alright. I didn't plan on being away from you the next few days anyway."

Pandora felt herself sigh in relief.

"Did you think I was going to be mad about needing a babysitter?" Abby smiled.

"I would be," Pandora admitted.

"You're a lot more independent than me though," Abby said. "Change. We need to get going. We still have to finish the garage."

Pandora changed into Abby's jeans and they headed out the door. Sam and Mason were leaning against Abby's truck, waiting.

"Hey." Sam smiled to Abby.

"Hi. Are you my watchdog today?" Abby asked Sam, causing Mason to laugh.

"Ha, ha." Sam rolled his eyes. "Yes."

"Me and the guys are going to get the garage done. If we find anything, we'll let you know," Mason assured Pandora.

"Thank you," Pandora said, hugging Mason before climbing into her truck, Abby next to her in the middle.

CHAPTER TWENTY-TWO

The Funeral

"Hey, Chief. Pandora Anput is here to see you," Joseph told Chief Richard.

Richard nodded, telling Joseph to let her in. Pandora entered his office with Abby and a man Joseph didn't know. He stood when they entered and stuck his hand out for the man to shake.

"Chief Richard," he introduced himself. "We didn't get to talk the other day."

"Sam Anubis." Sam smiled, taking his hand easily.

"Hey, Chief." Abby smiled to Richard as she gave him a hug.

Pandora hugged him next. Richard smiled at the two girls he had watched grow up fondly. They had been quite the troublemakers in high school. Richard would never tell anyone, but he was impressed with what all the girls had gotten away with through loopholes.

"What can I do for you, Pandora?" Richard asked.

"Well, I'm moving soon. My grandfather left me a cottage in Pennsylvania. I think Candace may have told you."

"Yes, ma'am, she did." Richard nodded.

"Well, before I leave, I was wondering if I could have a copy of the file about my parents and Apollo's accident. I know it seems weird, but I feel like I should have one."

"Well, of course," Richard told her. "There's a fee to print out the pages, though."

"That's fine," Pandora agreed. "I can run to the ATM and get the cash for you."

While Pandora, Abby, and Sam were at the police station, the pack and Mason were in the garage. There weren't very many boxes left, so they each grabbed one and got started. They went through the boxes slowly, finding mostly old clothes that needed to be donated. Nature grabbed the last box and opened it carefully. In the box, he found a briefcase, a black box, and a few files. He pulled the files out first, deciding to go through them. The files were mostly old tax papers, but the last file contained the number of a safety deposit box and the key for it.

Nature picked up the black box from inside the cardboard box carefully. He looked at the serial number that was on it and realized it matched the one mentioned in the file. He pulled the key from the file and opened the box. Inside the box were candles and seven wooden wolves. He looked at each one carefully, noticing how the wolves looked like the pack, except for the seventh one, which was a chocolate brown color.

He pulled a small cloth from the black box and inspected it. The cloth was black with a purple circle made out of small dots on it. He held it up to the light to get a better look and realized the dots were actually wolves. He folded the cloth and set it back into the box with the seven wolves and twenty white candles.

He picked up the briefcase next, feeling something inside of it slide a bit as he lifted it. He opened the briefcase and found an old journal. It looked like leather and was very worn. Nature guessed it was over a hundred years old. He opened it and found a wolf's face drawn on the first page. At the bottom of the page, there was a language that Nature recognized immediately. His father had beat the language into him when he was a child, making sure Nature could speak it fluently before removing his tongue.

The Iroquoian language that belonged to the Honniasont tribe was written neatly across the pages. Nature read quietly for a moment before standing suddenly and going into the house.

"Nature?" Jordan asked as the pack and Mason followed Nature inside.

Nature went into the kitchen and grabbed the notebook that he had seen in a drawer earlier that day. He took out a pen and sat at the kitchen table. He opened the journal and began to translate the journal slowly. The pack watched on as he worked.

"Should someone call Sam?" Warren asked.

"Already on it," Loren stated, showing he was already on the phone. "Hey, Sam. Nature found something."

Nature ignored the pack around him and continued, knowing that whatever was found in the journal may help Pandora with the dangers they were facing. Pandora arrived ten minutes later and sat next to Nature, reading some of what Nature had written already.

"How do you know this language?" Pandora asked Nature even though she knew he couldn't answer.

Nature just shrugged and continued writing.

"Did you find anything with it?" Sam asked.

Nature nodded and pointed to the garage. Sam and Loren left the kitchen and to retrieve the box. When they returned, Sam set the box on the table in front of Pandora. She pulled out the black box and opened it, studying the wooden figures, her eyebrows knitted together in concentration.

"I've seen this before," Pandora whispered.

"When?" Abby asked.

"Grandpa. He made them. Said they would be important one day. Also, there were some at the site where grandma died," Pandora stated, picking up the cloth. "Mom made this. She worked on it for weeks."

"What the hell?" Abby breathed slowly.

Pandora looked through the files and, finding nothing important, tossed them into the trash.

"Do you think your grandma went and got the box after your birthday?" Abby asked.

"Probably," Pandora said, checking the briefcase for any hidden pockets.

Pandora sighed when she found nothing else and went into the garage. Since the pack had finished the garage, Pandora began labeling the boxes as trash or donations. She needed to go pick up her grandmother's Beetle from the police impound lot before the hour was up, so she told the pack where she was going and left before anyone could try to tag along. Once at the impound lot, she paid a fee and was given the keys. She hooked the Beetle to her truck and headed home. Once there, she parked the Beetle in the garage and began rummaging through it, hoping to find more information. Sam joined her about half an hour later.

"Find anything?" he asked.

"No." Pandora sighed, shutting the glove compartment box. "I just wish I knew what she was doing there."

"Me, too," Sam said, kissing Pandora's head. "We'll figure it out. I promise."

Pandora sighed, leaning against him.

"We should get something to eat," Pandora stated.

"A few of the neighbors brought some food. We can snack on that if you want," Sam suggested.

"Or I can serve it all at the funeral home tomorrow at the reception to get rid of it, and we can eat not sad food," Pandora suggested.

"Whatever you want." Sam laughed.

"McDonald's is right around the corner. Let's grab everyone and get going."

Nature didn't seem thrilled about stopping what he was doing, so Sam, Mason, Loren, and Pandora figured out what everyone wanted and left. When they returned, Nature was freaking out.

"He just started throwing stuff," Jordan stated. "We don't know what's happening."

"Nature. Nature. Nature!" Nature finally stopped when Pandora yelled. "Show me what's wrong."

Nature picked up the notebook he'd been using and began scribbling on a new page. He showed the page to Pandora by shoving it in her face. Pandora took the notebook, giving Nature an annoyed look before reading what he had written.

"The golden wolf is a wolf that turns too soon for survival"

"Okay, so why is he trying to kill us?" Pandora asked.

Nature took the notebook back and began writing again. He passed it to her again and Pandora read.

"I don't know but it says the golden wolf has to go through a lot of abuse to turn and to attack anyone in the pack, wolf or not"

"So, we're looking for someone who's been abused so much that they don't trust other wolves?" Pandora asked.

Nature nodded and wrote again.

"The only way to stop him is to kill him or find him his mate before he turns 25"

"How are we supposed to do that? We don't know who he is or if he's already over twenty-five. He may not even have a mate," Pandora stated.

Nature threw the notebook in the air, showing that that was the reason he was throwing stuff. Nature picked up the notebook and set it back on the table. He began translating the journal again, feeling a bit better with Pandora in the room now. Pandora set food in front of him, giving him a smile as she sat next to him with her own. Nature ate it willingly, not paying much attention since he couldn't taste anything. He worked into the night, stopping only when Pandora took the pen from him and ordered him to bed. Nature did as he was told and laid next to Jordan, falling asleep quickly.

The next morning, everyone got up slowly, dressing for the funeral and waiting for Sam and Pandora. Sam came out of the room first, dressed in jeans, a white shirt, and black jacket, a thin, black tie around his neck. Abby came into the house in a black dress and heels, another pair of heels in her hand.

"She's in her room," Sam told her. "She's almost ready."

Abby nodded to Sam and headed to Pandora's room. Abby's parents and Mason came over and waited with the pack.

"Maybe I should go check on them." Candace stood.

Abby came into the room then, Pandora behind her. Pandora was wearing a black dress and the heels that Abby had brought over. Her hair was down, little ringlets cascading over her shoulders, framing her face that she had added makeup to.

"Ready?" she asked the room.

Everyone nodded and Jordan and Nature collected the food from the fridge to take to the funeral home with them. They drove silently, no one wanting to set Pandora off. Once at the funeral home, Pandora was greeted by the funeral director and Gregory. The director led the boys to where they could set the food. People would be arriving within the hour. Pandora just stood near the door, ready to greet anyone who came in.

The funeral home filled quickly. Being the only actual family member of her grandmother, Pandora spoke first. Once she was done, Candace took over, followed by Shannon, then the preacher who had married Pandora's grandparents. Almost everyone stayed for the reception, eating all of the food so that Pandora didn't have to take it home. Pandora felt as if she was being watched towards the end of the reception but shrugged it off since a lot of people had been watching her all day. Pandora accepted handshakes and hugs as people left, holding her head high with Abby and Sam at her side, offering reassurance by simply being there. Finally, there were enough people gone that Pandora could thank the funeral director and try to leave.

She walked outside alone, taking some time to gather her bearings in the fresh air. The sun had begun to set, and Pandora stood unmoving, watching it. She felt someone stand by her and looked over to see who it was. A man who couldn't be much younger than Pandora stood beside her. His skin was a light brown and his eyes looked black.

"Hello," he greeted with a small smile.

"Hi." Pandora smiled back politely.

"I'm Flynn." He held out his hand.

"Pandora." she shook it.

"I know. You're Dorothy's granddaughter."

"Yes, I am. How did you know my grandmother?"

"I didn't," he stated. "My grandpa did. He said she was his first love."

"Oh?" Pandora asked. "Where is he?"

"He passed away a few months ago. So, I brought him with me." Flynn smiled, pulling his necklace out of his shirt to show a small bottle with what Pandora guessed were his grandfather's ashes.

Pandora nodded, understanding.

"So, how did you hear about Grandma?" Pandora asked, curiously.

"I didn't," Flynn admitted. "I came looking for you."

Pandora took a step back, not trusting Flynn suddenly. Flynn continued smiling at her.

"I had a dream about you," Flynn stated, stepping towards Pandora and causing her to take another step back. "In the dream," step, "you were laying in the middle of a circle," step, "naked," step, "with candles all around you," step, "and you were gasping for air."

Pandora tripped over the curb, falling onto her back.

"Pandora!" Sam yelled.

Pandora looked around to her pack rushing towards her. She turned back to Flynn and gasped. Flynn was gone. Pandora stood quickly, holding the back of her head where it had hit the cement.

"Are you okay?" Sam asked, checking Pandora's head.

"Yeah," Pandora stated, looking around the parking lot. "Where'd he go?"

"Who?" Sam asked.

"Flynn. He was just here," Pandora stated.

"Flynn?" Abby asked.

"He was right here," Pandora stated. "He said his grandpa knew grandma and that he had a dream about me naked in some circle."

"What?" Sam asked, looking angry.

"Well, whoever he is, he's gone now," Abby stated. "Probably ran when he saw all the guys."

"Let's get out of here," Mason stated, wrapping his arm around Abby and heading towards the truck.

Sam did the same to Pandora, holding the driver's side door for her. He helped her climb inside and shut the door for her.

"You okay to drive?" Sam asked through the open window.

"Yeah," Pandora nodded. "I'll see you at the house."

Pandora kissed Sam gently before starting the truck. She waited until he was in his car before pulling out of the lot. Abby held Pandora's hand as she drove. It started raining as Pandora drove. At first it was just light sprinkling, but before they made it home, it was pouring. Lightning cracked across the sky as Pandora parked her truck. They ran towards the house, everyone falling into the living room once the door was open. Pandora went to the bathroom and pulled out enough towels for everyone and passed them around.

"Weird ass storm," Jordan stated, to which everyone nodded.

"Good thing we hit the liquor store on the way here." Warren smiled, pulling four bottles of rum from his suitcase.

"What in the hell?" Abby asked.

"We figured Pandora would need a drink." Loren smiled, pulling out two more from his own suitcase.

Sam laughed as Jordan pulled a bottle of gin from his suitcase and passed it to him. Sam popped the top of it and took a drink. He hummed as it went down easily.

"Dora?" Abby asked, passing a cup to Pandora.

Pandora smiled and took the glass, taking a drink of the dark liquor.

"Mmm." She smiled.

Soon, everyone was buzzed and laughing. Pandora had turned on a movie that no one was paying attention to for background noise. Mason, Abby,

Warren, Jordan, and Nature were playing Cards Against Humanity in the middle of the living room floor. Loren and Sam were telling Pandora about the time that they had gotten drunk in Mexico and ended up almost getting shot for hitting on some girls.

"So, Sam is trying to warn me that these big guys are walking up to us looking pissed, like he's really trying. I'm too busy trying to kiss this girl to notice though. Turns out the biggest dude was her boyfriend. He's tatted to the teeth, and his arm is as big as me. It's crazy. So, he pushes me and asks what I'm doing, and I tell him that I'm hitting on his girl, 'cause I'm drunk and an idiot...." Loren laughs as Sam takes over the story.

"So, I tell the guy we don't want any trouble and that we're leaving. I'm trying to drag Loren out of there, but he is still trying to flirt with this girl as we're going out the door."

"Oh my God." Pandora laughed, laying on the floor and holding her stomach.

"Dora!" Abby yelled, climbing on top of Pandora and laying on her. "I won!"

"Good job!" Pandora laughed, poking Abby in the side and causing her to giggle.

Mason crawled over and wrapped his arms around his girls and sighed.

"Mine." He smiled, hugging them both.

Sam let out a small growl.

"No!" Pandora yelled, pointing at Sam. "Bad Sam!"

Sam just rolled his eyes, a small smile on his face. Mason laughed and hugged the girls more. Abby cuddled into Mason and sighed. Pandora hugged them back and was about to sit up when the lights went out.

"Uh oh." Pandora laughed.

A few of the guys phones lit up and caused the room to glow. Pandora stood and went to the kitchen, Sam following with his light. Pandora pulled some candles from the black box and lit them with a match. She set the candles around the house so everyone could see and went back to the living room with Sam. Loren stood in the living room with the door open, looking out into the night.

"Looks like it's the whole block," Loren stated, shutting the door.

"What do we do now?" Pandora asked.

"We can play Truths," Abby suggested.

"No," Pandora stated. "You got pissed at me last time."

"Yeah, because you slept with Johnathon and didn't tell me until then," Abby stated.

"What is Truths?" Jordan asked.

"Who's Johnathon?" Sam questioned.

"Some guy from high school." Pandora laughed to Sam.

"Truths is a game where everyone goes around and tells secrets about themselves and everyone else decides if it's true or not," Abby explained.

"So, you can say anything?" Warren asked.

"Yeah." Abby smiled. "The catch is you only get one lie for every game."

"What does a game consist of?" Jordan asked.

"Three rounds where everyone says something. You don't find out which statement was a lie until the end of the game. Or you can be honest the whole time and really fuck with people." Pandora smiled.

"I hate your strategy." Abby glared. "I always end up losing."

"What happens if you lose?" Sam asked.

"You lose an article of clothing." Pandora shrugged. "It's a college game. Duh."

"That sounds interesting." Warren smiled.

"Let's play." Jordan smiled.

Everyone sat in a circle in the living room, each refilling their drinks before beginning the game.

"I'll start." Pandora smiled. "I had my first kiss when I was fourteen."

"Liar!" Abby yelled.

All the boys immediately agreed with Abby considering she knew Pandora better than anyone else.

"Maybe we should play teams," Pandora smiled to Abby.

"Or we cannot give each other away," Abby said, feeling bad.

"You didn't give me away," Pandora smiled. "That one was actually true."

"No, it wasn't," Abby argued. "It was at your fourteenth birthday party, but your birthday had been the day after the party, so thirteen."

"No," Pandora corrected. "My birthday was on Saturday, but grandpa threw my party a day late so that he and I could have my actual birthday together, so fourteen and a day."

"Oh," Abby stated. "Shit. Sorry guys."

"My turn." Warren smiled. "I got blue ribbon as Jr. Bull Rider in the town fair three years in a row."

"True," Jordan stated. "I've seen the ribbons at your mom's house."

Everyone except Pandora agreed. Warren and Pandora kept eye contact for a moment while she thought it over.

"Lie," she finally said.

"We'll see." Warren smiled.

"I have an older brother that I never talk to." Sam went next.

"I have had surgery thirteen times," Jordan stated.

"My mom thought I was going to be a girl, so she picked the name Lauren and just changed the spelling once I was born a boy." Loren smiled.

"I'm afraid of the ocean," Mason said.

"This isn't my real nose," Nature held a piece of paper up for everyone to see.

"I don't know how to do my taxes," Abby stated. "I just wing it and hope I got it right."

It was Pandora's turn again.

"I have never lied to anyone," she stated.

"Truth." Abby nodded. "Hiding things isn't the same as lying."

"True," Mason agreed.

"I've never been on a plane," Warren stated.

"I've never been out of North America." Sam smiled.

"I've never been out of the country," Jordan declared.

"I set things on fire for fun." Loren laughed.

"That sounds creepy," Pandora stated.

"I have no clue what I'm going to do with my life," Mason admitted.

"I can talk, it just sounds funny," Nature wrote.

"I can't have children," Abby nodded.

"Lie," Mason stated.

"Truth," Pandora corrected.

"What?" Mason asked, turning to Abby.

"Next!" Abby yelled.

"I've stopped taking my medications," Pandora stated.

"Truth," Abby stated.

"Wait, what?" Sam asked.

"I don't like this game," Mason stated. "You girls use it as a way to admit things you don't want to actually say."

"No, that's the alcohol's fault," Pandora stated. "Next?"

"I've never had sex," Warren stated.

"You are missing out," Pandora stated.

"I've only had sex with two people," Sam stated.

"What?" Pandora asked.

"I hate ducks," Jordan stated.

"I am terrified of losing you guys," Loren stated.

"Even me?" Pandora asked.

"Yes," Loren admitted.

"I've never dated a girl that my mom has liked," Mason stated.

"Truth," Abby scoffed.

"Nature isn't my real name," Nature scribbled.

"I am terrified of cars," Abby completed the round.

"Mine were all true, so everyone who said I lied has to take off one piece of clothing," Pandora stated. "Warren?"

"The first one was a lie. It was only two blue ribbons. Everyone except Pandora lost."

"The first brother one is true. The North America one isn't. He's my half-brother on my dad's side, and he's an ass. I did a lot of traveling right after high school, including South America."

"Damn it," Pandora took off the tank top she had on and her socks, leaving her in her bra and jeans.

"Fuck!" Abby yelled, stripping to her bra and underwear.

"Do I sound like I grew up in America?" Jordan laughed as Warren ended up in just boxers.

"Mine were all true." Loren sighed.

"I'm not afraid of the ocean," Mason admitted.

"I'm no liar," Nature wrote.

Abby let out a frustrated groan.

"I hate this game!" she yelled.

"We'll just agree that Abby lost, that way Mason doesn't have a heart attack," Sam laughed.

"Thank you," Abby mouthed to Sam, happy that she was keeping the remainder of her clothing on.

"We should be getting to bed," Pandora stated. "We've got quite a bit to do tomorrow."

"Yay for moving day." Abby smiled.

"Y'all can crash in Grandma's room," Pandora told Abby and Mason.

Abby picked up a candle and her clothes and led Mason to the room they would be sleeping in, hoping he wouldn't ask her questions until the next day. He didn't question her. Instead, he followed her to the room and held her as she drifted to sleep. He kissed her forehead before following her lead.

"I'll see you guys in the morning." Pandora smiled to her pack.

"Night!" they all called to her and Sam.

Sam and Pandora each carried a candle with them.

"Why aren't you taking your medicines?" Sam asked.

"They make it hard to feel," Pandora stated. "I stopped taking them after seeing Grandma's body. I knew if I kept taking them, I wouldn't be able to deal with her death."

"Okay," Sam sighed. "Are you going to start them again?"

"Not right now," Pandora told him, lying on the bed. "I'm going to wait. If I start getting bad, I'll start them up again."

"Okay," Sam nodded, lying next to her and pulling her close. "I like this bra."

"Oh, yeah?" Pandora laughed.

"I'd like it better if you had taken it off." Sam smiled.

"Well, why don't you take it off for me?" Pandora challenged.

"Gladly." Sam smiled.

CHAPTER TWENTY-THREE

Moving Day

Pandora made pancakes in the morning using dishes borrowed from Candace. After everyone ate, Mason and Warren took the donation boxes to Goodwill. While they were gone, the pack and Abby piled the few boxes that mostly contained clothes into Pandora truck. Nature connected Dot's Beetle to his truck.

"So, I have a present for you." Pandora smiled to Abby.

"Oh, yeah?" Abby asked. "What is it?"

Pandora handed a piece of paper to Abby for her to read.

"Wait," Abby said when she finished reading it. "Are you serious?"

"Yup." Pandora smiled, holding the keys to the Beetle up for Abby to take.

"Oh my God!" Abby yelled, grabbing the keys and throwing her arms around Pandora. "Thank you! Thank you! Thank you!"

Pandora just laughed at her friend and hugged her back.

"Everyone ready?" Shannon asked.

"Yes, sir." Pandora smiled, Abby nodding along.

Pandora climbed into her truck. Abby and Mason climbed in next to her. Pandora started her truck and pulled out of her driveway, leaving behind the home that she had lost so many people in and heading towards the one place that truly felt like home. They drove the hour and a half to Fuller's, stopping for an early lunch. Then they stayed on the road for seven and a half hours, only stopping for gas, until they reached their destination.

Pandora drove along the now familiar path, continuing through the trees until she reached the clearing. She pulled in front of the cottage and backed her truck up to the stairs to make unpacking easier. The boys all parked along the side of the house, each picking their own spot. Candace and Shannon parked next to them and stepped out of their vehicle.

Shannon looked at the cottage and nodded at the size of it.

"How many rooms are there?" Candace asked.

"Seven," Pandora answered.

"That's a lot of room," Shannon said, looking around at the group around him. "Do you boys plan on moving in too?"

"Yes," Pandora answered before they got the chance. "They wanted to wait until Abby, Mason, and I got settled though."

"So, you have family here?" Candace asked, feeling a bit better suddenly.

"Yeah." Pandora smiled. "This is my family."

The pack all smiled brightly. Nature picked Pandora up in a tight hug and set her back down gently, saying in a hug what he couldn't with words. Pandora smiled to him, and he went towards the truck, opening the tailgate and grabbing a box. The pack took the cue and began unloading the truck. They finished quickly as Shannon and Candace began looking around the cottage. Candace peaked into each room as Shannon went to the back patio. They met the girls back in the kitchen, finding Pandora had begun cooking dinner for everyone.

"What's on the menu?" Jordan asked Pandora, hoping on top of the counter.

"Tables are for glasses," Shannon said.

"Not for asses," Abby and Pandora completed together.

Jordan rolled his eyes and hoped off the island. Pandora threw him a sponge and made him wipe down the entire island. Once he had finished cleaning the island, he cleaned the dishes that Pandora had finished using, replacing the sponge when he was done.

"Where do you want this box, Pandora?" Loren asked, carrying a box that had no label.

Abby took the box from Loren and set it on the island. She opened it and looked inside.

"I don't know who this stuff belongs to," Abby told Pandora.

Pandora walked over, letting Jordan take over cooking as she went to investigate. The box contained Apollo's cradle and her mother's wedding dress.

"In my room please," Pandora told Loren, closing the box before passing it back to him.

He nodded and left with the box. Jordan told Pandora to sit as he finished dinner for her. Pandora smiled and sat at the bar stool closest to him, watching to make sure he didn't burn anything like he had in the past. Shannon and Candace sat at the island, smiling.

"Do you like it?" Abby asked her parents.

"Yes," Shannon smiled. "Very spacious."

"Well, it won't be for long. All these boys are going to take up too much room," Pandora laughed.

The boys all smiled as they came into the front of the house, taking up bar stools and the couches. They ate dinner there, talking amongst themselves before heading to bed. Shannon and Candace stayed in Sam's room, Pandora claiming it was a guest room so they wouldn't ask questions. Sam stayed in Pandora's room, content under the mountain of blankets while holding Pandora.

The next morning, Candace and Shannon headed home. The boys began moving their stuff into the cottage as Abby, Mason, and Pandora unpacked theirs. Pandora set Apollo's cradle up in front of her window, setting his faded blanket inside of it, folded with his name on top.

"I'll find you," Pandora promised the empty cradle. "I'll find you and bring you home."

Abby, Mason, and Pandora were the only ones in the cottage at the moment, so when Pandora heard a commotion in the living room, she ran out of her room, prepared to protect her friends. In the doorway was a woman holding up a familiar looking man.

"Help me!" she begged Pandora.

Pandora ran over and helped the woman drag the man inside. Mason and Abby came into the kitchen quickly. Mason helped the girls lift the man onto the kitchen island. Pandora recognized him immediately.

"Flynn?" Pandora asked.

"He's bleeding!" the woman yelled.

"Towels, Mason!" Pandora demanded, rushing to the first aid kit that Pandora had stashed under the kitchen sink. "Abby, call Sam!"

Abby pulled out her phone and called Sam quickly, explaining what was happening in front of her. She stayed on the phone as Pandora and Mason began working on Flynn.

"What happened?" Pandora asked the woman.

"Hunters," the girl cried. "They attacked us last night. We hid in the woods, but Flynn was bleeding so much."

"Did they follow you here?" Pandora asked.

The woman didn't answer, crying instead.

"Answer me!" Pandora yelled.

"No," the woman answered. "They didn't follow us."

"Who are you?" Pandora asked, pouring alcohol onto Flynn's gaping wound in his leg.

"Sasha," she answered. "My name is Sasha. Please, save him."

"I'll try," Pandora stated. "Nature is better at this than me though."

Pandora and Mason used every towel in the cottage to try to stop the bleeding.

"I can't find his pulse," Mason said suddenly as the pack finally arrived.

"Fuck!" Pandora yelled, climbing onto the island and starting chest compressions.

Nature ran over, dragging Warren with him. Nature grabbed a needle and bag from the first aid kit and set them on the kitchen counter. He wrapped a band around Warren's arm and stuck the needle in Warren's arm, pulling blood into the bag. Nature came to the island and began working on Flynn's leg just as Flynn's heart started again. Flynn gasped and his eyes flew open. He tried to sit up, but Pandora pushed him back down. Sam ran over and helped Pandora hold Flynn.

"Hold still!" Pandora demanded, causing Flynn to freeze.

The rest of the pack looked to Pandora, waiting to listen to her command as well.

"Get Sasha out of here," Pandora told Jordan.

Jordan pulled Sasha out of the cottage, shutting the door behind him so Pandora could finally hear herself think again.

"Keep working," Pandora told Nature before turning to Sam. "Don't let him move."

Pandora hoped off of the counter and went to Warren. She stopped his blood from flowing and changed the blood bag, letting his blood flow into the new bag. She brought the full bag to Nature, who pointed towards Flynn's arm, indicating that she needed it connected to him.

"Help me," Pandora told Loren.

Loren went to Pandora's side immediately, helping her place a needle in Flynn's arm. The blood began dripping into Flynn's arm. Loren held the blood bag up, making sure it didn't clot. Pandora went to Nature's side, helping him to close the wound. Once it was closed, Pandora wrapped Flynn's leg with bandages and looked to the wound on his arm. Nature was already stitching it up. Pandora set bandages next to him and headed out the door.

"He'll be okay," Jordan was telling Sasha.

"He's fine," Pandora stated. "Nature's got him bandaged up now, and Loren's helping with the blood. What happened?"

"The hunters," Sasha stated. "They burnt our house down yesterday. I tried to get Dylan out, but it was too late."

"Dylan?" Pandora asked.

"Our older brother. He had gone in to grab his notebook. Said it was too important to let burn. I went in after him, but he threw the notebook at me and sent me back out of the house. When I got back outside, they had Flynn surrounded. I turned and distracted them, but Flynn was hurt so badly he couldn't get very far. We made it to the woods on the other side of the mountain and hid there all night."

"I'm sorry about your brother," Pandora said. "What do you mean you turned?"

"We're wolves too," Sasha stated.

"He's asking for Sasha," Sam's voice said from the door.

Sasha ran inside, rushing to Flynn. She took his hand in hers and began whispering to him....

"I'm here little brother. I'm here. It's okay. We're with the Alpha now. It's okay."

"How did you find us?" Sam asked.

"The dreams," Flynn answered. "You have to tell them about the dreams."

"Flynn is psychic. His people skills aren't very good, so when he tried to tell Pandora, it came out all wrong. I'm sorry that he scared you," Sasha said. "Flynn's dreams led us here. I know you don't trust us, but we're a part of your pack, Pandora. We really are."

"Turn," Pandora told her.

Sasha nodded and went back outside. She stripped down and shifted into her wolf form, her red fur almost matching Nature's exactly. Pandora nodded and Sasha turned back. She dressed quickly and went back to Flynn's side.

"Warren," Flynn groaned in pain. "Need. Warren."

Flynn's ragged breath came out in pants as he reached in Warren's direction, eyes still closed. Warren looked confused but went to Flynn's side. Flynn took Warren's hand and Warren let out a sharp hiss through his teeth.

"What?" Pandora asked. "What's wrong?"

"It feels like lightening is going up my arm," Warren stated.

Pandora and Sam exchanged a quick look, familiar with what Warren was describing. Warren's eyes got wide as he studied the tattoo on Flynn's arm.

"We have a matching tattoo," Warren stated.

Nature walked to Pandora and held up a piece of paper for her to read.

"Mates have matching marks. It's in the journal," Pandora read.

"I have a mate?" Warren whispered the question, studying Flynn's face.

Sasha smiled fondly at her brother and Warren.

"He's been waiting a while to meet you," Sasha explained. "Dylan told us we couldn't come here unless we absolutely had to. He didn't want to put Pandora in danger."

"Dylan?" Abby asked.

"My older brother," Sasha stated. "He died in the fire."

"Fire?" Mason continued the questions.

"Were you not listening a minute ago?" Pandora asked her friends. "Hunters were after them."

"Oh," Abby said.

"We were a bit distracted by the dying guy," Mason defended.

"What do you know about the hunters?" Sam asked.

"Not much," Sasha explained.

"You said Flynn is psychic?" Pandora asked. Sasha nodded and Pandora continued her questions. "How did he not know the hunters were coming?"

"It doesn't work like that," Sasha stated. "Stuff comes to him in dreams. Like your nightmares. He doesn't just look into a crystal ball and get all the answers. Only you can do that."

"I can't do that," Pandora stated.

"Not yet," Sasha said. "All Alphas have true sight though. Your grandfather and Flynn only have half the gift."

"Which is how my grandfather knew how to set up the cottage," Pandora whispered.

"Exactly," Sasha shrugged.

"Well, at least we aren't the only girls anymore." Abby sighed.

"I didn't say they could stay," Pandora stated.

"If we leave, we're as good as dead!" Sasha exclaimed. "You can't abandon your pack!"

"You aren't my pack," Pandora said simply. "I don't know you. I don't trust you. The decision isn't up to you."

"Pandora," Warren pleaded.

"Everyone to the back patio," Pandora commanded. Sasha and Flynn remained in the kitchen as Pandora's pack followed her.

Once on the patio, Pandora shut the door behind herself so Sasha couldn't eavesdrop.

"Okay," Pandora breathed, turning to her pack slowly. "We need to talk about this."

"He's my mate," Warren stated.

"He's a creep who scared Pandora at her grandmother's funeral," Abby defended.

"He didn't mean to," Warren stated.

"Don't argue," Pandora demanded, making the pack flinch. "Sorry. Not used to that."

"Your commands are getting stronger," Sam commented.

"I noticed," Pandora said. "Not why we're here though."

"I vote they leave," Abby stated.

"Same," Mason said.

"I feel like the humans shouldn't get a vote since they aren't the ones who would be running with them," Warren stated angrily.

"Then you shouldn't get a vote because you're biased," Abby defended.

"Warren is right." Pandora sighed. "I'll count your vote as one instead of two for no, since your opinion still matters since they would be living with all of us. Warren is a vote for yes."

"I vote no," Jordan stated.

"Yes," Nature held up a piece of paper.

"No," Loren added.

"I vote yes," Sam said to Pandora. "I couldn't imagine taking someone's mate from them. The decision is yours."

Pandora sighed and thought for a moment.

"I'll decide later. They can stay until Flynn is healed. Until then, they're on probation."

Pandora opened the patio door and went to the kitchen. She told Sasha her decision and Sasha sighed in relief.

"Thank you," she said. "You won't regret this. I swear it."

"I better not regret it. If I do, I promise that the hunters will look like children with sticks. If you do anything to hurt my pack, I will rip you apart with my teeth," Pandora threatened, standing tall.

Sasha whimpered, cowering a bit. She nodded her understanding, and Pandora went to her room. She went back to unpacking her clothes, Sam watching her from the doorway.

"When you're done, the guys and I will go finish getting our stuff and be back before dinner," Sam promised. "I don't want to leave until you're done."

Pandora walked to Sam and kissed him gently.

"Have I told you how happy I am that you're here?" Pandora asked Sam.

"Not since last night." Sam smirked.

Pandora giggled and kissed Sam again.

"I have a question for you." Pandora smiled.

"Yes. Whatever you want, yes," Sam answered immediately.

"Okay," Pandora laughed. "Guess I'll finish unpacking in your room then."

"Wait," Sam gave Pandora a huge smile. "Really?"

"Yes." Pandora smiled. "I figure we'll be in each other's rooms anyways, and your closet is bigger than mine."

"I love you," Sam whispered, kissing Pandora before she could say anything.

Pandora laughed into the kiss.

"I love you too," she whispered once he released her, causing him to kiss her again.

"I'll help you move the boxes." Sam smiled, picking up the closest box and carrying it to his room.

"Are you two moving in together?" Abby asked, seeing the boxes.

"Yes," Pandora answered simply.

"About time," Loren mumbled.

While Pandora and Sam unpacked Pandora's things, Warren and Loren went and got their things. Sam, Jordan, and Nature left when they got back, returning within twenty minutes.

"What room will I be staying in?" Sasha asked.

"Mine," Pandora stated. "I want you close."

"Nature," Flynn moaned. "Stay with Nature."

Sasha rolled her eyes.

"No, Flynn," Sasha groaned. "Stop it."

"What's he talking about?" Pandora asked, feeling protective.

"Flynn seems to think I have a mate," Sasha stated.

"Nature?" Pandora questioned, stepping slightly in front of Nature in the process.

"Yes. I told Flynn I choose my own path. If I don't want a mate, then I don't have one. He thinks I'm fighting fate," Sasha stated.

"Girl power," Abby nodded. "Nice."

"I just don't think it's fair that wolves are forced to be with people whether they like it or not," Sasha shrugged.

"So, you're staying away from Nature. Good. Happy we agree," Pandora stated, walking past Sasha and into the kitchen.

Pandora's pack laughed lightly at her fondness for Nature. Nature stared at Sasha for a minute, catching her eye.

"What?" Sasha asked him.

Nature shrugged and looked away. He walked to Pandora and helped her as she began cleaning the blood. The pack followed his lead, working together to clean the mess. Warren gently lifted Flynn from the table and carried him to his room, laying him on his bed before covering him with a blanket. Warren stayed by Flynn's side, holding his hand and studying his face. Abby and Mason began ringing out the towels outside, trying to get as much blood out of them as possible before putting them in a basket.

Pandora took the basket of towels into her bathroom once Abby and Mason had finished. Sam had filled the tub with soapy water for her. Pandora dumped the towels into the tub, careful to not splash water everywhere. Sam brought Pandora a chair to sit in from the patio and watched as Pandora began hand washing the towels, scrubbing the stains with a wooden, bristled brush.

"We could go buy a washer and dryer if you want?" Sam suggested. "Loren knows how to set them up."

"I figure we'll do that eventually. I want to try scrubbing at these though. I might be able to get out stains that a washer couldn't. If Flynn stays, then I don't want a reminder of when he almost died in front of me."

"Technically, I think he was dead when we got here," Sam stated. "You were doing chest compressions, right?"

"Yeah," Pandora whispered. "We couldn't find a pulse."

"So, if it wasn't for you, he would probably already be dead."

"If it wasn't for Nature, he would be dead," Pandora corrected.

"Nature wouldn't have been able to help if you hadn't started his heart again," Sam argued.

"Why are you doing that?" Pandora asked, dropping the towel she'd been scrubbing into the tub.

"Doing what?" Sam asked.

"Giving me more credit than I deserve," Pandora answered.

"Why are you not giving yourself any credit at all?" Sam asked back. "You helped save Flynn, and you're acting like you had no hand in it at all."

"Because I don't want credit for saving someone when I couldn't even save Apollo, Sam!" Pandora yelled, wanting to break inside.

"Take your medicine," Sam stated.

"No," Pandora argued. "And you don't give me orders."

"As your beta I don't. As your mate, hell yeah, I do," Sam argued.

"I'm not taking the medicine, and you can fuck off," Pandora stated.

"Sorry to interrupt," Abby said from the doorway. "Loren needs you Sam. Something about you needing to learn to cook better."

"Yes, ma'am," Sam stated, rising and leaving the room quickly.

"Go easy on him, Dora," Abby stated. "He's just trying to help."

"I'm not taking my medicine," Pandora told her.

"I'm not asking you to," Abby shook her head. "I'm just asking you to go easy on Sam. He was scared on the phone. He thought you were going to get hurt, and he wasn't going to be here to help you. He went through a lot of emotions today and so have you. Don't take that out on each other."

Pandora remained silent, scrubbing the towels again. Abby left the bathroom, nothing else to say. Pandora went over Abby's words in her head a few times. She knew she was on edge and that it was coming out when she didn't want it to. She knew she should probably take her medication to help it. She just wanted to be stubborn for a bit longer first. She would take her medication after dinner. Until then, she would tough it out and try to not direct anything towards her family.

Pandora sighed as she finished scrubbing the towels. She pulled the plug on the tub and began to ring out the towels. She carried them onto the private porch and laid them over the bannister to dry. She sat on the small table outside and looked into the woods, taking a few breaths as she thought over the Sasha and Flynn situation. Flynn and Warren seemed like they would be inseparable now that they had found each other.

Sasha didn't want anything to do with Nature, which didn't bother Pandora one bit. That's what she told herself anyways. In her heart, it hurt her that Nature's mate didn't want to be with him. She understood that it should be a choice though. She was lucky that she and Sam had actually liked each other. What if they hadn't? What if they had hated each other?

Pandora sighed and stood, walking back into the cottage and meeting her pack in the kitchen.

"Where's Sam?" Pandora asked, looking around and not finding him.

"Loren and him went to go get something from the store." Abby shrugged.

"Oh." Pandora frowned. "Is Warren still with Flynn?"

"Yeah," Sasha answered. "They're in Warren's room."

Pandora nodded and headed down the hall, wanting to check on the boys. She smiled when she saw Warren watching over Flynn as Flynn slept. She knocked on the wall gently, alerting Warren that she was there. He smiled to her and she entered the room.

"I just wanted to check on you." Pandora smiled gently. "How's he doing?"

"Good." Warren smiled, sitting tall. "My mate is strong."

Pandora smiled and let out a small laugh.

"That he is." Pandora smiled. "Good thing, too. We almost lost him."

Warren shrunk a bit.

"He's okay though," Pandora assured Warren. "What do you think of Sasha?"

"She talks too much," Warren stated. "She also has a bit of an attitude."

"Kind of childish." Pandora nodded.

"Yeah." Warren nodded.

"It'll be alright." Pandora sighed. "I think I'm going to test her a bit."

"What do you have in mind?" Warren asked.

Pandora smiled, a sparkle in her eye.

Sam and Loren turned into the Home Depot parking lot.

"So, we're going to put the washer and dryer in the big bathroom, against the wall that the door is on," Loren stated.

"Okay," Sam agreed, not really caring.

"What crawled up your ass?" Loren asked.

"Pandora is in a bad mood," Sam stated.

"Why aren't you?" Loren asked.

"What do you mean?" Sam asked.

"Didn't you go through Pandora's stuff to see if she was dangerous not a month ago?" Loren asked.

"Don't remind me." Sam sighed.

"She's worried that these people are going to hurt her pack, and you're telling her to take medications to shut off her feelings," Loren stated. "How many times you going to fuck this up, Sam?"

"I didn't think about it like that," Sam admitted.

"Of course, you didn't." Loren rolled his eyes. "I bet Abby is telling Pandora to go easy on you right now, and Pandora is feeling bad when you're the one who messed up again."

"Shit." Sam groaned, pulling out his phone.

"What are you doing?" Loren asked Sam.

"Calling Pandora," Sam stated.

"Nope!" Loren took Sam's phone quickly. "You need to apologize in person. We'll get her a present while we're here."

"Another one?" Sam asked.

"The washer and dryer are for everyone," Loren corrected. "That's not a present. It's home appliances. What does Pandora like?"

"I don't know." Sam groaned. "We're still learning about each other."

"You are terrible." Loren sighed. "She likes sunflowers and dreamcatchers. Dude."

"How do you know that?" Sam asked.

"I pay attention," Loren stated. "So, we need to stop at the florist's on y through town. Call them now and make an order for a bouquet of ʳrs. We'll have to stop at Walmart and get something with dream- o."

"How do you know how to do shit like this?" Sam asked.

"Remember Anna?" Loren asked.

"She was a nightmare." Sam sighed.

"So was I," Loren stated. "We put each other through hell. Making up for the shit I did to her was something I was good at."

"Look at you, being an adult and shit." Sam laughed.

"Yeah, and now it's your turn. Let's get what we need and go."

CHAPTER TWENTY-FOUR

MATES

Sam and Loren returned home and called Jordan and Nature out to help carry the washer and dryer. Pandora and Abby laughed as Jordan got stuck in the door.

"Need help?" Warren asked, finally coming out of his room.

"Yes, please." Jordan gasped.

Warren took over for Jordan, allowing him to rest. Jordan sat at the island with the girls and Mason. Abby and Sasha continued their conversation from earlier. Pandora wasn't sure how she felt about how close the two seemed to be getting. Jordan bumped Pandora to get her attention off of Sasha and nodded his head to Sam. Sam smiled to Pandora and held his hand out to her. Pandora smiled and took his hand, hoping off of her stool and following Sam outside. Sam led Pandora to her truck. Pandora looked at her truck and gasped.

The bed of Pandora's truck was filled with sunflowers.

"When did you have the time to do this?" Pandora asked.

"We've been here for a little while. Loren helped me set everything up. I also got you this."

Sam held a long jewelry box out for Pandora to take. She opened the box and smiled to Sam. Sam took the box from her and told her to turn around. He placed the necklace around Pandora's neck, hooking it behind her neck. Pandora touched the necklace delicately. The dreamcatcher hung low on her.

"It's a locket." Sam smiled, opening it for her to see the pictures inside.

Pandora smiled at the picture of Sam on one side and the picture of Apollo on the other.

"When did you take that picture?" Pandora asked.

"While packing," Sam shrugged. "I was being an ass earlier. I'm sorry, Pandora. I wasn't thinking about how you're worried about the pack, and by telling you to take your medicine, I was basically telling you not to do what you're supposed to as an Alpha. I was telling you not to worry about your pack. I'm sorry."

"I'm sorry too. I shouldn't have taken my frustrations out on you." Pandora sighed. "I don't have a present for you."

"I think you'll come up with something." Sam smiled.

Pandora laughed, wrapping her arms around Sam's waist and pulling him close. He wrapped his arms around her and kissed her gently.

"I love you," Pandora whimpered.

"I love you too," Sam said.

"You didn't have to do all of this." Pandora smiled.

"Yes, I did." Sam smiled, kissing her again.

"Pandora?" Abby called from the front door.

"Yeah?" Pandora answered, heading towards the front of the house again.

"Nature needs you," Abby said. "Something about the journal."

Pandora and Sam climbed the steps quickly and entered the cottage. Nature was at the kitchen island, writing away in the notebook.

"What's up?" Pandora asked him.

He pushed the notebook towards Pandora for her to read.

"The strongest Mate bond will appear around the wedding finger as a wedding band. If these mates do not marry within a year of meeting each other, the mates will begin to fade. Within the next year of their lives, one or both mates will die. The only exception for this bond is the Golden Wolf, as it is already a danger to itself."

"What. The. Actual. Fuck," Pandora said each word angrily.

"What's wrong?" Abby asked.

Pandora passed the notebook to Abby to read. Abby read it carefully and began to smile.

"Are you telling me we get to plan a wedding?" Abby asked with a smile.

"What?" Sam asked.

Abby passed the notebook to Sam as the rest of the pack looked on curiously. Sam's eyes grew wide as he slowly looked to Pandora.

"No," Pandora stated, pointing at Abby who was bouncing around happily.

"I never thought this day would come!" Abby stated. "You hate everyone, so I figured you'd end up dying alone. I'm so happy!"

"You're happy?" Pandora yelled, cutting Abby's smile off. "You're happy that I'm being forced to marry someone that I barely know or else we'll die? Are you fucking serious right now?"

"I didn't think…"

"Of course, you didn't!" Pandora yelled. "Why would you think about it that way? Just because Sam and I get along so well and, as you put it, I hate everyone, you thought it would be fine! What the hell, Abby?"

Pandora walked out of the cottage and towards her truck. She stopped when she saw the flowers and realized she couldn't drive it around with it like that. She groaned in frustration, turning and almost running into Sam. He held up his keys for Pandora. She took them angrily and headed towards his car. He climbed into the passenger's side, not taking his eyes off of Pandora. Pandora drove towards the path into the woods. She took corners too sharply, ignoring the squeal of the tires in the process.

She drove for an hour, reaching Pittsburgh a bit faster than she should have. She pulled into a Chevy dealership and parked, smiling politely to the salesman that approached Sam and her.

"My name's Chuck. Welcome. How can I help you today?" Chuck asked.

"We're looking to buy a new car." Pandora smiled.

"Are you going to trade the Impala in?" Chuck asked.

"No," Pandora and Sam said immediately.

"Alright," Chuck smiled. "What are you interested in? What's your price?"

"Is it okay if we just look around for now, Chuck? I'm not sure what I want yet. I have an old truck at home, but I think I'm going to turn it into a lawn ornament."

"What kind of truck is it?" Chuck asked.

"It's a '66 F-150. My fiancée here filled the bed of it with sunflowers and I can't really drive it with them in there." Pandora smiled.

"Good man." Chuck nodded. "I'll let you look around. Just ask for Chuck when you're ready."

"Yes, sir, we will." Sam smiled as he and Pandora headed down one of the aisles. Once they were a good distance away, Sam turned to Pandora.

"Fiancée?" he asked.

"Well, if we don't get married before my birthday next year, we're going to die. I might as well call you my fiancée." Pandora sighed. "I always said I would never get married."

"I've always wanted to get married." Sam shrugged.

"Why?" Pandora asked.

"Because I like the idea of two people loving each other so much that they want the people they care about to celebrate their love with them," Sam stated.

"Yeah, well, when you're married you aren't your own person anymore. Everything turns into a 'we' or 'us' thing. I don't want to belong to someone else. I'm not furniture," Pandora stated.

"You don't like marriage. Got it," Sam stated. "This isn't exactly what I want either, Pandora. When I propose to you, I want it to be some big, grand thing. I don't want it to be a life or death situation."

"When you propose?" Pandora asked. "Have you already thought about it?"

"No. I mean, yeah. Kind of," Sam stuttered.

"That was a lot of different answers," Pandora joked.

"Shush. What kind of car do you want?" Sam changed the subject.

Pandora ended up choosing a 2019 Tahoe that could fit eight people and had four-wheel drive to help with the shaky path through the woods and to the cottage. The outside was shadow grey, and the interior was a light cocoa color. The vehicle would cost around sixty thousand dollars, so Pandora set up payments twice a month to build up her credit, paying ten thousand dollars up front. Chuck waved goodbye to the couple as they drove away, Sam following close behind Pandora.

"So, how's it driving?" Sam asked over Pandora's speaker.

"I like it." Pandora smiled. "I feel big."

Sam's chuckled vibrated through the Tahoe.

"So, want to get lunch?" Pandora asked.

"You're a big spender today," Sam commented.

"I feel like I deserve a break. Plus, we should talk about the whole marriage thing."

"Deal," Sam stated. "I'll follow you."

They pulled into a Mexican restaurant and headed inside. They were sat quickly and both ordered drinks. Once the waiter was gone, Pandora smiled to Sam.

"So, how would you have proposed?" Pandora asked.

"Can't tell you." Sam smiled. "Might still do it."

"You don't need to," Pandora stated.

"I want to," Sam told her.

Pandora just sighed and leaned back in her chair.

"I feel like I need to apologize to Abby. I shouldn't have yelled at her like that," Pandora said.

"She'll be fine," Sam said. "You can apologize to each other later. You were both in the wrong, so it'll be okay."

"I know it'll be okay. I just hate fighting with her," Pandora said.

"She's basically your sister. Of course you hate fighting with her. You probably don't fight that often."

"We really don't," Pandora stated. "We've fought twice ever."

"Well, you need to make up before the year is over. Someone has to be your maid of honor," Sam joked.

"Ha." Pandora fake laughed. "So, we really should talk about that."

"We should." Sam nodded.

"We really don't have a choice in the matter." Pandora groaned.

"So, we're getting married?" Sam asked.

"Are we?" Pandora asked.

"Pandora." Sam smiled. "Will you marry me?"

Pandora rolled her eyes at Sam.

"I don't know." Pandora sighed. "You didn't even give me a ring or get down on one knee."

Sam climbed out of his seat and got on his knees next to Pandora.

"Oh, God. No. Get up. I was kidding."

"Pandora Williams-Anput!" Sam yelled, causing people to turn and watch them. "Will you do me the honor of becoming my wife? I promise to spend the rest of my life making you as happy as I possibly can. I will fill your truck with flowers and help you keep the boys in line. I will learn to cook so that you and Loren don't have to all the time. I will be completely over dramatic at the worse possible moments just to get you to laugh. Please, be my wife."

"I am going to murder you when we get home." Pandora laughed. "Yes, Sam, I will marry you, if I don't murder you first."

Sam kissed Pandora, holding her close in the process. Pandora could hear people cheering around them and pulled away from Sam. Sam smiled brightly at her and sat back in his seat, keeping Pandora's hand in his. The waiter returned and congratulated them, bringing them their food. Pandora and Sam ate quickly, ready to get home to their pack.

"Can we get the check?" Sam asked the waiter.

"It's on us today." The waiter smiled. "Congratulations again."

Sam and Pandora thanked them and headed to their vehicles. Pandora stopped for gas and promised Sam she'd meet him at home. She somehow still beat him there and parked her Tahoe next to her truck. Abby met her outside.

"New car?" Abby asked.

"Yeah." Pandora sighed. "I think it's time to retire the truck. Plus, it's kind of hard to drive it when there's a bunch of flowers in it."

Abby smiled at that.

"I'm sorry for yelling at you," Pandora said.

"You don't need to apologize," Abby stated. "I'm sorry. I didn't even think about the fact that you hate the idea of marriage. I should've been angry for you instead."

"I still shouldn't have yelled at you." Pandora sighed.

"Let's just agree that we both suck." Abby laughed.

"Yeah." Pandora smiled. "Did I miss anything?"

"No." Abby sighed. "Flynn woke up. Warren and him are by the water." Pandora smiled.

"Where's Sam?" Abby asked.

"I'm not sure," Pandora said, pulling out her phone and dialing his number. "He should've beat me here."

"Hey, babe," Sam answered his phone. "I'm almost there."

"What took so long?" Pandora asked curiously.

"You'll see when I get there." Pandora could hear Sam's smile.

"You're not going to embarrass me again, are you?" Pandora joked, walking into the cottage with Abby.

Sam just laughed.

"I'll see you soon. Love you," Sam said.

"Love you too." Pandora smiled, hanging up her phone and turning to her pack. "Hey, guys."

Sam smiled at his phone as he hung up with Pandora. He turned back to the man in front of him.

"I'll take it." He smiled.

"Excellent choice." The man smiled.

When Sam got home, he found everyone in the front yard. He smiled as he approached the group, but then frowned when he heard yelling. He rushed to the group quickly, standing next to Pandora and Loren quickly. Sasha was red in the face from yelling and Pandora had a small grin on her face.

"What did I miss?" Sam asked.

"Your mate tried to kill me!" Sasha yelled.

"If I had tried to kill you, you would be dead." Pandora shrugged.

"We were racing, and she jumped from a one mountain to another! She knew I couldn't make that jump!" Sasha stated.

"How the hell was I supposed to know that?" Pandora asked. "And you would've been fine if you hadn't made it anyways. Also, no one said you had to follow me."

"Maybe you should breathe, Sasha," Flynn suggested.

"She did it on purpose!" Sasha stated.

"I wanted to see how strong you were," Pandora stated. "I actually did think you could've made it."

"Bullshit!" Sasha yelled. "You don't like me, and you don't want me in your pack."

"Not right now I don't. You're really dramatic."

"No! You're a bitch!"

"Sasha!" Flynn yelled. "Calm down!"

Sasha huffed and walked away from the pack, heading towards the water. Pandora let out a low breath, trying to figure out how to deal with the situation.

"It was a little mean." Loren smiled.

"I know. I'll talk to her later." Pandora turned to Sam and hit his arm. "Where have you been?"

"How am I in trouble?" Sam asked.

Pandora just smiled at him.

"You want to tell them?" Sam asked.

"Tell who what?" Loren asked.

"You can tell them." Pandora smiled. "I already told Abby. She's freaking out."

"I bet." Sam laughed.

"Tell us what?" Warren demanded.

"Pandora and I are getting married." Sam shrugged.

"I thought we knew that," Jordan said.

"Willingly," Pandora corrected.

"Oh." Jordan smiled. "Good."

"Yeah, we're happy y'all aren't dying." Warren smiled.

"When's the big day?" Loren asked.

"No clue," Pandora said.

"Two months." Flynn smiled.

"That's so weird," Loren mumbled.

"Two months?" Pandora asked. "Abby's going to be pissed."

"Yes," Flynn responded. "Not for the reason you're thinking though."

"Shit," Pandora groaned, heading towards the cottage.

Sam smiled and followed Pandora inside.

"Were you messing with Sasha for a reason?" Sam asked.

"I was testing her reactions." Pandora smiled. "I feel like we should make her play Truths with us."

"Can we never play that game again?" Sam groaned.

"Deal," Mason said, coming down the hall. "Abby and I still haven't talked about that night."

"In some defense, we've been a bit busy," Abby stated, joining them in the kitchen.

Mason said nothing as he looked to Sam.

"Where were you?" Mason asked curiously.

"Nowhere," Sam shrugged. "Stopped for gas and got stuck behind someone going really slow."

"That sucks," Abby commented.

Sam just shrugged again, noticing how Mason wasn't wrapping his arm around Abby like he normally would. He ignored the thought as soon as he had it though and went to the fridge to get something to drink. The pack joined them in the kitchen along with Sasha a few minutes later. Sasha glared at Pandora for a moment before sitting next to her brother on the couch. Pandora walked past Sam and grabbed two bottles of water from the fridge before going into the living room. She sat on the coffee table in front of Flynn.

"How are you feeling?" Pandora asked him, passing Flynn one of the bottles of water.

He took it with a smile.

"Kind of sore," he admitted.

"At least you aren't bleeding anymore," Pandora commented. "You should get some more rest. Warren will bring you some dinner once it's ready."

Flynn nodded and stood, walking down the hall to Warren's room. Warren followed him closely, not wanting any distance between them. Pandora looked to Sasha next and held out the other bottle of water.

"We agree that we don't like each other?" Pandora asked Sasha.

"Definitely," Sasha stated, arms crossed over her chest.

"We agree to get over it in order for our pack to stay whole?" Pandora asked.

"Agreed," said Sasha, finally taking the bottle of water.

"Good. You can stay," Pandora stood from the table.

Pandora didn't stay in the living room to see Sasha's happy reaction. Instead, she headed towards hers and Sam's room, grabbing Abby's hand and dragging her along with her in the process. Once in the room, Pandora shut the door so no one could hear them.

"What's going on with you and Mason?" Pandora questioned.

"I don't know." Abby sighed. "He's been acting all distant ever since the game."

"Have y'all talked about it yet?" Pandora asked.

"No. Every time I try to bring it up, he says he has to go do something. He's avoiding me," Abby admitted.

"What a dick," Pandora commented. "Want me to talk to him?"

"No." Abby smiled. "I'll talk to him tonight."

Pandora smiled to her friend before wrapping her in a hug.

"Flynn said the wedding is in two months," Pandora said.

"That's not long." Abby laughed. "You don't want anything big though, so that shouldn't be hard."

"He said you were going to be pissed, but wouldn't tell me why," Pandora told her.

Abby released Pandora from her hug and cocked her head to the side.

"I wonder who's going to piss me off," Abby finally said.

"My money is on Mason," Pandora nodded.

"Mine was on Sasha." Abby laughed.

"You two seem to get along pretty well," Pandora commented.

"She's alright." Abby shrugged. "Talks too much."

"I've noticed." Pandora laughed along with Abby.

The two girls went back into the kitchen and found everyone. Pandora sat at the island, watching her pack. Nature was cutting vegetables and Warren was peeling potatoes. Flynn was in the living room, laying across one of the couches with his head in Sasha's lap as she read quietly to him. Mason was on the other couch, reading to himself as Abby sat next to him and played on her phone. Jordan sat next to Pandora with his laptop open, scrolling through his Tumblr. Sam and Loren were standing over the stove top, Loren explaining how to cook something to Sam.

Pandora smiled, content.

CHAPTER TWENTY-FIVE

Fight

"Can we talk?" Abby asked Mason, standing in their bedroom doorway so he couldn't run off again.

"I'm tired, Abbs. Can it wait?" Mason urged to Abby to let him rest instead of having the conversation he had been dreading.

"No," Abby said sternly, shutting the bedroom door. "You will not keep avoiding me, Mason. I've been your girlfriend for two years, and it isn't fair to do that to someone that you say that you love."

"It isn't fair to keep a secret from someone you love either, but you did," Mason commented and immediately regretted.

"I didn't keep a secret from you, you idiot. I just found out that I can't have kids right before graduation. The only person who knew was Pandora, because she went with me to the doctor," Abby stated angrily.

"Wait. Why did you go to the doctor?" Mason asked.

"I thought I was pregnant," Abby stated.

"But you weren't?" Mason asked.

"No," Abby answered. "They told me that I was having signs of early menopause."

"How is that possible? I thought only old women get menopause?"

"I thought that too," Abby stated. "It's rare, but it happens."

"I'm sorry," Mason told Abby, rubbing her arms.

"For?" Abby asked.

"For being an ass. For not talking to you sooner," Mason said.

"You're forgiven." Abby smiled. "Let's go to bed."

Mason kissed the top of Abby's head and led her to the bed. They cuddled in close to each other. Abby fell asleep quickly, happy that she and Mason had finally talked. Mason stayed up, thinking about his and Abby's future, ignoring the pang that he felt in his heart when he thought about never having children of his own.

The next morning, Abby woke alone in bed to the smell of blueberry pancakes. She smiled and sat up in bed, stretching. She brushed her hair and headed into the kitchen, smiling when she saw Pandora dancing around the kitchen in a shirt that belonged to Sam and pajama shorts, her hair in a messy bun on top of her head. Mason sat at the island, eating a few pancakes already.

"I see a lot of blueberry pancakes in our future." Abby smiled.

"I'm not complaining." Sam smiled, coming into the kitchen barefoot and wearing long pajama pants.

"Of course, you aren't." Mason smiled. "You get pancakes and sex. What more could a guy want?"

"Can we not?" Pandora asked, her face turning red.

Mason, Abby, and Sam all laughed a bit as Pandora continuing cooking. She set plates in front of Sam and Abby, giving them both two pancakes and then continuing to pile the rest of the pancakes into two big piles on the cutting board. The rest of the pack joined them a few at a time until everyone had finally eaten.

"What's your plan for today?" Sam asked Pandora.

"I am going into town to look at available shops." Pandora smiled. "Do you have work?"

"We all do, unfortunately." Sam smiled. "I also have to prepare for my show next month, so I won't be home until late tonight."

"I'll save you a plate of dinner." Pandora smiled.

"Thank you." Sam smiled, kissing her forehead before heading back to their room to change.

"What's on your finger?" Abby asked Pandora suddenly.

"Nothing," Pandora insisted, hiding her hands behind her back.

"Bullshit!" Abby yelled, running over to Pandora and grabbing her hand.

On Pandora's left hand, just barely covering her mate tattoo, was an engagement ring. The ring had a blue sapphire in the middle of it, a silver circle incasing it. On each side of the circle were crescent moons, making the sapphire appear to be a full moon. Abby smiled at the ring, knowing Sam got it because of the moons.

"Why a sapphire?" Sasha asked curiously.

"It's the birthstone for September," Pandora told Sasha. "September had been my little brother's birthday and my grandmother's birthday. He picked it for them."

"Oh." Sasha nodded. "Nice."

"That's so sweet." Abby smiled. "Good job, Sam."

"My boy can pick a ring." Loren smiled.

"Can we all stop staring at my hand now, please? It's getting weird."

Abby laughed and let go of Pandora's hand. The pack all began leaving to get to their jobs. Sasha and Flynn were staying at the cottage since neither felt safe and it would give Flynn more time to heal. Sam kissed Pandora goodbye as he went out the door, promising to text her throughout the day. Pandora, Mason, and Abby loaded into the Tahoe once the pack had been gone for a bit, deciding to finally head into town.

Pandora drove through Main Street slowly, parking once she was in front of city hall. Abby, Mason, and Pandora walked up and down Main Street, looking into empty windows and saving numbers into their phones as they went. Pandora hadn't been paying attention and had accidently bumped into someone at one point. She had apologized about a thousand times to the guy she had run into before he finally got the chance to tell her it was okay and to have a good day.

"That poor kid didn't know what hit him." Abby laughed.

"Kid?" Mason asked.

"Yeah." Abby shrugged. "He looked like he was still a teenager."

"He had to be, like, twenty," Mason stated.

"I don't think so." Abby laughed.

They continued on their way, Mason and Abby bickering a bit more than normal as they went.

"Are you two going to kiss and make up anytime soon?" Pandora finally asked. "I love y'all, but this is getting annoying."

Mason and Abby stopped arguing after that. In fact, they seemed to just stop talking in general at that point. Pandora sighed and rolled her eyes, wishing Sam was there to help diffuse the tension around her. Pandora's phone vibrated in her pocket, causing her to smile.

"Need me?" the text from Sam read.

"Always, but not right now."

Pandora sent her text and put her phone back in her pocket. They walked down the street until Abby spotted a wedding shop.

"Let's go in!" Abby told Pandora, dragging her through the door.

"How may I help you?" a woman greeted the three friends.

"Hi. I'm Abby, and this is Pandora." Abby took over. "Pandora here is getting married in two months and we just realized she needs her mother's wedding dress altered a bit. Do y'all do that here?"

"Yes ma'am, we do, but it's by appointment," the woman answered. "Our tailor is free in two weeks. Would you like me to write you in?"

"Yes." Abby smiled.

"Great! Have you gotten your bridesmaid dress yet? I'm assuming you and the gentleman are the wedding party."

"Mason." Mason stuck out his hand for the woman to shake politely.

"Dakota." She smiled, shaking his hand.

"Yes, they are." Pandora smiled. "Abby is the maid of honor and Mason is, well, I'd say bridesmaid, but he's a guy."

"We'll call him a bridesmen." Dakota smiled. "What colors will we be looking for?"

"Good question." Pandora laughed. "Let me ask Sam again. We're kind of rushing this."

"Oh?" Dakota looked like she wanted to ask why.

"We have family members who are fading quickly," Abby whispered to Dakota.

"Oh," Dakota said in an understanding tone. "I got you."

Pandora pulled out her phone and texted Sam.

"Abby dragged me into a wedding store. This lady asked me about a color scheme. I have no clue what to say"

Sam didn't text back, making Pandora feel a bit awkward as she stood in the store. The bell over the door tinged, causing everyone to turn. Sam strode into the shop and went straight to Pandora, smiling.

"Hey, babe," he whispered to Pandora, kissing her head before turning to Dakota. "Sorry I'm late. Had to wait for my lunch break."

"Hi, Sam." Dakota smiled in surprise. "I didn't know you were getting married."

"I haven't told much of anyone yet." Sam shrugged. "Loren and Warren will be here in a few minutes."

"Did they fight over who was going to be best man?" Dakota laughed.

"No." Sam smiled. "Warren already knew it would be Loren. Jordan seemed a little butt hurt that he wasn't going to be included though."

"Poor guy." Dakota laughed. "How is he?"

"He's good. You should give him a call sometime. Get that second date you both keep trying to avoid." Sam smirked.

Dakota turned red and was saved by the bell above the door as Loren and Warren came in, laughing at something from before. The group of six greeted each other happily before giving their attention back to Dakota.

"The colors?" Dakota asked.

"Oh, yeah!" Sam smiled. "Just black and white. Maybe off white."

"Okay." Dakota smiled. "Follow me."

The group of six followed Dakota happily.

"Is it more casual or dressy?" Dakota asked.

"A bit more casual," Pandora told her, getting a smile from Sam.

"So, we'll look for something simpler than a tux. Maybe just a long sleeve, button-up shirt for the men with black dress pants?" Dakota questioned.

"That sounds perfect." Sam smiled.

"Can I ask the color of the wedding dress?" Dakota asked Pandora, eyeing Sam.

"It's off white." Pandora smiled. "A little on the tan side. I have a photo if you want to see it to get a better idea."

"I can work with a picture." Dakota smiled. "Then, in two weeks when you come in for the alterations, I can make sure the color of Sam's shirt is correct."

"Sounds good." Pandora smiled.

"Do you want the maid of honor in black or white?" Dakota asked.

"I'd like to see a few of both and then decide," Pandora told her. "Just depends of which one I like more."

"Long or short length?"

"Short."

"Style?"

"Boho chic."

"Shoes?"

"Barefoot."

"So, boys go that way, and Jamie will assist you." Dakota pointed the men in the direction of another woman. "Ladies follow me. I think I have a few ideas."

Dakota got Abby's dress size and disappeared for a few moments, letting the girls look through a few racks before returning with four dresses for Abby to try on. The first dress was an off-white dress that reached Abby's knee. The dress had a white lace pattern as the top layer and a black ribbon around the waist. Pandora liked it but felt like it wasn't quite what she was looking for.

The second dress was a short black dress that was made of satin and silk. It zipped up in the back and also had a clasp behind the neck. It was very elegant and much closer to what Pandora wanted. The third dress was a white knee length dress with long sleeves. Pandora shook her head immediately, causing Abby to turn right back around and shut the door of the dressing room.

The final dress was a lace, vintage dress. It was black and the front of it reached Abby's midthigh. The back of it went just pass her knees. The sleeves were translucent and went to her elbows. There was an embroidery of small, white flowers on the right side of the dress that stretched from her hip up to her shoulder and went from the middle of the dress down her right sleeve. Pandora stared at Abby for a few moments, speechless.

"That's the one," Pandora whispered. "You look amazing."

"Thank God, because I really like this one." Abby laughed.

Pandora smiled to Abby as Dakota helped Abby out of the dress in the stall. Dakota rang up the dress and the men's clothes and Sam paid, not giving Pandora the chance to. Pandora sighed, letting Sam know that he didn't need to pay when she could have without making a dent in her banking account. Dakota smiled as the group left the store, happy that Sam had found someone that made him so happy but wondering how long the couple had actually known each other.

"Are we going to be doing anymore wedding shopping today?" Pandora asked Abby.

"Yes," Abby answered simply.

"Can we take me home first?" Mason asked. "No offense, but this seems a little bit too girly for me."

"But who will help us carry stuff?" Abby asked.

"Pandora has super strength," Mason pointed out.

"Clark Kent can't tell the world he's Superman!" Abby argued.

Mason sighed and rolled his eyes before agreeing to go with. Pandora just looked to the sky, hoping to not get a headache by the end of the day. Sam kissed Pandora goodbye as he headed back to work, Loren and Warren leaving at the same time as him. The three friends got into the Tahoe and headed towards Walmart, Abby demanding they go through the wedding aisle at every store that had one.

They ended up spending the rest of the day looking at decorations. Pandora had decided on a mixed theme. It would be woodlands and moons and wolves decorated everywhere, combining everything that felt like home to Sam and Pandora. Pandora smiled, knowing Sam would love it. She took a picture of the cake topper she had found and sent it to Sam. It was wooden and had two wolves howling at the sky. There were trees on both sides of them and mountains above them. Sam sent back smiling emojis as his response, causing Pandora to place it in her cart.

"Have you called Mom and Dad yet?" Abby asked Pandora seriously.

"No," Pandora admitted. "I feel like Shannon is going to be mad that he wasn't asked permission."

"He'll probably drive up here just to yell at Sam." Mason laughed. "Candace, too."

"You should call them." Abby smiled.

"That way you can ask Shannon to give you away like you've been trying to figure out how to do in your head ever since we started talking about weddings." Mason smiled.

"Actually, I wasn't going to have anyone give me away. I'm not property that can be given to someone else. Sam said he doesn't even expect me to give up my last name when we get married," Pandora stated, understanding more and more what Sasha meant when she had gone on her rant about mates.

"I think Sam is perfect for you." Abby smiled before whispering low, "Mates or not."

Suddenly, there was screaming coming from a few rows over. Pandora, Mason, and Abby froze as the screaming got closer. Pandora came out of her trance first and looked around the aisle they were in. She grabbed Abby and

Mason by their arms and pulled them in the opposite direction of the screaming. She ran down a few different aisles before ending up in the baby stuff. Pandora pulled Mason and Abby to the floor so no one could see them. Pandora then moved a few of the stroller boxes from the bottom shelf and then ushered Mason and Abby into the shelf before replacing the boxes, hiding her friends. She then slowly began moving towards the screams that had multiplied, trying to see what was happening. She froze again when she finally found where the screaming was coming from.

CHAPTER TWENTY-SIX

THE GOLDEN WOLF

All he could feel was pain. His heart felt like it was going to explode from his chest, and his brain was splitting. His eyes were both swollen shut, and he was trying to not choke on his own blood. His skin had grown around the chain on his ankle, making it a part of his body at that point. He had never known life off of the chain, off of the concrete floor. He could just barely remember the face of a woman that he wanted to call his mother. Her face had been beautiful, her voice soft. He wondered where she was, then he remembered that she had sold him to these people, the people with the chains who beat him until he was almost dead every chance they got.

Sometimes he would hear them talking. They mentioned a girl, her name sounding almost familiar to him, providing him some comfort before the beatings would start again. The beatings he could handle though. Those were the easy nights, a break from the worst of these people. The worst didn't use their hands. They used sticks with lightning at the end of them, shocking him until his whole body buzzed.

They used the sticks on his face, his chest, his privates, anything they could reach. He hated those sticks. He hated those people. They wanted information from him, information he didn't have. They asked about the girl with the comforting name. He didn't know her. They asked about creatures he had never heard of. He didn't understand the questioning. He had grown up on his chain, his floor, his body just barely surviving after all this time.

One night, the people were angrier than normal at him. It was strange, because he felt calmer than he ever had before. The sticks were used and so we're the people's hands. They kicked and punched and shocked him repeatedly, but he couldn't feel it anymore. Somehow, he had grown used to it. It only angered them more when he didn't whimper or cry like normal, having stopped screaming when he was still a child. Now, he wished he'd just cried as he lay dying on the floor.

"Please," he whispered to anyone who may listen to him. "Please, help me. Don't let me die here. Let me die somewhere peaceful."

He felt more pain then. It tore through his body. He looked around but didn't see the sticks or the people. He wondered where the pain was coming from when he felt his spine crack. He screamed in agony, catching the attention of people in the other room. They came running in but stopped when they saw him. He didn't know why they stopped, but the pain blinded him before he could think anymore.

"This is how I die," he thought to himself, giving in to the pain.

The pain faded once he gave up, and he briefly wondered if he was dead. He heard the people screaming, pulling out their sticks and pointing the lightning at him. He tried to hold his arms above his head, thinking he couldn't handle any more pain that night but then realized his arms weren't his arms anymore. He looked down at his body and felt himself begin to panic.

His body was no longer his own. It had been replaced by that of a dog.

Someone jabbed him with a stick, and he growled, jumping at the man. His chain fell off of his foot that was now a paw once he jumped. The man fell to the ground, and the now wolf bit into the man's neck, ripping his throat out. Two more men stabbed at him, so he attacked them as well. He could feel himself growing stronger with each man that he killed, their lightning useless against him now.

He went through the building, killing anyone who got in his path without mercy. He jumped on one man and ended up falling out of a window, rolling and landing on his two feet again. He looked down and saw his naked body, scars all over his body.

"Find him!" He heard someone yelling.

He began running. He ran as far and as fast as he could, hoping the men wouldn't find him. He ended up in some woods, mud drying to his feet as he continued to run. When he stopped, he could feel his heart pounding in his chest. He looked down to his ankle and was happy to find the chain was truly gone. His ankle had almost completely healed, as if he hadn't been cuffed just hours ago.

He heard a low rumble in the distance and followed the sound. He found a guy standing next to a strange looking machine. He saw the man climb on top of it and ride it around in a few circles. He wondered if he could do it, too, and studied what the man had done. Once the man stopped again, he turned into his beast form and attacked the man, killing him quickly before turning human again. He stole the man's clothing, figuring that he would need them more, before climbing onto the motorcycle and copying the man's movements from earlier.

He figured out the motorcycle pretty quickly and rode it around in a few circles as he had seen the man do before. He then pointed the bike towards the main road before taking off. He didn't know where he was going. He just knew that he needed to be somewhere else. He rode for hours before stopping. He hid the bike in some woods and began walking.

He found clothes hanging on a line and grabbed some that looked like they would fit him. He threw them on and began walking along the road, determined to go back for the bike eventually. He stopped at a building with gas pumps in front of it. He went inside and looked at the man behind the counter. The guy smiled to him and asked if he needed help. He nodded before breaking the guy's neck. He grabbed the money in the register, knowing from the people with the lightning that it was called money and would get him things. He also grabbed a gas can and filled it outside, knowing machines ran on gas.

The people had taught him a few things while he'd been chained down, hoping he would help them. When he refused, they began to hurt him. He tried to offer to help once the beatings and lightning had begun, but they had told him it was too late, and his kind deserved to be tortured and killed. They told him that they would find the others like him and torture them too.

"There are others like me?" he had thought to himself. "Why aren't they helping me?"

He grew angry at the people like him and the people with the lightning, vowing to kill both if he ever got the chance. He was not a gentle soul, and he was on a mission. He was ready to destroy everything and everyone in his path as he set out on the bike again, the money stuffed into his pockets and the now empty gas can was thrown into the woods. He raced past the gas station that now had police surrounding it and continued on his way. He drove over a stated line that read South Carolina and went deep into the marshy woods, laying low until he was strong enough.

He fed on rabbits and squirrels, eating them raw when he hunted in his wolf form. In human form, he made a fire and cooked them. He often ventured into the town nearby for water, buying huge packages of them with the stolen money.

One day while in the store, he smelled something that was almost too sweet. He followed the smell, his wolf instincts taking over for the new hunt, until he found the source. He found a group of men and one woman laughing in one of the aisles. He realized that the sweet smell was coming from the red-haired woman, and he tilted his head curiously. He kept his distance and watched the group carefully. He followed them throughout the store, his water resting on his shoulder easily with the new muscles he had grown. They did their shopping and went to pay. He did the same and followed them until they got into their cars.

He walked past them and headed back towards his woods. He put his water where he had been hiding in the woods and hoped on his bike. He went back into town and began searching for her. He found her and her group in the farmer's marker, speaking to an older woman who was selling tomatoes. The woman smelled dully like all but one of the men around the sweet-smelling girl. He was curious to say the least, but then recognized what the men and old woman smelled like. They smelled like him.

He growled, wanting to attack the people who hadn't protected him from the lightning. He calmed himself when he heard the girl laugh though, reminding himself he was surrounded by people.

He continued to watch the group from afar, finding that there were two more like him in their group. The group left in their vehicles that night at separate times, and he went back to his woods. As the weeks went by, he continued to watch the sweet-smelling girl, wanting to growl every time the human touched her. It was maddening, not being able to get the girl alone. He wanted to take her to the woods and figure out what the hell she was and why she smelled so strongly to him. He wanted to taste her, to see if she was just as sweet as she smelled.

One morning, the old woman left her house alone on an odd day. She headed towards his woods, and he followed her. He walked along a narrow path, not wanting to alert the woman that he was going to be upon her soon. He shifted halfway along the path, preparing himself for a fight if need be. She laid naked on cement, candles around her. He watched curiously as she spoke to herself before she turned her head towards him. He froze, not wanting to be found. She sat up and looked more closely. He couldn't stop himself. He was just so hungry.

He left the woods that night. He hid in town, wondering if he would finally be able to get to the sweet girl now that he had taken care of part of the problem. He laid low for a few days, not going near her home until the coast was clear. When he went to her house, he discovered that she was gone. He looked next door and found the house empty. He groaned in frustration and climbed on his bike, heading north for some reason.

He rode for eight hours, stopping for gas once. He continued until he was in a small town. He climbed off of his bike and began walking along the sidewalk. He heard laughter and found the sweet girl, the human, and the girl who smelled like him. He wanted to growl but forced himself not to. The human and sweet girl seemed to be arguing, the girl who smelled like him seemed annoyed by it. He walked pass them, bumping the woman in the process.

"Shit. I'm so sorry. Are you okay? I wasn't paying enough attention. I'm so sorry. I'm sorry..." she babbled on for a bit before he finally got a word in.

"It's fine," he told her. "Have a great day."

He walked away, just barely brushing the sweet girl in the process. He felt a sharp pain in his arm that reminded him of the lightning sticks and recoiled from her skin. She stared at him for a moment, confusion on her face before she turned back to the woman who smelled like him and began talking. He kept a steady pace even though everything in him told him to run. Once he turned a corner and was out of sight, he began panting, trying to ignore the flashbacks in his head.

The flashbacks always came and went as they pleased, always causing him to feel like he was still chained to the floor before the wolf in him had been set free. He fought the urge to shift and headed back to his bike. He went to the woods that he had found there and sat on a rock, calming himself and wondering why the sweet girl had had that power over him. He didn't like it, not one bit. He felt that she made him weak, so he came up with a plan.

The plan was to go back into town and find the sweet girl. He would find her and take her. He would bring her to the woods and interrogate her. He would figure this out and he would figure it out now. He got back on his bike and left the woods, heading back into town. He followed the scent of her into a few different stores, following her and the other two for a bit. He needed a distraction. Something to get the one who smelled like him away from her.

He waited until they were all smiling about something before he set up his distraction. He walked a few aisles away and killed three men in the clothing aisles, leaving their bodies for someone to find. He walked a few aisles away, knowing the she-wolf would hide the sweet girl and the human somewhere before going to investigate. He found them a few aisles over and hid behind a shelf.

When the screaming began, the wolf did exactly as he thought she would. She hid them behind some boxes and left them alone. He was about to approach when the human came out of the boxes, putting them back in place before leaving the sweet girl alone and following after the wolf. He couldn't believe his luck as he went up to the boxes. He moved them quickly and found the sweet girl looking at him, terrified.

"Come on," he whispered. "We need to get out of here."

The sweet girl nodded, following him out of the store quickly, not knowing that she had just fallen into a trap.

Once outside he knocked her out, grabbing her and ignoring the lightning feeling as he put her in front of him on the bike and raced away, holding her up easily as he drove. Instead of going to the woods, he carried her to an empty apartment above the empty shop where he had bumped her for the first time. He tied her to a chair that was already up there with duct tape from inside his bike's seat compartment. He patted her face, rousing her from the sleep she had been in.

She opened her eyes and looked at him, the confused look on her face again, her lips parted. She realized what must have happened and looked around the room wildly, trying to find a way out. Finally, she screamed.

"Help!" she yelled. "Someone help me!"

He backhanded her across her face, forcing her to be quiet except for a small whimper.

"Who are you?" he questioned.

"Abby," she answered quietly.

"You are not a wolf," he said simply.

She shook her head no.

"Are you a hunter?" he asked.

"No," she told him, feeling more confused.

"Why do you feel like the lightning sticks?" he asked her.

"What?" she asked.

Instead of saying anything, he grabbed her neck, choking her as his hand felt like it was catching fire. He released her a moment later.

"Why does it feel like that?" he asked.

"I don't know," she lied.

"I can hear your heartbeat," he told her. "Lie to me again, and you will regret it. Why does it feel like that?"

"I don't know," she lied again.

He pushed her chair over, letting her head smack against the hardwood floor. She whimpered again, and he hated the sound.

"What are you doing to me?" he questioned. "Why do I feel so weak?"

"Please," she begged him. "Please, just let me go. I won't tell the pack or the police what happened or where you are. Just let me go, please."

"Shut up," he told her, choking her again.

He couldn't ignore the lightning anymore and let it wash over him. He pushed his lips against hers hard, feeling her kiss him back. His hand left her throat and caressed her face. He heard her let out a small moan and lost himself for a moment. He ripped the tape from her body, tearing her shirt open and scratching her chest a bit from his carelessness. She didn't seem to mind as she gasped from pain and pleasure.

He pushed the chair away and climbed on top of her, pushing his body into hers and taking his mouth with his own. She moaned into him again as he pinned her hands above her head and ripped her shirt open the rest of the way and broke the contraption that held her breasts in place. He took one of his nipples in his mouth, not being gentle at all as he sucked and nibbled her chest. She wiggled underneath him, bucking her hips into him to create friction. He groaned at the feeling.

He let go of her hands as he moved lower. He pulled her pants and underwear down her legs quickly, pulling her shoes free in the process as well.

He dipped his head between her legs and smelled the sweetness the was pooling there. He finally tasted her, realizing the sweetness there was somehow even better than the smell. She moaned loudly and wrapped her hands in his hair, losing herself to the feeling.

He couldn't take it anymore. He had to have her. He pushed his pants down quickly and climbed back up her. He looked into her eyes and saw that, while her body was enjoying everything that was happening, her eyes looked terrified. She asked him to stop, tears coming out of her eyes. He froze like that, not wanting to move as his head suddenly exploded. He felt a battle happening in his soul and laid against Abby. He couldn't move from the pain he felt. The pain lasted for a few minutes, finally ending and causing his to breathe raggedly. He looked into Abby's eyes and found that she wasn't crying anymore, nor did she look terrified. She put her hands on both sides of his face and held him there.

He felt shame suddenly. Guilty. The feelings washed over him as Abby looked into his eyes. He pulled away from her quickly and crawled away from her to the other side of the room. He began to cry, wanting to curl up and die right there. The sweet girl pulled her pants back on and pulled on his shirt. She crawled across the floor to him, wincing a bit at the effort it took.

"I'm so sorry," he cried. "I'm just as bad as them. It was the wolf. He did this to me. He did this. I would never…"

"Shh," Abby told him, wrapping her arms around him. "I know. Wepwawet told me. I know."

"Wepwawet?" he asked her.

"He's a god. He created the wolves. While your wolf and the golden wolf were fighting for your soul just now, Wepwawet came to me. He told me what had happened to you and who you are. He told me he was sorry for everything that we both went through, you for your whole life and me in the past hour. He said you're healed now. He said you can come home with me, and that you'll be safe. I won't tell anyone what happened, and you can't either. We'll tell them that you were the golden wolf, and that I healed you with just a touch. The pack will protect you. Abby will protect you," Abby explained.

He felt so confused and ashamed of himself. He could feel a slight buzz where Abby touched him, but nothing like it had been before. He never wanted to hurt her again. How could she be so calm?

"How do you not hate me?" he asked her. "How are you holding me right now?"

"Wepwawet told me that you will face consequences for what has happened," Abby explained. "We can't have children. You will always get your flashbacks. You will never be able to touch me like that again unless I say so," Abby stated. "He told me your name, though."

"I have a name?" he asked.

"Apollo."

CHAPTER TWENTY-SEVEN

Apollo

"What the hell were you thinking?" Loren bellowed. "How could you just leave her alone knowing she's been in danger! Pandora trusted you watch over her and instead you leave her alone, knowing there's danger around!"

"I was trying to figure out what was happening," Mason explained.

"Don't blame him!" Sasha yelled. "He feels bad enough."

Pandora was shaking. She had looked through Walmart, practically tearing it apart searching for Abby. The police claimed they were doing the best they could, but it had been hours and they still hadn't found her. Pandora had taken to the forest then, searching everywhere for signs, only to find none. Pandora's heart dropped in her chest, worry and despair evident on her features. Sam rocked her back and forth on the living room floor, trying to calm her, but failing.

Pandora stood and walked to the door again, ready to search more. Loren called after her, but she ignored him, shifting the moment she stepped out the door. She ran through the woods, searching for Abby again. The sound of a motorcycle turning onto her path caught her attention. She ran to it and jumped onto the road, giving the motorcycle time to see her and come to a stop. She growled at the two people as they stepped off of the motorcycle, ready to pounce.

The woman took her helmet off, her red hair falling out of it and cascading down her shoulders. Pandora stopped growling and stared into Abby's bright eyes. She let out a whimper as she nuzzled against Abby, pushing her fur against Abby's face. Abby let out a slight laugh and then winced in pain. Pandora whimpered again.

"Let's get to the cottage," Abby told Pandora, her voice sounding husky. "We'll follow you there."

Pandora looked to the driver who still had his helmet on. She nodded to him and began running towards the cottage. She could hear the motorcycle revving behind her, keeping up with her easily. They made it to the clearing easily, stopping when they reached the cottage. The pack exited the cottage, Sam holding clothes for Pandora. Pandora shifted and pulled the clothes on quickly, turning to the motorcycle. Abby took off her helmet again and was greeted by the pack. Warren picked her up and squeezed her, causing her to yelp in pain. The man who had driven the motorcycle punched Warren in his rib, causing him to drop Abby. The man caught Abby and threw his helmet off.

"Are you okay?" he asked her gently.

She nodded and stood up with his help. He kept his arm under her elbow, assisting her. Pandora walked over to Abby quickly and began examining her. She looked at the bruises on Abby's neck, as if someone had choked her. The bruise on her check that stretched over her eye and to her temple was a deep purple. Pandora felt her heart sink and grimaced.

"What happened?" Pandora asked softly, guilt ripping through her voice.

"I found the golden wolf," Abby stated, her voice scratching.

She put her hand on her throat, trying to keep it from hurting. Pandora wrapped her arm over Abby's shoulder and began leading her inside. The man followed them, keeping his hand on Abby's elbow to steady her. Sam stopped the man at the door, causing him to let go of Abby. He let out a low growl with the loss of contact.

"Who are you?" Sam asked him, standing tall and looming over the man.

"I'm Abby's," He growled, trying to get pass Sam and to Abby.

Sam stood his ground.

"Sam," Abby's voice called. "Please."

Sam stepped aside, allowing him to pass. He went to Abby quickly, taking her arm again. The human, Mason, glared at him. Pandora led Abby to the couch, sitting next on her right with the man on the left. Nature brought the first aid kit over, sitting on the table in front of Abby. Nature opened the small box and poured some alcohol onto a cotton ball. Gently, he dabbed the small cut on Abby's cheek, causing her to hiss. The man growled low, a warning to Nature.

"Growl at my pack again, and I will throw you out," Pandora told him. "What's your name?"

"I don't have one," he said, glaring at Pandora, green eyes staring into equally green.

"Yes, you do," Abby said. "Tell her."

He bowed his head to Abby before looking at Pandora.

"Apollo," he stated.

"He was the golden wolf," Abby told Pandora.

"Was?" Sam asked, going to Pandora's side as she was silently staring at Apollo, her eyes wide in disbelief.

"Not anymore," Abby gave Sam a small smile. "We checked before coming here."

"Checked?" Jordan asked.

"I watched him shift," Abby shrugged. "His fur is brown now."

"Did you kill him?" Pandora asked Abby, confused.

"No." Abby laughed. "He's your brother, Dora."

"I am not Dora's," Apollo stated. "I am yours."

"Why does he keep saying that?" Mason asked.

Abby met Mason's eyes, a sad expression on her face. She gaped at him for a moment, not knowing how to explain. She closed her mouth and her eyes, turning her head down, trying to figure out how to tell Mason what was happening. He deserved the truth. They had been together for so long.

"I am her mate," Apollo told Mason, feeling Abby's inner turmoil.

"She's not a wolf," Sasha stated. "Wolves are the only ones who receive mates. It's in the journal."

"Well, Wepwawet told me himself," Abby stated. "He came to me and told me who Apollo was and what was happening to him and to me."

"You spoke to Wepwawet?" Sam asked.

"Yes," Abby nodded. "He told me not to worry and that Apollo would be my protector now. He told me that mates are only what we need, and I don't need a lover."

"So, you think you get both?" Mason asked in disbelief.

"No," Abby stated. "I'm just saying that Apollo isn't suddenly replacing you. He's simply my protector unless I ever want anything more."

"So, like a guard dog?" Mason asked bluntly, giving Abby more attitude than needed.

Apollo growled at Mason then. He rose from his spot next to Abby and took a step towards Mason. The pack moved quickly, blocking Mason for his protection. Pandora had put her arm in front of Abby, shielding her in case a fist went flying.

"I may no longer be the golden wolf, but I am still a wolf and you, human, will not speak to her like that," Apollo said before sitting back down, knowing this was a fight he could not win.

Mason glared at Apollo, keeping his mouth closed. Pandora could feel the tension in the air.

"Mason, will you go get the blanket from y'alls' room please. Abby's freezing."

Mason left the room quickly, anxious to get away from Apollo.

"Apollo, will you wait outside for a few minutes, please? I just need to talk to Abby alone, and I don't think she'll speak freely with you in the room."

Apollo looked to Abby, asking her what she wanted.

"Go," Abby smiled to him. "I'll join you in a moment."

Apollo stood and went to the front porch, sitting in the porch swing and waiting. Mason came back with the blanket and wrapped it around Abby's shoulders gently, careful not to hurt her. She thanked him, and he went back to their room. Abby turned to Pandora.

"Guys?" Pandora asked them. "Give us a minute?"

The men dispersed quickly, Sam going outside to keep an eye on Apollo while the rest of the pack went to their rooms. Sasha sat across from Abby on the coffee table, passing her an ice pack. Abby placed it on her cheek, flinching a bit in the process.

"What happened?" Pandora finally asked.

"I need you to promise not to hurt him or tell the pack what happened," Abby said to Pandora.

"Abby, he's my brother," Pandora stated.

"Promise me," Abby insisted.

"I promise," Pandora told her.

"You too," Abby said to Sasha. Once Sasha nodded, Abby began her story.

"He was the golden wolf, but he had no true control over his actions. Everything was about survival for him. Now, he has some control, but it's going to take time and patience. He's not supposed to be a wolf yet, so his maturity and emotions are all over the place. The journal said that we would have to kill him or find his mate. You bumped into him earlier today and he just barely touched me in the process, which started to change him.

"He came to find me when he started getting weaker. He knocked me out and took me to an abandoned apartment and taped me to a chair, and he asked why I felt like the people with lightning. I think…I think the hunters had him. They tortured him and beat him and had him chained to the concrete ground somewhere down south. The used stun guns on him his whole life, simply because he refused to help them track down the descendants.

"He touched me, and the mate bond got stronger and…"

"Touched you?" Mason asked, coming back into the room. "Touched you how?"

"He kissed me," Abby lied, deciding not to tell anyone what really happened. "Then, his head started to hurt, and he ran from me. When his head started hurting, Wepwawet came to me. He had a dog head and was wearing all gold. He called me a child and told me everything would be alright. He told me that the golden wolf was your brother Apollo, and that he was my mate. I asked how it was possible when I wasn't a wolf, and he told me that, for the golden wolf, that doesn't matter. Wepwawet explained that Apollo had no control over himself before, and that he would be punished for hurting me. He said that's why I can't have kids. It's part of his punishment."

"Bullshit," Mason spat.

"What?" Abby asked, standing and turning to face Mason.

"I said, bullshit. Wepwawet didn't say shit to you. That guy isn't Apollo. You're just trying to protect him because you're his mate," Mason stated.

"Mason," Pandora warned, but Mason ignored her.

"Admit it, he didn't kiss you. He fucked you and now you're using Apollo as a reason to keep Pandora from killing him. All of this is an excuse to get rid of me because you're still mad at me."

"It had literally nothing to do with you," Abby said. "Why are you acting like this?"

"I'm acting like my girlfriend was gone for hours with a guy who claims to be her mate!" Mason yelled getting in Abby's face.

Pandora heard the front door slam open. Apollo was in between Abby and Mason in an instant, his body vibrating as he growled protectively. Sam managed to wedge himself between them, pushing Mason back too hard and knocking him to the floor as he faced Apollo.

"Mason!" Abby yelled, running over to him.

Apollo stopped growling when he saw how concerned Abby was.

"I'm sorry," he apologized to her.

"It's okay," Abby told him. "Mason, are you okay?"

"No, I'm not okay!" Mason yelled. "You're telling me you're supposed to be with this guy! He can't even control himself!"

"Yes, he can," Abby stated. "He's still learning. You need to calm down."

"Calm down?" Mason asked, standing up. "How am I supposed to calm down when you suddenly belong to someone else? Someone who gets angry way too fast! He's going to end up accidentally killing you!"

"Mason," Abby went to argue.

"No!" Mason yelled. "I'm not going to stay here and watch him hurt you!"

Mason left the room, Abby chasing after him. Pandora let out a long sigh as she could hear a bedroom door slam, open, and then slam again. Sam was holding Apollo in place in the living room as the rest of the pack joined them, not wanting to eavesdrop on the couple. Apollo sat on the couch with a huff, wanting to get to Abby, but knowing he needed to wait until Mason calmed down.

"Has he ever acted like this before?" Sam asked Pandora.

"Once," Pandora admitted. "It was about a year ago. Abby was planning a surprise birthday party for Mason, and the guy who brought the kegs said he gave them to Abby for free because they had sex. He got all angry and jealous, claiming the surprise party was an excuse to sleep with that guy. That's why his mom doesn't like her."

"I never would have guessed it," Jordan said.

"No," Pandora commented. "But Flynn might have."

Pandora turned to Flynn with a glare.

"Did you know that she was okay this whole time?" Pandora questioned angrily.

"No," Flynn assured her. "I haven't seen anything beyond us joining you here. I swear it. It's like my visions only show me enough to give me hope, like the knowing Sasha and I have mates."

"Okay," Pandora said. "I believe you."

Mason came down the hall then, a suitcase in one hand and his keys in another. Everyone got out of his way as he went out the front door, Abby nowhere behind him.

"Someone go check on Abby," Pandora ordered, going after Mason.

Pandora didn't need to look to know Apollo had run to the room. She followed Mason down the steps and to his car. He threw his suitcase in the trunk before turning to her.

"I'm sorry, Pandora, but I won't be here for your wedding," he stated, getting into his car and driving away before Pandora could respond.

"Mason!" she called after him. "Mason!"

She watched as his taillights faded into the trees. She called for him a few more times, tears rolling down her face as one of her two best friends drove away from her, abandoning here like her family had. Pandora crumbled to the ground. Sam came to her and wrapped her in his arms, rocking her back and forth as she cried. He whispered quietly into her ear as she let her emotions flow out of her. Soon, she felt exhaustion wash over her and fell asleep in Sam's arms. He carried her inside and laid her in bed, tucking the blankets in around her in the process. He left the room, nodding to Abby as she went into the room to be with Pandora, her face wet with tears as well.

He watched Abby climb into the bed and cuddle into Pandora's back. He sighed, watching as the girls who Mason had claimed as his not a week ago, suddenly became his.

CHAPTER TWENTY-EIGHT

Not Quite Whole

Abby and Pandora threw themselves into wedding planning, ignoring the fact that Mason was now gone from their lives. So far, all Pandora had heard from him was that he was safe and working with his mother. She had sent them both invitations. They had both marked their boxes no. Pandora had begun throwing things and completely trashed her and Sam's room in one fell swoop. She had cleaned up the mess after sitting in the disaster she had made for a bit, enjoying the feeling of release while it lasted.

Nature had happily taken Mason's place in the wedding, going to the wedding shop with Sam to explain the situation to Dakota. She had just nodded with understanding, getting Nature fitted quickly. Pandora went up there two weeks after to get her mother's wedding dress altered. Apollo and Abby had accompanied her, Apollo excited to get to know his older sister. He felt pride when he had found out that she was the first Alpha in 150 years.

When Pandora walked out of her stall in her dress, Abby cried. The dress had a deep V-neck and was backless. There were sequins covering the whole thing and it was transparent on most of the dress. The cloth under the dress that covered her was a light champagne color that stood out on Pandora's tanned skin. The long sleeves billowed out a bit before becoming tight with a small band around her wrist.

"Our mom got married in this?" Apollo asked.

"Yeah." Pandora smiled. "I'll show you pictures when we get home. I've been hiding them, so Sam won't see the dress."

"Now we just need a veil," Abby smiled, standing up and walking somewhere else in the shop.

She came back a few moments later with a champagne-colored drape veil. She pinned it to Pandora's hair, which had been left down for the day, with pearl clips that were connected to it.

"Perfect." Abby smiled, showing Pandora herself in the mirror.

Pandora smiled widely, feeling like she was about to cry. Apollo stood next to her and smiled. Seeing him by her side in the mirror, she got an idea. She would save it for later though as Abby began ushering Pandora back into her stall to change so that they could do more shopping.

Once changed, Pandora, Apollo, and Abby set off to search for flower ideas. Sam had picked the boutonnieres already at the floral shop, so all Pandora needed to do was pick a few more flowers for her bouquet. The boutonnieres were a single anemone flower with a sprig of statice behind it. Pandora chose the two flowers along with scabiosas, spray roses, and escimo roses to go with them. They paid for the flowers and moved on to decorations.

They were having the wedding outside the cottage, next to the pond, and the reception would be in the back patio. Loren and Nature had dug a circle in the ground, lining it with rocks from the forest, for the couple to stand in during the ceremony, where Jordan would marry them. Jordan had felt left out and had gotten ordained online once Nature had taken Mason's place. Now, almost the whole pack was participating in the wedding except for Sasha, Flynn, and Apollo.

The guest list had been very small. Sam invited his mother and sister. Pandora had invited Mason, his mother, and Abby's parents. Everyone except Mason and his mother had marked their invitation yes. Candace and Zuri had been speaking on the phone almost nonstop since, being the mother of the groom and placeholder mother of the bride. They had color coordinated their dresses and everything.

They had ordered macaroons that looked like the moon phases special for the wedding. Pandora had gone to the same bakery that Sam had driven her to the hotel on her birthday from and had special ordered a two-tiered cake. The cake was white and designed to look like mountains and trees, like their Wolf Rocks trail view. Pandora had gone back to the store where she had seen the cake topper with wolves and bought it one day when Abby and

Apollo weren't with her, not wanting to remind them of what the golden wolf had done there.

For the food, Pandora had decided to cook. She would start her jambalaya the night before, letting it simmer overnight. She would soak pork tenderloin in Italian dressing, soy sauce, and brown sugar for a week before hand, sticking it on kabobs for the grill the night before as well, allowing Loren to take over the cooking portion for that. Abby had picked the cocktail to serve. It was a simple glass of champagne poured over a small ball of cotton candy. There would also be water, beer, and tea.

Inside the back patio, the boys had been hanging up bulb lights and star streamers. Over the long table where they would all eat dinner, Warren had hand carved a moon from a tree that had fallen over during a storm. After Warren had sanded it down, Sasha and Jordan had painted it before hanging it up. Warren had also used the tree to make stump chairs for outside during the ceremony.

Sam had found black plates and white silverware for them to use for dinner. Loren found black napkins and a white twine with stars on it. When he had gotten home and showed Pandora his find, she had taken the white silverware and wrapped each set in the black napkins, using the twine to hold it shut and setting it in a safe place until the day of.

As the wedding got closer, Pandora spent more and more time with her brother, wanting to get to know him better. There wasn't much to him, except that he had been tortured all of his life and was trying to figure out how the world worked. Pandora happily answered any questions he had. Pandora wasn't shocked when she learned that he didn't have much of an education. Abby had begun teaching him a lot of different things such as math and history. Learning basic things was difficult for him, and whenever someone used a word he didn't know, he would get frustrated. Pandora and Abby were patient though and would sit with him, explaining everything that they could to him. Two weeks before the wedding, Pandora and Apollo were sitting on the front porch steps, watching the sun rise above the trees.

"I want to ask you something," Pandora told Apollo.

"What is it?" Apollo asked.

"Will you give me away at the wedding?" she asked.

"What do you mean?"

"Like, you would walk me down the aisle and give my hand to Sam. Jordan will ask who is giving me away, and you'll respond with the words, 'I am.' It's an old tradition, but you're the only person that I want to do it," Pandora explained to him.

Apollo smiled.

"It's a family thing?" he asked.

"Yes." Pandora smiled. "It's a family thing."

"I would love to," Apollo smiled.

They sat quietly, watching the sunrise together, sipping on their coffees.

Two days before the wedding, Pandora's phone rang.

"Hi, Candace." Pandora smiled.

"Hi, Dora. I have some bad news." Candace sighed. "We won't be able to make it to the wedding dear. I'm so sorry."

"Oh," Pandora said sadly. "What's wrong?"

"We have to go to France for business. There's an emergency with a client and they asked for us specifically. We leave tomorrow. I'm so sorry."

"It's okay," Pandora assured her. "You have work. I completely understand. Let me know how it goes?"

"I will, Hun. I'm sorry again," Candace apologized.

Pandora assured her it was alright a few more times before they got off of the phone. Abby had been angry with Mason and his mother already, but now her parents weren't coming, and she was furious. Flynn had sighed, having sensed that Abby would be angry about something. Pandora had turned to Flynn with an amused smile at dinner.

"Are you sensing anything bad to happen at the wedding by any chance?" Pandora asked him.

He had laughed and told her no, feeling in his chest that he might be wrong, but not wanting to worry the bride. Abby and Sasha had dressed Pandora up that night and they drove to Pittsburgh, Loren and Warren going with them just in case they had the same issue as the last time they had gone drinking in the city. The group of five barhopped all night, gaining free drinks when people saw the sash around Pandora saying she was a bride.

By two in the morning, all three of the girls were drunkenly being led to Pandora's Tahoe, Loren carrying Pandora as Warren escorted the other women. They drove the giggling girls home and helped them inside. Pandora had refused their help though and remained in the Tahoe until Sam came out to get her. Unfortunately, Jordan and Nature had gotten him almost as drunk as Pandora was and they ended up making it to the small bed on their private porch. They slept under the stars, making love and not caring if anyone could see them.

Fortunately, Sasha had gone to Nature's room when she'd gotten home. She didn't have to worry about seeing the two lovers near her window. She had tiptoed to his bedroom door as quietly as she could in her drunken state and knocked. He answered it after a moment and stared at Sasha in confusion. She had surprised him with a kiss that made him want to sink to his knees from the fire that buzzed through his body. He pulled her into the room and kicked his door closed, not caring if it alerted the pack with its sharp noise.

Apollo tucked Abby into her bed and went back to the living room, lying across the couch that faced the front door. He had taken this spot as his own since the first night of being there. He faced the door so he could see any danger that tried to enter the cottage, prepared to protect Abby with his life. In the morning, he woke up to find Pandora cooking blueberry pancakes and starting their coffee. He sat at the island and smiled at her as she hummed to herself, her messy hair in a bun on her head.

Their mornings always consisted of one of two situations. Either Pandora and Apollo would watch the sunrise while drinking coffee, asking each other questions about their lives, or Pandora would hum and teach Apollo how to cook breakfast. They were almost always the first to wake, Sam sometimes joining them.

Pandora told Apollo to come over, so he stood and walked around the island to her. She talked him through how to mix everything for pancakes and showed him how to make sure the blueberries didn't burn and stick to the pan. They worked together, falling into an easy pattern. Apollo smiled, very happy with how his life had changed. He worried that the hunters would come looking for them soon though. So far, everything had been quiet and much too easy for them. He kept waiting for something to go wrong.

He shook the feeling off and smiled to his older sister and Alpha as more of the pack woke and joined them. Nature and Sasha wondered into the kitchen together, both looking a little more satisfied with themselves than normal. Apollo smiled and rolled his eyes when he smelled their scents on each other, knowing immediately what had finally happened. Pandora eyed them for a moment, a small smile on her face before turning back to the pancakes on her plate.

The pack began leaving for work, Sam kissing Pandora goodbye before heading out the door. Around noon, Pandora and Abby headed into town to meet with a realtor about a shop space on Main Street. The building itself was old, but spacious. Pandora smiled at all of the shelves that lined the walls. She would need tables for in the middle sections, the checkout counter needed to be sanded down, and everything was in need of fresh paint. Pandora smiled around as she did a slow circle, checking out the store.

"I'll take it." Pandora smiled to the realtor.

They took the next hour to fill out paperwork. Once it was done, the realtor handed the keys to Pandora, the check having already been accepted by the bank. Pandora and Abby began laughing once the realtor left, too happy for words. They went back to the cottage and picked up Flynn, Sasha, and Apollo, taking them to lunch before enlisting their help with the shop. Once they agreed to help for the day, they all headed to the shop so Flynn, Sasha, and Apollo could see it. They looked around as Pandora and Abby headed to Home Depot to buy supplies.

Once there, they split up, each taking a cart and a half of the shopping list. Pandora got tables, paint, paint stripper, and a varnish to stain the cabinets with. Abby got tarps, sandpaper, painter's tape, and tablecloths. They met at the register, and Pandora paid for the supplies. They loaded up the Tahoe and went back to the shop. Flynn and Apollo unloaded the Tahoe, leaving the tables and tablecloths for later. They laid out the tarps and got to work. Flynn and Abby began sanding down the main counter. Pandora, Sasha, and Apollo began painting the shelves and cabinets. They left the walls white and made the shelves Water Baby Blue.

As the pack got off of work, the joined the crew in the store, helping paint the shelves and cabinets and sand and stain the main counter. They finished quickly since there were so many of them working on it. The men brought in the tables, Sasha and Abby carrying the tablecloths as Pandora directed the pack on where to put the tables. Sasha and Abby put the tablecloths on the tables as Warren, Loren, and Nature hung the chandeliers that they had surprised Pandora with, lighting the store up once they were all wired into the ceiling.

Pandora looked around the store and felt herself about to cry from how happy she was. Abby took one of her hands, and Sam wrapped his arm over her shoulder, kissing the top of her head. She smiled and thanked her pack, buying them dinner at IHOP as her thanks. The waitress that had hit on Sam previously barely looked at him as she got their orders, knowing that Sam and Pandora were getting married soon. Sam's mom and sister joined them before they had finished ordering.

"It's so nice to finally meet you, Pandora," Zuri greeted her with a hug.

"It's nice to meet you too," Pandora smiled, releasing Zuri and turning to Sam's younger sister. "You must be Nala."

"I am," Nala smiled, hugging Pandora as well before turning to her brother. "She's prettier than I thought you would ever score."

"Nala!" Zuri warned as Sam laughed.

"It's okay, Mom. She's right." Sam smiled, pulling out his mom's chair for her. Zuri took the seat next to Sam that was offered, and Nala sat next to Jordan.

"Hi, Jordan." Nala blushed.

"Hi, Nala. How's college going?" Jordan asked with a smile.

"Good." Nala smiled. "I really like all of my classes."

"You're a freshman in college, right, Nala?" Abby asked.

"Yes," Nala answered. "Are you Abby?"

"Yes." Abby smiled and pointed to Apollo next to her. "This is Apollo, Pandora's brother."

"Nice to meet you." Nala smiled to them.

They ate dinner, smiling and laughing, Zuri and Nala telling stories about Sam when he was younger. They all headed to the cottage. Zuri and Nala were going to stay in the front bedroom that had once been meant for Pandora but was available now that Sasha had moved into Nature's room earlier that day. Sam would be sleeping alone in his and Pandora's room, while Pandora slept in Abby's room with her. They all headed to bed, Sam kissing Pandora goodnight about a hundred times before Abby finally sent him away.

Pandora fell asleep next to her best friend and sister, feeling happier than she ever had before.

CHAPTER TWENTY-NINE

Wedding

Pandora woke to Abby opening and closing the bedroom door. Abby came to the bed and sat down next to Pandora, passing her a cup of coffee. Pandora thanked her, sitting up and taking the cup from her. Pandora sipped the coffee, smiling as she stared at her wedding dress hanging on Abby's mirror.

"You ready for this?" Abby asked Pandora. "We could always grab the keys and run away."

"Ha, ha." Pandora rolled her eyes. "Strangely enough, I don't think that will work out for me in the end."

"Because you'll probably die?" Abby asked.

"Because I'd miss him." Pandora shrugged. "Weirdly enough, I actually like the guy."

"Just like?" Abby smiled to her friend.

"Shut up." Pandora smiled. "Let's go eat some actual food, please. I'm starving."

"No can do," Abby stated. "Sam's out there and can't see you until wedding time."

"I don't believe in that superstition." Pandora sighed, standing up and walking out the door.

Abby sighed and followed Pandora into the kitchen. Sam smiled and kissed Pandora's head when he saw her.

"I thought y'all weren't supposed to see each other until later," Warren commented.

"Shush," Sam told him, refilling Pandora's coffee cup.

Pandora leaned against the counter and turned to the small group in the room. "What's the plan for today? Anyone have plans?" Pandora joked.

"I think I'll go for a drive today." Sam smiled. "Get some fresh mountain air."

"I was thinking of taking a train ride to Philly," Sasha said.

Abby looked at Pandora and glared.

"Stop that," Abby told her.

"Calm down, Abbs." Pandora smiled. "We're just playing. I'm going to go put some clothes on and start the meat."

Pandora left the room with a smile, knowing Abby would calm as the day progressed. She threw on some jeans and one of Sam's shirts before throwing her hair up and going back into the kitchen. Everyone was up and moving now. Jordan and Apollo were in the kitchen, Jordan showing Apollo how to make scrambled eggs. Pandora smiled, pulling bacon and sausage out of the fridge to cook. Sam started making toast. Abby grabbed the meat for the kabobs and began sticking it on skewers for Pandora, Sasha joining her. Warren, Nature, Loren, and Flynn went outside to begin decorating the circle that had been made for the ceremony. Zuri and Nala sat in the living room, watching as the pack worked together.

Jordan brought the marriage certificate in, having Sam and Pandora sign it early, Abby and Loren as the witnesses.

"Technically, you're, like, half married now." Jordan smiled.

Once breakfast was made, the boys came back inside to eat before heading back outside again, taking Sam with them so that Abby could begin getting Pandora ready. Pandora sighed as she stepped into Abby's shower, feeling the hot water wash over her, relaxing her tense muscles. She had told everyone that she wasn't worried about today, but she was. She wasn't worried about marrying Sam, just that he would regret marrying her one day. She was worried that he would end up leaving her, like Mason had left Abby. She let out a shaky breath and began washing her hair, using the shampoo that Abby had put in the shower for her.

She took her shower quickly, ready to get to Sam again. Abby pushed her into a chair as soon as Pandora had her robe on. Abby blow dried Pandora's hair and pulled it back with a clip so that she could begin her makeup. Abby used a light brown on Pandora's eyes, giving Pandora a natural look before adding a wing with eyeliner. She used a light lipstick, adding a pink tint to Pandora's lips. Next, Abby let Pandora's hair down before pulling a few strands from the front and braiding them into a crown around the top of Pandora's head.

Abby refused to let Pandora see herself until Pandora was dressed, that way the whole look would be complete. Abby helped Pandora into her dress, careful not to mess up her hair or makeup. Apollo came into the room with the veil and smiled as Abby clipped it to Pandora's crown. Pandora then put on her locket from Sam, having taken it off before her shower.

"How do I look?" Pandora asked her brother.

"Perfect." Apollo smiled brightly.

Pandora smiled to him as Abby finally told Pandora that she could look. Pandora turned to Abby's full-length mirror and gasped.

"How did you turn me into that?" Pandora asked Abby.

"Magic," Abby joked, stealing Pandora's joke.

"You look beautiful." Apollo smiled.

"I wish grandma were here," Pandora thought to herself and then shook her head to keep from crying.

Pandora took a deep breath and asked for the time.

"We have about twenty minutes." Abby smiled. "I'll get dressed."

Pandora smiled as Apollo left the room so that Abby could have privacy. Abby changed into her black dress quickly. She had done her own hair and makeup while Pandora had been in the shower. Abby smiled to Pandora and asked if she was ready. Pandora smiled brightly and nodded. Nature, Loren, and Apollo came into the room, smiling at the girls.

Nature kissed Abby's cheek before kissing the top of Pandora's head. Loren smiled brightly to Pandora before brushing her cheek with his lips and telling her she was beautiful. Apollo held his arm out for Pandora to take. Pandora smiled and took his arm. Abby passed Pandora her bouquet that the boys had gone and picked up for her when they went to get the cake. Pandora took the bouquet and let out a low breath.

"I'm ready," she assured the small group.

Nature led them to the door before holding his arm out for Abby. Abby took Nature's right arm and Loren's left arm, walking out of the cottage and towards the circle. Apollo led Pandora out the door and down the steps of the cottage. Pandora smiled at the rock path that was lined with candles and her flowers, leading to the side of the cottage and the small pit that had been built. Pandora found Sam as she and Apollo came around the side of the cottage and smiled brightly. He saw her and gasped before smiling brightly. Their eyes never left each other as Pandora walked to him.

Apollo passed Pandora's hand to Sam and took his seat next to Zuri and Nala, Sasha and Flynn behind him.

"Pack, we are gathered here today to join Pandora and Sam together in marriage. Who gives this woman away?" Jordan asked.

"I do." Apollo smiled, and Jordan continued.

"I haven't known Pandora for long, but I know that Sam has never smiled so much before. The two of you bring so much brightness into a room when you're together. I have never seen two people more in love before. Sam calms Pandora, and Pandora forces Sam to see things from more than one perspective. They have helped each other become better people in such a short amount of time. It is amazing to watch, and I hope we all find someone just as perfect for each of us.

"Sam, do you take Pandora to be your lawfully wedded wife? To have and to hold? To protect and love, as long as you both shall live?"

"I do." Sam smiled.

"Pandora, do you take Sam to be your lawfully wedded husband? To have and to hold? To protect and love, as long as you both shall live?"

"I do," Pandora promised.

"The rings?" Jordan asked.

Loren passed Sam his ring, and Abby passed Pandora hers.

"Sam, place the ring on Pandora's finger."

Sam did as he was told.

"Pandora, place the ring on Sam's finger."

Once she had, Jordan smiled.

"I now pronounce you husband and wife. You may kiss the bride."

Sam grabbed Pandora's face in his hands and brought her into a deep kiss. Pandora laughed a bit as the kiss broke.

"I love you," Sam whispered to her.

"I love you too," Pandora promised.

"We're married," Sam told Pandora.

"We're married," Pandora repeated, laughing a bit more.

Sam kissed her again before turning to their applauding pack. There was a loud crack heard in the sky, and Sam felt a pain in his chest. He looked down and was confused by the red stain that was growing on his shirt and the hole in his shirt over his heart. He heard Pandora call his name as he fell to his knees. Pandora's arms were around him and his head was in her lap. She pushed on his chest, telling him he was going to be okay and to stay with her. He saw spots in his vision before everything went black.

"Sam!" Pandora yelled as the pack around her shifted and ran at the hunters that came through the trees. "Sam! Wake up! You have to stay awake!

"Dora!" Abby yelled to get her attention.

"Get inside!" Pandora yelled to Abby, Zuri, and Nala.

Apollo, not having shifted yet, kneeled in front of Pandora.

"Stay with Abby," Pandora told him. "Shift and protect her and Sam's family."

Pandora looked back to Sam. His eyes were still open, but they weren't shining like they had been a moment ago.

"Sam?" Pandora asked, feeling her voice crack. "No. No. Sam, baby, I need you to breathe, baby. Please."

Pandora begged Sam to breathe for her. She checked his pulse and found that he didn't have one.

"No!" Pandora yelled, starting chest compressions. "Come on, baby. You can't do this to me. Not today. Not right now."

When his heart didn't start, Pandora knew he was gone. She kept trying when Apollo took her hands.

"He's gone, Pandora," Apollo told her. "He's gone. The pack needs you."

Pandora looked into Apollo's eyes and then to the scene behind him. The hunters were attacking her pack, hurting them. They had killed her mate. Pandora felt herself rise from the ground. She walked towards the battle happening around her when she felt a scream rip through her body. The hunters all fell to the ground, covering their ears as the earth trembled beneath Pandora.

"She's a banshee!" one of the hunters yelled, his voice not high enough to be heard over the scream though.

A few of the hunters fell to ground, dead from their eardrums exploding. The rest remained on the ground, unable to defend themselves as the pack descended on them. Pandora stopped her scream and shifted, destroying her wedding dress in the process, her necklace still hanging from her neck, the chain being just long enough to wear as a wolf, as Sam had planned. Pandora ran through the hunters, ripping their throats with her teeth and tearing into their stomachs with her claws. When the hunters all laid on the ground, most torn in multiple pieces, Pandora shifted back into her human form, letting out a wail for Sam.

 She didn't know how long she laid in the middle of the battle ground, the hunters' blood soaking into the soil. She screamed more and more, crying as she felt her heart breaking into smaller and smaller pieces. She slowly stopped crying, turning her feelings off and retreating into herself. She felt a blanket being placed around her and looked up just enough to see Loren's face, covered in tears at the loss of his brother. He sat next to her, not speaking and looking at the bodies around them.

 "We need to get rid of the bodies," Sasha whispered to someone.

 Sasha, Flynn, and Apollo walked around the bloody mess before them, picking up limbs and putting them into a pile in the large clearing. Warren and Jordan joined them at some point. Nature drove off in his truck, returning within ten minutes with a full can of gas and matches. Pandora turned away as the fire was lit, burning the dead hunters.

 She stood, holding the blanket around her and went to where Sam's body still laid. She sat next to him and took his hand in hers, his wedding ring shining on his hand. Pandora didn't cry anymore as she looked at him. She felt empty, like everything in her had died with him. Abby came to her and told her that they needed to figure out what to do. Pandora let out a low breath before turning to Abby.

 "We take him to the city. We go into an alley, and I call the police. I tell them we were mugged, and they shot him when he tried to protect me," Pandora stated. "We need to go now the time of death needs to be as close as possible."

 Loren didn't need to listen to anyone's arguments. He lifted Sam easily and carried him to the Tahoe. He set Sam gently into the trunk and took the keys. Pandora threw on a blue sundress and took Sam's car and followed Loren as he drove her Tahoe. They sped the whole way, making it to Pittsburgh within a half hour. Loren stopped the Tahoe in a location with no traffic cameras before pulling Sam out of the car. He set Sam gently on the concrete while Pandora called the police. Loren left quickly, going a few streets away to a convenience store to get bleach and a scrub brush. He climbed into the Tahoe's trunk and began scrubbing at the carpet, getting Sam's blood out the best he could.

Pandora held Sam in her arms, getting more of his blood on her dress and starting to cry again. The police arrived quickly and took the scene. They wrapped Pandora in a warm blanket in the back of an ambulance. She heard them say something about shock and asked if there was anyone they could call. She nodded and pulled out her phone, dialing Loren and telling him where she was. Loren waited a half hour before going to Pandora. He drove her to the police station, where she gave a statement, saying that everything happened too fast for her to get any details.

They released Pandora and Loren led her back to Sam's car. She drove it home, following Loren again. This time they drove the speed limit, not getting back to the cottage until after dark. Once there, Pandora noticed that Nature and Warren were filling the hole where Sam and Pandora had gotten married just hours ago. Pandora ignored the pain in her chest as she stepped into the cottage.

She looked around the room at the eyes that went to her immediately. Loren stepped next to her.

"It's done," Loren stated. "Mugging gone wrong. They probably won't find the guy who did it, but they'll try. They said they would hand the body over to Pandora within the next few days for a funeral service."

Pandora walked through the cottage and went to Sam's room, closing and locking the door behind her as she looked around the room. Everything in the room smelled of Sam. His shoes were next to the door, lined up in the order he liked. His grey blanket was thrown across the bed as he had rushed to make it this morning. His clothes were still in the hamper, waiting to be washed.

Pandora walked to his hamper, pulling out of the shirts he'd worn that week. She breathed in the scent of Sam and lay on his side of the bed, burying her head into his pillow while cuddling his shirt. She let out a loud sob, ignoring the incessive knocking on the door. She curled into a ball, retreating into herself again as she let her sobs rock her whole body.

How was she supposed to do this? She couldn't lead the pack alone! How was she supposed to go on without her mate? What was she supposed to do now that the one person in the world that she was made for was gone?

Pandora remained in Sam's room, feeling hopeless and ignoring every person who tried to talk to her. She stayed in her room for three days, only rising when the police called her to tell her that Sam's body was available. She called the Somerset funeral home, setting up Sam's funeral for a few days from then. She exited her room, finding only Loren awake. He was standing in the doorway to the cottage, staring out at the sunrise. Pandora grabbed a cup of coffee and joined him. He looked to her, surprised.

"The police released Sam's body," she explained. "I called the funeral home in town. They're on their way to get him and prepare the body. The funeral will be in three days."

Loren nodded, not saying anything. The two stood in the doorway, a small breeze entering the cottage. Soon, the pack began to join them. Pandora stepped outside and sat at one of the rocking chairs. Loren stood by her side, keeping his gaze on the sunrise, but keeping Pandora company with his presence.

Pandora looked at her pack, all having their own spots on the front porch, still wiping the tired from their eyes. They all seemed older now. Abby and Apollo were on the porch swing, Apollo making sure not to make contact with Abby as they swung gently. Flynn and Sasha sat on the top step, each leaning against a different banister. Warren sat in front of Flynn, his arm resting on his mate's leg. Nature sat in the rocking chair next to Pandora, not saying a word as he drank his water. Jordan was sitting on the bannister, one leg kicking a bit.

"This," Pandora thought to herself. "This is how I survive."